Viking Enemy

Book 14 in the Dragon Heart Series

By

Griff Hosker

Contents

Published by Sword Books Ltd 2016
Copyright © Griff Hosker First Edition

Cover by Design for Writers

Prologue

We had been forced to abandon my son's former stronghold at Elfridaby. With Wolf Killer dead and many of his hearth-weru slain, it was indefensible. We had destroyed the walls, burned the buildings and filled in the ditches so that no enemy could use it against us. When we had finished it was as though it had never existed and soon nature would reclaim the black scars which remained. It would be remembered only in our songs. With my son and grandson dead along with most of his oathsworn, there was no reason to hang on to that outpost of our land. I did not wish to risk losing Elfrida or my two grandchildren. My grandson, Ragnar, and my son, Gruffyd, were now my future. Although we had killed my son's killers it had not eased the pain of their loss. Wolf Killer and Garth were in the Otherworld; they had died bravely, but a father should not out live his son. The fact that those who had paid the assassins still lived ate at me. King Egbert had always hated my son for he had taken Elfrida from him. The other, who would pay, was Grimbould of Neustria. He had hired and given gold to those who killed my kin. One day I would have my vengeance and he would die.

I had not slept well since the two deaths despite the fact that my own hall was secure and Elfrida and her family lived with me. I woke, suddenly, in the middle of the night. Something had disturbed my sleep but I knew not what it was. This was the third night in a row when I had been awoken. I knew I would not be able to sleep again. Something was calling me and, in an effort to see a little clearer, I took myself to the top of Old Olaf. I had done this before but not for some years. I left before dawn and told no one where I was going. I strapped on Ragnar's Spirit and slipped from my hall. I did not think I would be in danger but I was closer to the spirits and the gods when I wore it. The night watch opened the gate for me. My silent nod told him I had no wish to speak.

The mountain started soon after the last hut just four hundred paces from my walls and my legs began to burn within the first five hundred paces of the climb. They would soon adjust but I needed the pain. It helped to focus my mind. I had thought my days as a warrior were long gone but they were not. I had to become Ulfheonar once more. That meant being able to keep going when others faded. It meant enduring greater pain than other warriors and it meant becoming the best of warriors. This pilgrimage to the top of the Old Man was the start of a journey of rediscovery. I had become soft. A home free from danger, good food and ale would do that to a man. My sword belt was now tighter than it had been. I had mocked Windar who had grown fat in his home on the Mere and now I was in danger of becoming him.

I knew the track well. The hardest part was the higher part of the journey for the path insinuated itself around the mountain. Our miners and slaves had worn the lower path smooth. I passed the Blue Water and then turned south. I could have gone directly to the top but I wanted the longer journey along the path to clear my mind. It enabled me to think as I trudged up the mountain. We had made peace with Northumbria. They were no longer our enemies. We respected our mutual borders. Our enemy was Wessex for since King Coenwulf had died the Mercians were too busy fighting both Wessex and the East Anglians not to mention their constant border wars with the Welsh. The Hibernians were kept in their place by Jarl Gunnstein Berserk Killer in Dyflin and the men of Strathclyde had been quiet for some time. Our other enemy was our own people, the Vikings who lived in Eoforwic. They were Danes, and it was they who were too close for comfort for they were untrustworthy. They did not seek land to farm as our people did but they sought to take what others had worked for.

The path twisted back upon itself but, as the dawn broke over the water of Cyninges-tūn I reached the top and was rewarded by a view almost to Wyddfa in the south and Dyflin to the west. In between them was our former home, Man. The view always inspired me. I looked to the east and saw the water that was Windar's Mere on the far side of Grize's Dale. Beyond that were the high hills that divided this island in two.

I took out my sword and planted it a hand span into the earth. I knelt and held the hilt with both hands. Closing my eyes I began to empty my mind. I could have asked my daughter, the volva, for a potion to help me speak with the spirits but I never liked that approach. If the spirits chose not to speak with me then I could live with that. I was only raised a Viking. I had enough Saxon and the blood of the old people coursing through my body to choose my own path.

As soon as my eyes were closed I could hear far more than before. I heard the gulls far to the south. I heard the chattering magpies lower down the slopes. I heard the wings of the skylarks as they flitted above my head. By concentrating I heard the wind blow the longer tufts of grass which struggled to grow from between the rocks. It was then I heard my heart beating rhythmically in my ears. It reminded me of a chant by which we would row. Pictures emerged. A ship appeared in my head and I saw that it was my ship; it was the *'Heart of the Dragon'*. I saw her sail north to the rocky islands of the northern Vikings. I saw the wild Scots as they plundered and feasted upon the carcasses of dragon ships. The voice I heard in my ears was not my son, as I had expected, but my mother. She had been murdered by Hibernian raiders. I had avenged her but her spirit wandered our land still. Her voice was like a chant in a drekar, *'Guard the land and guard your home, Beware the enemy who do roam, Guard the land and guard your home, Guard the land and guard your home'*. The voice faded and disappeared and was replaced by my heartbeat once more.

I opened my eyes and saw that the sun had fully risen and bathed my valley with the harsh blue cold light of morning. By evening it would have become golden, almost red but at that moment, as I stood it was blue. The vision came to me of the people who had attacked Jarl Thorfinn Blue Scar on Ljoðhús. They had blue skin and they were Scottish. It was a sign. I would watch my northern borders. I would heed the word of the spirits. I did not know why but the enemy I had to fear, was the Scots. They had been quiet for some time and I had not expected to look north. I felt the danger would come from the Danes in the east. I was happy that I had come up to the mountain. If I had not done so then I would have looked in the wrong direction. Such mistakes were always costly.

We would prepare for war. I would seek news of the men of Strathclyde. I had already planned on visiting my wrath upon Grimbould the Mayor of Neustria for he had been complicit in the murder of my son. If my vision was a false one then we would travel to Neustria but first I would seek the advice of my daughter and her husband. The spirit world would guide us.

Part One

King Dumnagual

Chapter 1

The journey down the mountain was almost as hard as the one up. My knee jolted each time I put it down. Old war wounds never went away. I met my miners ascending as I descended. I smiled and spoke with them. The interruption to the jarring journey down was a relief. I was in no hurry.

Ragnar, my grandson, and Gruffyd, my son, were sent to find me. I met them by the Blue Water. Gruffyd said, "Mother was worried. I was not for I knew where you would be."

I nodded and drank a handful of the blue water to refresh myself. Ragnar said, "My father often told me of this place. He said the water was the same colour as the stone in your sword, grandfather." I was pleased that he was able to talk of his father. I had done the same when Old Ragnar had been killed. "I now see what he meant. You can feel the presence of the old ones, here in the rocks, just as you can by the Water."

"Aye, that would be your grandmother and great-grandmother. Their spirits are always by the Water. Here is the spirit of Old Olaf. He never saw this land but we always feel closer to him here."

He nodded, "What do you do on the mountain top, Jarl Dragonheart?"

"I find peace and sometimes the spirits speak with me."

Gruffyd asked, "Did they speak this time, father?"

I stood and stretched, "They did but first I need to speak with Kara and Aiden. I may be interpreting this dream badly. I am no galdramenn. I am a warrior."

As we walked down the track to Cyninges-tūn Water Ragnar asked me about the Water and the mountain. He had visited many times with his father but he had never lived here and now it was to be his home. He wanted to know all about it. His home had been in the flat and wooded part of my land. He had just had a river. In truth, I had never liked it but my son had chosen it as his home. That had been when he had been wilful and had fallen out with his sister. Ragnar's curiosity was understandable. I was pleased that Gruffyd volunteered so much information. It showed that he had listened and learned. This was his land and one day he would rule in my stead.

"So do you go to war again, grandfather?"

"A Viking is always a sharpened sword away from war, Ragnar, but I do not seek war. I never have. You two are like me. Neither of you are true Norsemen. One of you has a Saxon mother, I had a Saxon father and the other has a Welsh mother as I did and the blood of others runs through your veins. Those like Haaken and Snorri are Norse through and through. They enjoy war and they seek war. I suffer war. It marks me as different."

"Yet they all follow you and would die for you."

"They would, Ragnar, and that is a great responsibility."

When I reached my hall Brigid's frown was the only sign that she was upset. Later, when we were alone, she would tell me her worries. Since the death of my son, she had become more fearful. "An early morning walk, my husband?"

I smiled, "I knew it would be a good sunrise and I wished to see it. The view was worth the climb. And now I could eat a horse with its skin on!"

It was a phrase I often used and the two boys laughed. Uhtric brought in a platter of pickled fish along with fresh bread. The Water provided us with food all year round. It was said to be as deep as the ocean although how the fishermen knew that was beyond me but it teemed with fish. We only fished what we needed but Brigid had the slaves brining and pickling the surplus every few days. Brigid brewed good beer and the combination of salty, pickled fish and golden beer was one I savoured.

"I will go and see Kara and Aiden."

The innocent words made my wife turn. Her eyes asked the question. I smiled in answer and kissed her forehead. "I will not be away long."

Although my wife was Christian she was aware of the dreams, voices and visions which we experienced. She had learned to accept them but they were always a portent of danger. She did not understand them. Her religion came to her through the words of priests in a language they could not understand. Our way was simpler. Ragnar and Gruffyd tagged along behind me. I would not exclude them from my meeting. Both would be warriors. Ragnar would be ready for his first raid soon for he was already old enough even if he had not grown into his warrior body. Boys younger than he already sailed as ships' boys on my drekar. Both my son and grandson had swords, little more than double-bladed seaxes, and they practised with them constantly. That was how we bred our warriors. The weapons we used were part of us.

My daughter had a house of healing and many widowed women worked with her. Two former nuns, Deidra and Macha, made cheese for us and organised the women for Kara. It was in direct contrast to my warrior hall which was filled with young, unmarried warriors.

In the last year my granddaughter, Ylva, had begun to show powers inherited from her parents. If Ragnar and Gruffyd had warrior skills from me then Ylva had the power of a volva from my dead wife Erika as well as her parents. She was old beyond her years. She seemed not like a girl of but seven summers; she was more like a young woman. My own daughter, Erika was only a year younger and yet she still played with other children. Ylva spent her time with her mother learning to be a volva.

It was Ylva who greeted us, "Welcome grandfather. We have been expecting you."

My son and grandson both had a wolf token around their necks for protection and I smiled as their hands went to the wolf. "It is not to be feared, Ragnar. Those in this house have powers we do not understand but they will never harm us."

Ylva shook her head as though she were the elder and Ragnar the younger, "We are family!"

I waited until Kara and Aiden were present before I asked the question to which I already had the answer. "You dreamed?"

"We did." Kara looked at Ragnar and Gruffyd and then back at me.

"Would you have them excluded from something which affects them as much as any? They have both faced death and survived. They will be warriors."

She smiled, "You are right. This is *wyrd*." She gestured to seats and nodded to her servant who fetched beer. "We saw but a glimpse of your dream."

"I dreamed not."

"Then why did you wake and go to see Old Olaf? You had a dream and it woke you and sent you to the mountain. Your mother spoke to you did she not?" I nodded. "The dream woke you so that she could speak with you. What did she say?"

"She chanted, as though she was rowing a drekar. She sang, *'**Guard the land and guard your home, Beware the enemy who do roam, Guard*** *the land and guard your home, Guard the land and guard your home'*."

Aiden nodded. Although he now had flecks of grey in his beard I still saw in his sparkling blue eyes the young Irish slave we had rescued all those years ago. "The dream which woke you was filled with wild men from the north. They flooded south like a blue wave. In your dream, you tried to stop them but you sank below them."

I saw Gruffyd start. "These dreams are not a picture of what will happen, my son, but what may happen if we are not prepared." He nodded. I turned back to Aiden and Kara, "You will dream again?"

"Tonight is a good night for there will be a full moon and the skies will be clear. We will dream but it seems clear that the enemy will be coming from the north."

It was what I had thought already. "Then I will ride to Ketil Windarsson and Ulf Olafsson. I will travel the wall. I need to speak with my jarls."

As we left I mentally prepared for the journey. I would take Snorri with me, not as protection but I might need his eyes. He was the best scout I had. Haaken One Eye would also wish to come. He had had a month with his wife and his daughters. That was always enough for him and Olaf Leather Neck had no family but still yearned for action. When we were not raiding or fighting he was drinking and that was not a good thing.

I was aware of my son and grandson squabbling about something behind me. "What is it?"

"We will be coming with you won't we, father?"

"It may be dull. I will just be talking to my jarls. There will be no fighting."

Ragnar said, "We know but we will be jarls one day will we not? We need to know how to be jarls."

"You will only be jarls if men are willing to follow you. I was a slave. The sons of the jarl did not become the leader of the clan, I did. Think on that. It does not come to you by birth. You have to earn the title."

"All the more reason for us to come with you," Ragnar was confident enough to argue with me.

"Very well but I will need to speak with your mothers."

Snorri and Olaf lived in the village but Haaken had a farmstead south of it in the forest. He kept sheep on the fell side. When he was away his family could easily manage them. He had a dog which had been a pup of

Wolf, my first sheep dog. I sent Ragnar and Gruffyd to summon my oldest friend while I braved the women.

Elfrida and Brigid were working with their women to knead the dough. My daughter, Erika, was helping them. The air was thick with flour dust and the room filled with the sound of dough being slapped on wood. I smiled, "Such industry!"

"You men all have big bellies which need filling."

Nodding I said, "I will take the boys north with me. I wish to visit with Ketil and Arne. We will be away for a few days."

Elfrida and Brigid stopped kneading. Erika frowned as they did so. "Why?"

As soon as my wife spoke I knew that she was not happy. My early morning walk and now this added up to only one thing, trouble. She might not be a volva but she was clever. "I have not visited with them for a while." Brigid cocked her head to one side. I sighed, "And my daughter has dreamed of danger to the north."

My wife began kneading again but this time it was to channel her anger into the dough. The bread would be good! Elfrida said, "It will be safe, Jarl, will it not? Ragnar..."

"Ragnar will be with me and we will not cross the river. I go to use the eyes of those who watch the north. We will not even take mail. I promise that no harm will come to either of them." Satisfied she nodded. "But they would both be warriors and there will come a time when they will be in danger. I will not lie to you." That showed my nature. A Norseman would never have explained his actions.

Brigid slammed the dough down so hard that a cloud of flour rose like fog. "But they are boys!"

"They are Vikings and Viking boys become warriors."

Brigid did not agree with that but she had chosen to live amongst us and had to accept our life. I could see that she was angry. A man might vent his anger in words but Brigid would keep it within. The only sign that she was upset was the punishment she dealt the dough. I left them. They would talk about my words when I had gone. I had no doubt they would be critical of me but they would accept my words for I was Jarl Dragonheart. When Haaken returned with the boys I knew that he was already bored with life on the farm. His month had been enough. We found Olaf and Snorri and went to the Water. It was a pleasant morning and we could sit beneath the shade of the trees and watch the deep waters of Cyninges-tūn as we spoke.

I told them of my dream and the words of Aiden and Kara. "So we will see what Ketil and Ulf know. Snorri, I would have you slip north and see if the men of Strathclyde prepare for war. If the dream is false then we will soon know for they will tend their fields and not gather for war. I will ask Raibeart to travel north to Ljoðhús and speak with Thorfinn. I will visit him tomorrow. We will leave the day after."

Olaf was whetting his seax on a stone, "We should have Karl One Hand begin to train more warriors. The last battles cost us dear. I know we might only face Scots but they are like fleas on a dog. They keep coming when all hope is gone."

"You are right. I will ask Ketil to send us men from Windar's Mere. With Elfridaby abandoned they need to do more of the fighting."

We rode down to Úlfarrston early the next morning. Raibeart Ap Pasgen was not Norse but he had the heart of a Norseman. He was a fine seaman and captained *'Red Snake'* when we went to war. He also took my knarr, *'Weregeld'* to trade and to spy for us. He was with Erik Short Toe at the shipyard on the river. Erik had lost an eye in the recent wars and his son, two fingers. It did not diminish their desire to serve me.

"What brings you here Jarl Dragonheart? Do you wish me to prepare *'Heart of the Dragon'* for sea?"

"Not yet Erik but that day may come soon enough. My daughter has dreamed and there may be danger from the men of Strathclyde." They both nodded. "Raibeart, I would have you sail north and visit old Thorfinn. He normally knows what the Scots are up to. We also need seal oil. Go trade with him and use your nose to sniff out danger."

"I will Jarl. When should I sail?"

"When the knarr is ready."

"She is ready now. We have goods here. I was going to sail to Dyflin but Ljoðhús will do just as well."

"Good. I will travel on the morrow up to the Eden and the Esk. We will see what Snorri can sniff out." I turned to Erik who wore a black patch over his damaged orb. "How is the eye?"

"I am used to it now but my wife still finds it difficult to look at. I have taken to wearing this patch. I told her that Haaken lost his eye when he was much younger and people do not even notice now. I can still steer, even with one eye!"

As we headed back north Gruffyd asked me about the wounds men suffered and said, "You have no wounds, father."

"I have but you cannot see them. My knee ached when I came down from the mountain. I have been stabbed and cut many times. My skull has been cracked more times than enough. It is the lot of a warrior. A Viking fights even though he is hurt. It marks us different from many warriors. Your body becomes harder. Scars on a warrior's body are a measure of his survival. The Allfather sets us challenges and we must meet them."

We reached the lake and saw the fishing boats dotted around. There was plenty of room and those who took the fish had their own favourite places to gather them. As we were not at war many of the fishermen were my warriors. Like me, they took the opportunity of spending time with their children. These were precious times and were not to be wasted.

"We will not need mail for this journey tomorrow but bring your shields. You should get used to carrying them. And watch Snorri. He has skills which you can learn. They are as valuable as the lessons with the sword which Karl One Hand gives to you."

"Our bows too?"

"Bring your bows and the hunting arrows. We may find some game and that, too, is good practice for a warrior." Everything we did with the young was to prepare them for war. They played roughly and had many a bloodied nose to show for it. They worked hard and that built bodies into oaken flesh and they made bonds and friendships which translated into a shield wall and an oar on a drekar.

We left at dawn for we had far to go. We stopped at the Rye Dale to speak with Audun Thin Hair. His crops would keep us through the winter. We used his rye to make the bread which, along with the fish, was often our only food in winter. He commented on the peace we were enjoying. That was good for it meant there were no strangers in my land. He lived close to the pass which led to Windar's Mere and Cyninges-tūn. We headed, first, for the stad on the Eden. It had been attacked many times and Ulf Olafsson had improved its defences. Ulf Olafsson had been Ulfheonar and chosen to live here on the northern border. With Audun, the Builder the two of them had a warband that was more than capable of defending the walls of their home. We reined in on the Roman Road to look down at the walls of his stronghold. Formerly we had used the old Roman Fort but, over the years, it had fallen into disrepair. We were not masons and so Audun and Ulf had built a stronghold of earth and wood surrounded by water diverted from the Eden. The former fort lay in ruins.

Olaf cast a critical eye over it. With his mighty war axe, Olaf knew how to breach the defences of such places. "Ulf and Arne have done well. That ditch has water in it. I am guessing that they have put stakes at the bottom. That double earth bank upon which the wood has been planted is a good idea. It gives them a fine fighting platform. If we had less stone at Cyninges-tūn then we could build one too. I might have made the walls higher and put towers at the gates but it is strong enough."

Haaken laughed, "If you were attacking it, Olaf Leather Neck, then I might worry but the barbarians who come from the north do not come mailed. Ulf and Arne can defend it easily enough."

We were spied from a distance and recognised. We rode over the bridge and dismounted to walk our horses under the earth walls into the heart of the stronghold. My visits were rare and warriors came out to speak with me. Those who chose to live here were amongst the bravest of my warriors for they faced enemies from the north and the west. I had fought alongside many of them. Arne and Ulf strode over to us.

"Welcome, Jarl Dragonheart. What brings you from your home?" Ulf was Jarl; it was his right to ask such questions.

"I thought to show my son and grandson the extent of the land of the Wolf and I was anxious to see the stronghold now that you have finished."

"We have not quite finished, Jarl. We have two towers to build over the main gate. We have a guard house there at the moment." I saw Olaf nodding. "Come we will show you." He waved over a thrall, "Feed and water these horses for the Jarl."

It was Ulf who showed us the defences even though Arne had had the task of building them. "We used the slaves we captured to dig out the ditch and to make the earth ramparts. We wanted a large and flat fighting platform. The double bank means that if an enemy managed to scale the lower wall they would have a second one to climb and there would be but a narrow walkway for them to use. I know there are some who would think we could have made our walls higher but we were limited by the size of the trees."

Haaken said, "We have taller trees by Cyninges-tūn."

"I know but it would have added time to the building and we were keen to have it finished sooner, rather than later."

The hairs on the back of my neck stood up. "Why was that?"

"We have seen signs of enemies. There have been scouts around our land. A boat came from Hibernia. It was not our brethren but some of the clan mac Murchad. We know them. When we sent horsemen to watch them out they fled. Then our men found scouts who crossed from the Esk. They were the men of Strathclyde. We slew some of them but others escaped."

"When was this?"

"A moon or two back. We have kept a close watch." Ulf was watching my face. "Speak what is on your mind, Jarl Dragonheart, for I can see that this is not news to you and this visit is more than a courtesy."

"There has been a dream and the spirits warned us of an attack from the north."

"This visit was not just to show your son and grandson my home then?"

"No, your words have confirmed my fears but you have done well with the stronghold. I came here for confirmation and you have given it to me. Snorri will sniff out the intentions of our neighbours."

"If an enemy comes, Jarl, then they would find it hard to breach our walls but there are many who live in remote farms. Some are even north of the Esk. Loc and his family have a farm at Loc-hard's by. If the men of Strathclyde came they could destroy many of our farms and take our animals."

Olaf said, "They chose to live there."

Ulf said, "But I am Jarl and my hersir deserve my protection."

I sensed an argument and I put an end to it quickly. "You are both right but there is an answer to this. We bring warriors here and keep a good watch north of the rivers. Snorri will ride forth tonight and scout out the enemy. Perhaps the killing of their scouts has deterred them. It has been some time."

Ulf shook his head, "The delay was understandable. When they came to scout our sheep had not lambed. Now they have lambed and the cattle calved. That is what they will come for. They covet our animals."

I nodded, "And that is why Loc is safe for he does not have animals."

"That is right, Jarl. You know the land well there. He grows crops and when they are harvested he will become the target. They can ignore the farms north of the river. It is my belief that they allow them to prosper to harvest them at their leisure and to dull our guard."

"Then we shall show them the error of their ways. Tomorrow I will ride to Ketil and Snorri will scout. It seems the spirits are watching over us still."

My two leaders were keen to show their hospitality and laid on a feast for us. It was a measure of the richness of the land that we ate and drank so well. The rivers and waters here produced a beer that tasted different from ours. We enjoyed it. Snorri left before dawn and Ulf himself led some of his men to venture north of the river and visit the isolated farms. As we rode Ragnar pointed out landmarks he remembered. He had been with me when we had gone with Ketil to make the peace with King Eanred. I was impressed that he had remembered so much.

Ketil still lived close to the Roman Fort we had first rebuilt many years ago. Like Arne, however, he had added wooden walls and ditches to accommodate his halls. He and his men used horses far more than any other of my warriors. Like Ulf, he had signal towers that warned him of our arrival.

"Jarl Dragonheart, an unexpected visit. Is there trouble?"

"I am not certain. There was a dream which warned of an attack from the north and Ulf has had his lands scouted. How about you?"

"Our border with Northumbria is secure. King Eanred has kept his word and we have kept ours but I too have had to keep men watching the border with Strathclyde. There has been no major attack but we have seen evidence of the Scots close to our land." He led me into his hall.

"Then we must plan our response. Do your people have crops to harvest?"

"There are a few but here we raise animals. That is the danger. I worry that the Scots will raid and rustle them."

"Then I would fetch them down from the high pastures early. I intend to bring my men north ready to respond to any invasion. With you and Ulf on a war footing, we should be able to send these men back to their homes and wary of attacking us in the future."

"We will do as you suggest. It would help if we knew what they were up to."

"I have sent Snorri north. He will ferret out where they hide and their plans."

Seara his wife had managed to organise food and ale quickly and we were welcomed as though royalty. We were accommodated in the old stone buildings the Romans had built.

I planned on spending two days with Ketil. We rode out the next day with six of his warriors. We rode north and east. We would be heading towards the land which bordered King Eanred's land and that of the Scots. The land over which we travelled was bleak in places. Great high bare mountains were devoid of anything save the most hardy of animals. The tracks which crossed them were tortuous. We stopped at Aldeneby. It was high and it was remote. It was in the land of Northumbria. Ketil was known and respected well enough that they allowed us inside their palisade.

It was Ketil who spoke with the headman, "Have you had any animals taken or seen strangers, Alden son of Athelstan?"

The headman nodded, "Aye, lord; ten days since one of the shepherd boys was found with his throat cut and his dog killed. They took a small flock of sheep belonging to my son, Aed."

Ketil could not help his honesty. I admired that trait in him. He asked the hard and uncomfortable questions."Did you think it was us?"

Alden stared back and then shook his head. "No, Jarl. We knew it was not you. The tracks led north. We wondered if it might be those men who live on the Eden."

I spoke, "I am Jarl Dragonheart and those men on the Eden are mine and they have orders to keep the peace. I fear it is the men of Strathclyde."

His face fell, "May God save us from those wild blue men. Are you certain, lord?"

"If it is not us then it can only be the men of Strathclyde, especially if the tracks led west. Do not worry, we will deal with them."

We turned and headed due west to bring us along the valley of the Eden. The path twisted down through stumpy trees clinging to the high stone. Lower down, the fertile valley was filled with trees. It would be a longer journey back to Ketil's home but a more pleasant ride for we would be out of the wind. Had we had Snorri with us we would not have been surprised but Ketil and his scouts were so preoccupied with the idea of Scots in the valley that Beorn son of Eriksson was hewn from his saddle by an enormous Scot before we knew there was an ambush.

"Ambush! Ragnar, Gruffyd, behind me!" I had no shield with me but I did have my sword. I drew Ragnar's Spirit and kicked my horse in the ribs. "At them!" Haaken and Olaf rode by my side.

The barbarians were in the trees and they burst forth with their curved swords. We were not used to fighting from horseback but we had to get to grips with them quickly or they would soon gain the upper hand. As the Scot raised his sword to decapitate Beorn son of Eriksson I galloped at him and swung my sword at head height. He had no mail and my sword bit into his neck. However, he was like a rock and I was knocked from my horse by the blow. I rolled and quickly got to my feet looking for the next barbarian. I held my sword in two hands while looking for danger.

Two warriors ran from the trees towards me. Instead of waiting for them to strike the first blow, I ran at them. I pulled my sword back and then swung it across me as I approached them. I ducked as the one on my left tried to take my head. I did not look at the weapon but at the warrior on my right. I felt the sword waft over my head as my own bit into the side of the warrior on my right. His own sword was in mid-air, scything towards me. I pulled back on my sword and it sawed through his flesh, grating on his ribs. I then spun to my right. The move caught the other unawares. His own sword struck the air where he thought I would have been. Ragnar's Spirit hit him in the back. Mail would have been better protection than tattoos. My sword shattered his spine.

"Father! Behind you!" Gruffyd's urgent voice was a timely warning of danger.

I instinctively dropped to my knee and thrust my own sword, blindly, point first at whoever was attacking me. The axe flew harmlessly over my head and my sword found flesh and then bone. I pulled and turned. My sword had struck the warrior in the thigh. Bright blood spurted. It was a mortal wound. I made sure of his death by taking his head. Another jumped from above me. He had been in a tree. I sensed him and moved out of the way. I slashed at him with my sword and its edge rasped against his ribs. I smacked the flat of my sword against his head and he fell unconscious.

Haaken and Olaf were magnificent. They had leapt from their horses and, although without mail, thrown themselves at the wild men from north of the Esk. In a whirl of swords and axes, their weapons found flesh and warriors who were not as well trained or as experienced as my Ulfheonar. The ground around them was littered with body parts and dead barbarians. I looked around for more enemies. There were none who were alive save the last one I had struck whose life pumped away on the rich grass beneath the trees. I saw that Beorn had not been the only loss. The man who had tried to take my head with an axe had slain

Thrand the Merciless. Ketil had lost two men. We had proved that the dream was true but at a cost.

Chapter 2

Ketil was angry at the loss of his two men but I think part of that anger was that it could have been avoided. The leader of his hearth-weru, Oleg Strong Arm, was angry with Beorn Eriksson for he had been the scout and should have seen the enemy. On the way back he and Bergil Sharp Eye rode ahead and made sure we were safe.

Ketil said little until we were safe within his walls. He had been responsible for protecting us. If it had not been for Haaken, Olaf and myself the result might have been tragically different. "I thought my land was safe because of the peace with the Saxons. I have learned a harsh lesson. We must return to the days when we were vigilant and wary."

"It is the same at Cyninges-tūn. Now that we no longer hold Elfridaby our defence from the south and east are the fly-filled forests of Grize's Dale." He nodded and I turned to Gruffyd, "Thank you for the shout. You did well but I fear I have realised that you are not ready to ride to war." I looked at Ragnar, "If aught had happened to you how could I have faced your mother?"

"And yet, grandfather, one day we will go to war and we might not return."

"But then you will be ready. When you can defeat Karl One Hand in single combat then you may go A-Viking."

Gruffyd burst out, "He has but one good leg! It will be easy."

Ketil laughed, "One-legged or not he was Ulfheonar. I think Jarl Dragonheart has given you a fair test."

"And besides," I added, ominously, "war is likely to come to our home sooner rather than later. You may find yourself defending our home."

Ketil said, "Perhaps not, Jarl. When last I met with Prince Aethelred he told me that since our peace he and his father had managed to reclaim Eoforwic from the Danes who were gaining power. He has appointed a strong Eorl and it is now a well-garrisoned burgh. He told me that many of those who lived there have left for the land of the East Angles. There they fight as hired swords against Mercia. There should be no threat from the east. Your dream of danger from the north seems to present the greater threat."

"Danes are like that. They will go to the land of the Angles for they smell weakness. They are like the carrion circling a dying stag. Mercia, since the death of Coenwulf, has been weakening. They go to enjoy the spoils."

"But that helps us, does it not, grandfather?"

"It does until Wessex swallows Mercia. Even though your father is dead King Egbert hates us for your mother was his wife once. He has not forgotten that. The threat from the east may be diminished but the danger from Saxons is ever-present."

We left the next morning for the stad on the Eden. Ketil wished to send warriors with us as an escort but I refused. "You need to begin the weapon muster. I need your people protecting but I also need a warband. I will send a rider to you when I need them. We will meet at Pyrlweall. The village there is sheltered and hidden from the north."

"You have a plan, Jarl?"

"I have the beginnings of one but it will depend upon the news and information which Snorri brings."

"Farewell Jarl. We will be there."

"One last thing, send to you brother, Harland, at Windar's Mere. Without leaving your land there undefended we need some of his warriors too. It is time they shouldered the defence of this land. He and Arne Thorirson need to improve the defences of their stad."

"Aye, Jarl. I will visit him myself."

There was no sign of Snorri when we reached the stad on the Eden but I saw the evidence of work by Audun and Ulf. When I had left there had been a couple of sections of the upper ramparts which had had no wooden palisade. It was now complete. As I walked the ramparts I said, "This is a stronghold which will be hard to take."

"But for one thing, Jarl, the walls are extensive and if we are to man it completely then we have no reserves. An enemy could wear us down. We have men to man the walls but we do not have a large number of warriors here."

"It may not come to that."

"I hope that you are right, Jarl Dragonheart."

I had begun to worry that harm had come to Snorri for he had been away longer than I had expected. Then he arrived late one night appearing like a wraith from the dark. He looked tired and I waited until he had drunk beer and swallowed some bread before I questioned him.

"Your dream was accurate, Jarl. I travelled deep into their land. It is why I was away so long. I went north to Alt Clut. They are raising an army. Men from Hibernia are coming with hired swords. King Dumnagual is exhorting his warriors to take back the land that was rightfully theirs."

"Theirs?"

"He claims to be descended from King Ridderch of Alt Clut. They ruled this land after the Romans left."

"How did you discover this?"

"There was a gathering of warriors. It was like the Saxon wapentake. Their chiefs and their warriors were called together and they drank and had games of wrestling and feats of strength. I played a trader from Northumbria. I was able to get close to their camps. I also fell in with a merchant who travelled south. He told me much too."

"And did you discover when this King Dumnagual will launch his attack?"

"They were waiting, it seems, for some kinsmen to come from Hibernia. They are related to the clan mac Murchad. As the army travels on foot I cannot see them being ready until Tvímánuður."

"Hay time."

"Aye. His chiefs wanted their crops gathered before they went to war. They see our animals as treasure."

"Good, then my plan might just succeed. How many men will he have?"

"I cannot give an exact number for I know not how many will come from Hibernia but I would say he has over two hundred warriors already. They wear no mail and few have shields but they are wild. Some of the ones I saw have the limed hair of the Hibernians and they like to fight with bare chests. They think their inked bodies will protect them and they do not use war bows or arrows. They use hunting bows."

I turned to Arne. "You have time but get your people inside before they come. Even if you have to leave crops in the fields bring in your people. I will return."

Ulf nodded, "Aye Jarl. I see now that the ships and the scouts were part of the same danger. How do we defeat them?"

I had thought this through and I gave them the outline of my plan. It had still to be refined but for that, I needed Aiden and Kara. However, they knew my signals and they knew my mind. They were both satisfied. The ride south was faster than our leisurely journey north. Haaken and Olaf were full of our plans and strategies. They were thinking of the weapons and supplies we would need. They ran through the muster of men we would take. We were Ulfheonar and we led on the battlefield. Men might follow their hersir or their jarl but all were subservient to the Ulfheonar. Any one of them could have been a Jarl but they chose to stay with me.

I was acutely aware of the silence from my son and grandson. I could have ignored it but, as I had found to my cost, with my son Wolf Killer, that merely stored up problems. I dropped my horse back to ride between them. "Let us clear the air between us. You are both unhappy with my decision not to take you to war." They looked at each other. "If you cannot answer me now how will you have the voice to fight? Speak. I will not bite your head off."

Ragnar plucked up the courage to answer me, "Yes, Jarl Dragonheart, you are right. We are unhappy. You will be taking boys to war with you who are younger than we are."

"That is true and might be a good argument. The boys who will be coming to war and are younger than you will be using their slings and guarding the horses. You are both good with a sling?"

Ragnar said, "I have used one."

"And you Gruffyd, you would be happy cleaning the horses and ponies? Feeding them? Can you use a sling?"

He said nothing. Ragnar said, "We might not be able to use a sling well but we can use a sword."

"Against a warrior twice your size? It would be a slaughter." He said nothing. "Ah I see it, you wish me to have a warrior guarding you so that if you get into trouble he could save you. Perhaps two, one each?"

"We could fight at your side. We saved you from ambush."

"Aye, you did and my first thought was not for myself or my men but for you two. That cost one of Ketil's men his life. If you are on the battlefield my mind will be on you and not the battle. Is that what you wish? You want our clan to lose the battle?"

This time I allowed the silence to sit upon their shoulders all the way back to the pass leading to Cyninges-tūn. There it was broken by Ragnar. "You are right we would not be able to fend for ourselves yet upon the field of battle. I am sorry, grandfather. I was thinking of me and not the clan. We will train and become worthy of you so that you do not need to worry about us on the battlefield."

"And already you have grown for one day you two will be jarls and the clan will be in your hands. Then you think of them first and yourself last."

When I broke the news of my intended action to Brigid and Elfrida I had a mixed reaction. Both were pleased that their sons would be spared the war but Brigid wondered why I had to lead my men again.

"If I do not lead them then I do not deserve the title of Jarl. So long as I can lift a sword then I will lead my men to war."

"Then I hope some barbarian takes your hand. A stump and a husband is better than a corpse."

Her words shocked even Elfrida. I smiled and took my wife in my arms. "Aiden has not dreamed my death. I will live a while longer."

Shaking her head she returned to the servants brewing the ale. Elfrida said, "Thank you, Jarl. I know that Ragnar will go to war one day. I cannot stop that. He is his father's son; but not yet." She kissed me on the cheek.

"When he goes to war he will be ready as his father was. Wolf Killer would be alive today if it had not been for assassins. There was no warrior alive who could best him. We need to go to war to keep the folk in the north safe. Our land is shrinking and there comes a point where we say 'enough', This is that point."

We did not have long to prepare. I wanted to be close to the border a week before Tvímánuður. My warrior farmers harvested their crops early and brought their animals down to lower pastures. When we returned they would go to the higher meadows and harvest the hay. The animals would still be able to eat but we had to be ready to go to war. Bjorn Bagsecgson's smiths rang all day and into the night as he made spearheads, arrows and swords. There was not enough time for mail. Only my Ulfheonar had mail byrnies. Those who returned with treasure would, no doubt, have one made by Bjorn.

While this was going on Raibeart ap Pasgen arrived. "I bring news Jarl. Jarl Thorfinn Blue Scar is dead. His people were raided by the Scots and they were slaughtered. Some survived by hiding and we found them, half-starved. I brought them back with me. They are resting at our home. When they are fit to travel they will journey here."

"Does his son know?"

"The last his son heard his father was unwell. That was last year. The next time we sail close to Raven Wing Island we will tell him. He can do nothing about this."

"Thank you. So you did not trade?"

"We sailed further west and found more Vikings. We traded but they said that there is a king called Dumnagual who wishes to make Strathclyde a great kingdom once more. He has sworn to drive the Norse from his lands. He calls himself the Enemy of the Vikings. He has skulls of those he has killed adorning his hall at Alt Clut. The jarls of the northern isles are preparing for war."

"I thought he followed the White Christ."

"He excuses his practice by saying he is carrying out God's will and the heads are the heads of pagans."

"I thank you for your efforts. Tell Erik Short Toe that when we have met this King we will raid his lands."

"Good. My men yearn for action again."

Although they were not Norse the men whom Raibeart led had, like me, adopted the dress and values of the Viking. They sailed my drekar, *'Red Snake'* and were worthy warriors who followed my standard.

I sought out Karl One Hand. "I have two tasks for you. I need you to keep a good watch on our people. With no one at Elfridaby, there is danger from the south and east. I am leaving the older warriors with you."

He smiled, "But not you, Jarl, even though you have a grey beard now."

"No, Karl, not me. The second task is that I wish you to train my son and grandson to become warriors. I have told them that they cannot go to war until they have defeated you in single combat. Do not make it easy."

He laughed, "Trust me, Jarl I will not. Do you wish them to be fully trained? They will stand in a shield wall as did Ragnar's father. Just because they may lead the clan does not mean that they should have an easy time of it. They need to know how to use the slings too. They are fair archers but they have not used a spear."

He rubbed his hands, "Good and they can help to watch the walls. That is a good skill to learn but not one the young warriors relish."

The days passed far too quickly. We had too many men for us all to go to war mounted and so I would lead my Ulfheonar while Asbjorn the Strong led the rest of my men. Sigtrygg Thrandson would not be coming to war. I needed him to watch the south and east. He was the warning of danger from Mercia and Wessex. The day before we left men oiled their mail if they had it. They sharpened their swords and their spear heads. They added more studs to their shields and repainted their designs. Mine was the only one that could be recognised. It was the wolf. It marked me on the field of battle and that was as it should be. Many men made sacrifices to Odin for their safe return. As I was taking Aiden with me I did not need to make a blót. We would save that until just before the battle.

The only tears shed as we left my hall were shed by my wife. All the rest of the women accepted that they were married to a warrior. They knew that if their men died they would go to Valhalla and that the rest of the clan would care for them. Brigid was a follower of the White Christ. She thought that if I died in battle I would not go to heaven and she would never see me again. I leaned down to kiss her, "I will return. I promise!"

We headed for Windar's Mere to pick up the warriors waiting there with Harland Windarsson and Arne Thorirson the hersir. Harland would not be coming to war. Like his father and unlike his brother he was no warrior but he and Arne ran the village well and they were prosperous.

"Jarl, will this battle end the danger for us?"

"No, Harland. I fear that your people will have to endure more of this. Look to your defences! See what Audun the Builder has done at the stad on the Eden and make sure that every man and boy can fight!"

"Aye Jarl Dragonheart." His voice suggested that he would procrastinate. That had ever been his father's way. When time allowed I would have to make sure he obeyed my commands.

Ketil and his men were already at Pyrlweall. We headed west to wait close by the old Roman fort. We travelled without too much talk. I think he was still brooding. I knew that he felt bad about the ambush and was keen to make up for his mistakes. Oleg Strong Arm made sure that his scouts kept a good watch this time. We were between the Irthing River and the Roman Wall. We would just be eighteen miles from Arne and his stad. He would be the bait. That night we set sentries and lit fires. We were in a valley and there was little chance of being seen. We had well over a hundred and thirty warriors. With the boys who would watch the ponies and horses and use slingshots, it was nearer a hundred and fifty. We would still be outnumbered. Snorri and Beorn the Scout had left us at Pyrlweall. They would be our eyes and ears. We would wait, in our valley, for their news.

I went through my plan with my jarls and hersir. My men cooked our food over open fires and we drank sparingly of the beer we had brought with us. As we sat around the fire we spoke of those warriors who would be in Valhalla now: warriors like Sven Svensson. Bjorn Beornsson, Eystein the Rock, Cnut and, of course, my son Wolf Killer.

When we had spoken of them Olaf said, "Haaken One Eye, give us a song. Let us hear of the sword touched by the gods. Haaken stood and began to chant. We all joined in with the chorus. Cnut Cnutson looked particularly proud for we sang of his father.

The storm was wild and the gods did roam
The enemy closed on the Prince's home
Two warriors stood on a lonely tower
Watching, waiting for hour on hour.
The storm came hard and Odin spoke
With a lightning bolt the sword he smote
Ragnar's Spirit burned hot that night
It glowed, a beacon shiny and bright
The two they stood against the foe
They were alone, nowhere to go
They fought in blood on a darkened hill
Dragon Heart and Cnut will save us still
Dragon Heart, Cnut and the Ulfheonar
Dragon Heart, Cnut and the Ulfheonar
The storm was wild and the Gods did roam
The enemy closed on the Prince's home
Two warriors stood on a lonely tower
Watching, waiting for hour on hour.
The storm came hard and Odin spoke
With a lightning bolt the sword he smote
Ragnar's Spirit burned hot that night
It glowed, a beacon shiny and bright
The two they stood against the foe
They were alone, nowhere to go
They fought in blood on a darkened hill
Dragon Heart and Cnut will save us still
Dragon Heart, Cnut and the Ulfheonar
Dragon Heart, Cnut and the Ulfheonar
'Ulfheonar, warriors strong
Ulfheonar, warriors brave

Ulfheonar, fierce as the wolf
Ulfheonar, hides in plain sight
Ulfheonar, Dragon Heart's wolves
Ulfheonar, serving the sword
Ulfheonar, Dragon Heart's wolves

"This will not be as glorious a battle for we fight Scots and we all know that they are brave but wild and cannot be controlled!"

I shook my head, "Haaken, do not think that way. This king has gathered a large army. He has defeated Thorfinn Blue Scar. Do not think this will be easy for that invites disaster. Let us catch this game before we dine upon his flesh!" Thus chastened, Haaken sat down. "What we do not know is the exact time they will strike. We may be here for some days."

Olaf laughed, "I think it is the married men who might find that hard! Haaken One Eye will miss his wife's arms around him at night. He likes his soft bed."

Haaken sniffed, "I have earned it, Olaf Leather Neck, and the reason you are still without a wife is that no woman can bear your smell!"

Olaf nodded affably, "That may well be true. I had not thought of it." He lifted one cheek and let fly a loud fart. "On the other hand that may be the reason!"

The banter and humour told me that they were in good spirits. I went to the other side of the fire and sat with the last of my son's oathsworn, his boars. There were just six of them left after the last battle for his men had thrown themselves into the battle, keen to avenge their lord. "Einar I want you and your brothers here to fight for Ragnar tomorrow. He is not here but fight for his future."

Einar frowned, "I do not understand you, lord."

"When my son died his boars tried to avenge him by being reckless. Just six of you remain. If you are reckless against the Scots who will be there to fight for my grandson when he goes to war? Or perhaps I will find warriors to fight for Wolf Killer's son."

They looked at the ground. Einar the Tall said, "You are right, Jarl Dragonheart. We did wish to join Wolf Killer in Valhalla. We did not think what he would have wished. You are right. He would want us to protect his son. But he is not here, Jarl."

"No, he is not so when we fight you will survive. That way you can return to Cyninges-tūn with me and help to make him a warrior his father would be proud of. I would have you as the hearth-weru of my grandson in honour of his father."

They nodded, "We swear that we will."

"Good. When the battle comes and we fight, you six will guard Leif the Banner. I have no doubt that King Dumnagual will send his best warriors for me. The Ulfheonar can guard me if you guard the banner. That way my plan might succeed."

"We are honoured that you have chosen us for this task."

Aiden sat with me. "Well galdramenn, do you see anything I ought to know?"

"I have not dreamed anymore. But in my mind, I see a rider in silver on a white horse and he leads men in blue. The swarm around the stad like flies but I do not see the outcome. I saw ships but whose I knew not."

"Perhaps we may not need your magic. It is good that you are here though for your skill can save lives."

"Kara said that she would come."

I laughed, "My daughter is strong but I am glad she is at home. Cyninges-tūn needs her hand when I am abroad."

Two days later Beorn the Scout rode in not long after dawn. "Jarl Dragonheart, the Scots have crossed the river. They will be at the stad by noon at the latest."

I turned to the warband, "Now is the time, let us show these men of Strathclyde how a Viking can fight."

We rode the horses and ponies at the pace of a man walking. We were mailed and the ponies would ensure we reached the battle-ready to fight. We moved in a column. The Roman Road made it easier to make good time. Snorri would be waiting for us close to the ambush site. Ulf and his defenders would have to hold on until the Scots were totally committed to an attack. We would use the defences of the stad and the river to make a killing ground. We reached Snorri before noon. The boys took our horses away and we prepared for battle. Shields had their straps tightened. Helmets were secured and whetstones put an extra edge on our spears.

We headed through the woods which lay to the east of the stad. They ended less than five hundred paces from the wooden walls. Once in the eaves of the woods, I saw the massive warband as it hurled itself at the defences. Ulf had taken up the bridges across the ditch. Hidden in the black and brackish waters were sharpened stakes covered in animal dung.

A wounded warrior would not last long if he tried to cross it. The Scots had brought a few horses. I saw, from the torcs around their necks, that they were ridden by their chiefs and leaders. King Dumnagual was on a white horse and he wore mail which had been oiled and polished so that it looked like silver. I knew it was not. That would be a waste and would not be as good as iron. It told me much about the man. He was vain and patently not a warrior. A warrior wore mail and carried weapons that did the job. He did not wear mail merely because it looked good. This was the vision Aiden had seen.

I saw the king ride up and down shouting to his men. I could not hear his words but from what Snorri had told me I guessed he was extolling them to acts of valour against the pagan invaders. A priest behind him carried a standard upon a cross. He was making it a war of Christian against pagan. When he stopped he pointed his sword at the walls of the stad. His men sounded the horns and pipes they carried and a third of the warband raced towards the water-filled ditch. As they did so I was able to estimate the numbers of his army a little better. It was more than three hundred warriors we would be facing and fighting.

My galdramenn stood next to me. He too had observed their numbers and identified their type."He keeps his Hibernian mercenaries close by his standard. The ones he sends in now are the ones without skill and good weapons. He is clever. They are expendable and will find the strengths and weakness of the stad and then he will exploit it with his better warriors."

"Then let us hope that Ulf and Audun have made it hard for them. However, there seem to be but twenty or thirty Hibernians there. From what Snorri told me I expected more."

Aiden nodded, "I, too, would have expected more."

I turned to Snorri, "Were there more than thirty Hibernians at the wapentake?"

"Aye, jarl Dragonheart. There were at least a hundred."

"Then where are they?" I worried about the missing Hibernians but we had to deal with the attack before us.

Amazingly some of the warriors ran so fast that they were able to jump the ditch. I had not thought it possible but at least eight managed it. None had shields and carried just a short curved sword. Ulf's men waited until they had landed before they slew them with their arrows. The ones who fell into the water shouted and cursed as they were impaled on the hidden stakes. The slightly slower ones saw the fate of their comrades and looked for easier ways in. They held up their shields as they peered into the water. Their shields were not as big as ours and offered less protection. Then a chief began to berate them and he struck at them with the flat of his sword. They braved the water. Although we were some distance away I saw that they used the bodies of the dead as stepping stones. Some still fell to the arrows from Ulf and his men for the path was not stable.

There were so many men, however, that eventually, they had a toe hold on the lower bank. They had two ramparts to ascend and the wood had been made slippery with seal oil. The arrows, stones and javelins from the defenders began to take their toll. A horn sounded and the survivors made their way back across a ditch which now had many islands of bodies upon which they could clamber. It was as we had expected when I had discussed the plan with Ulf.

The King gathered his chiefs about him. I was tempted to change my plan and make an attack there and then. Aiden said quietly, "Your plan is a good one, Jarl. Hold to it and do not be impatient. We have lost no men yet and they are bleeding."

I nodded. I had forgotten that Aiden knew me as well as I knew myself and could read my thoughts. It was sometimes disconcerting. The King shouted and waved his arm. Horns sounded and a second wave moved forward. This time they approached more slowly behind a wall of shields and I saw that they had archers with them as well as slingers. Then the horn sounded three times. None of those on the battlefield reacted and I wondered what it meant.

Aiden said, "See, he does just as you predicted. Perhaps you are becoming galdramenn."

"No, but I know how to make war. It was predictable and see, he keeps his oathsworn and mercenaries close to him. He protects himself. He is not committing to the attack yet."

The slingers and archers of Strathclyde began to send their missiles at the defenders on the walls. Although they did little damage they forced Ulf and his men to shelter behind their shields. A fourth horn sounded from the men of Strathclyde and I heard a reply... from the north and west.

Just then Beorn the Scout shouted, "Jarl, I see the masts of ships beyond the stad. They are on the Eden."

Aiden shook his head, "I have been blind. The ships are Hibernians. This King Dumnagual is clever. He attacks both sides of the stad at once."

Chapter 3

The plans I had made would have to be changed. Ulf would have to shift some men from the wall facing the enemy to face the ships. The enemy would be able to find somewhere to scale the walls. I had counted on the enemy being committed to an attack on a well-defended wall before I launched my men. We would have to attack early. I turned, "Form line! Swine array!"

We stepped from the woods and my jarls and hersir led their men into their appointed positions. With the Ulfheonar in the centre, we were a line with small wedges protruding. It was an easier formation for moving and allowed my slingers and archers to tuck in behind the last rank and use their weapons to harass the enemy. Against men without armour, the lead balls and arrows could prove crucial.

"Leif, raise the banner!" Leif and Wolf Killer's oathsworn were behind the rear rank of Ulfheonar. As the banner rose my men cheered. I heard a horn from within the walls of the stad. Ulf had seen the banner and understood the signal. "March!"

As we marched we chanted,

'Ulfheonar, warriors strong
Ulfheonar, warriors brave
Ulfheonar, fierce as the wolf
Ulfheonar, hides in plain sight
Ulfheonar, Dragon Heart's wolves
Ulfheonar, serving the sword
Ulfheonar, Dragon Heart's wolves
Ulfheonar, serving the sword'
'Ulfheonar, warriors strong
Ulfheonar, warriors brave
Ulfheonar, fierce as the wolf
Ulfheonar, hides in plain sight
Ulfheonar, Dragon Heart's wolves
Ulfheonar, serving the sword
Ulfheonar, Dragon Heart's wolves

Ulfheonar, serving the sword'

The rhythm helped us to march and the words gave my men, all of them, purpose. Those who were not Ulfheonar felt honoured to be part of them, albeit briefly. As we headed across the level ground every warrior felt himself to be oathsworn with me. Some banged their spears on their shields and the loud, rhythmic cracks echoed and rippled before us. Our sudden appearance had upset the King of Strathclyde's plans just as the arrival of the Hibernian ships had upset mine. I had a plan to deal with such a surprise. Had King Dumnagual?

His men sounded their horns. The ones who had crossed the ditch and begun to ascend the lower walls stopped. Ulf and the ones who remained on the north wall took advantage of their inattention and they slew many before the men of Strathclyde began to filter back across the body-filled moat. King Dumnagual's men began to reorganize their lines to face the new threat that was us. To give them time to do so the Hibernians detached themselves from the rest and began to race towards us.

Aiden, who was at the rear, shouted, "Archers and slingers!"

There was no sudden flight of arrows. My archers knew their own range. My best archers loosed first and I saw one Hibernian struck in the shoulder. Even though he was bleeding heavily he ran on. They were hard to kill. Aiden told me that they took a draught that had something in it to numb the pain and induce euphoria. Certainly, the ones who charged us looked to be almost berserkers. More arrows flew and then stones and lead balls. The lack of helmets and armour meant that our missiles did serious damage when they struck. Even with the drug-induced numbness many received mortal wounds and fell. The ones who hurled themselves at us had already suffered wounds.

When they were ten paces from us I shouted, "Halt! Brace!" Our spears were held over our shields. Behind me, Olaf and Haaken's spears appeared above my shoulder and those of Rollo Thin Skin, Rolf Horse Killer and Finni the Dreamer poked too. With our left legs forward and braced we waited for the Hibernians to hit. They jumped high into the air to try to bring their weapons down on our heads. The wall of spears was their welcome. They were impaled upon them. This time no drug could save them and they died. We lowered our spears and shook them to shake the bodies to the ground. I stepped forward to slay one of them who wriggled still. Finni and Haaken did the same. They died. But the wild men of Hibernia had slowed us down and allowed King Dumnagual to organize his men into a defensive formation.

"March!"

The brave Hibernians had been sacrificed to give his men time to form their own battle lines and they were ready for us. We had slaughtered many already but the men of Strathclyde still outnumbered us. We approached their serried ranks. Their king had arrayed his men in three lines. This time most of the ones in the front rank had a shield. His oathsworn, however, his mailed men and his mounted men, were still in the rear rank. His second rank was made up of his poorer armed warriors. Another horn sounded and the men of Strathclyde came towards us. His Hibernians had done their job. They had died well.

As they came towards us they showed their lack of discipline. Unlike us they did not march in step nor were they tight together with locked shields. They came in a loose line and some eager warriors encouraged, no doubt, by our small numbers raced forward for glory. I saw three such men run at Ketil's wedge and hurl themselves piecemeal at him. They were easily slain but, more importantly, the gap they had created was filled by men who did not have a shield.

We were approaching rapidly and I had to time my next order well. When we were twenty paces from each other I yelled, "Charge!"

We were marching together and each wedge was fighting with brothers in arms. We moved as one. We did not run but moved quicker. I raised my arm to strike downwards with my spear. Our shields were held high to protect as much of our bodies and heads as possible. The enemy tried to match our charge but they were not as one. Some were ahead of others and there were gaps between them. Even though they outnumbered us we had more men to meet them in the front rank and we were all well-armed warriors. The chief who jabbed at me did so with an upward motion. His spear clanged off the side of my helmet. I struck down with my own spear and found flesh just below his shoulder and neck. Bright blood spurted and sprayed as he fell dead. We smashed through their front rank. Some of their men were struck by two spears.

I heard Aiden shout, "Archers and slingers, aim at their flanks!"

They outnumbered us and would be sweeping around Asbjorn the Strong's men on my right and the men of Cyninges-tūn led by Cnut Cnutson on my left. Those two bands would have to hold. My wedge was slicing through the men of Strathclyde as though they were not there. The men in the second rank had neither shields nor helmets. Our spears darted out and each blow found flesh. Our danger was in blunting our spears on bone and breaking the shafts. Our wedge was also a little out of shape. Olaf and Haaken were almost on my shoulders now. Finni the Dreamer was close too. Still, we powered through them. The danger for the ones behind was tripping over the bodies which lay strewn over the ground.

I was about to order a halt so that we could reform when a horn sounded three times and the men before us, turned and fled. I was too wary and wise to risk just hurtling after them. The King of Strathclyde still had a hundred men who had not fought with him and half of them were mailed.

"Halt! Reform!"

I heard Olaf say, "Change sides with me, Haaken One Eye. My spear is broken. It is time for Odin's Daughter to be unleashed!"

Odin's Daughter was his war axe. Standing to the left of Haaken he could not swing his weapon. Rolf Horse Killer shouted, "Rollo, change places with me too. Let the Horse Killer join the Daughter and give these barbarians a reason to curse us." The two men with axes would give us a deadly edge to our right side.

Olaf laughed, "Aye they might fight with an arrow or two in them but when they are cleft in twain they cannot!"

"Ready!"

As one, my clan shouted, "Aye Jarl Dragonheart!" It was so loud that it must have carried to the stad.

"Then march!"

'Ulfheonar, warriors strong
Ulfheonar, warriors brave
Ulfheonar, fierce as the wolf
Ulfheonar, hides in plain sight
Ulfheonar, Dragon Heart's wolves
Ulfheonar, serving the sword
Ulfheonar, Dragon Heart's wolves
Ulfheonar, serving the sword'
'Ulfheonar, warriors strong
Ulfheonar, warriors brave
Ulfheonar, fierce as the wolf
Ulfheonar, hides in plain sight
Ulfheonar, Dragon Heart's wolves
Ulfheonar, serving the sword
Ulfheonar, Dragon Heart's wolves
Ulfheonar, serving the sword'

Their voices were even louder as we headed towards the enemy. King Dumnagual had deepened and narrowed his lines. He had put half of his mailed warriors in a block in his centre and his whole army was now four ranks deep. This time we would be facing mailed men. They had learned their lesson and were now tightly locked together to mirror us. If the king thought we were evenly matched he was sadly mistaken. My Ulfheonar were better than any oathsworn and the weapons we used were superior. As we closed with them I saw that their shields were smaller and their byrnies did not cover their arms. They only went to their waists. They looked to me like the type the Roman legionaries had used but were not as well made. Their spear heads were broader and shorter. Ours tapered to a point that allowed them to slip into the mail easily. Such small differences could affect a combat.

They waited for us this time. The men of Strathclyde had run, raced and charged at least three times and retreated three times too. They were tiring. We had also charged once. We had one more charge left in us. As my men chanted, ' *Ulfheonar, serving the sword'*, I yelled, "Charge!" And we ran the last ten paces into their line.

As I had expected the four warriors before me all aimed their spears at me. My shield was held high. Two struck my shield and one my helmet. Only one managed to hit my mail. It glanced off the rim of my shield and scored a line along my mail. I stabbed into the screaming open mouth of one of King Dumnagual's oathsworn. At the same time, Olaf's axe hacked below the smaller shield of the next warrior to hack through his leg. He fell to the ground pumping his life away. Haaken's spear found flesh too. The last of the four was bowled over by the weight of our wedge and I heard his scream as Rollo Thin Skin speared him on the ground. I thrust my spear downwards towards the warrior behind. He had been taken by surprise at the sudden disappearance of the ones before him. My spear struck his mail high on his shoulder. He twisted as he fell and his sword hacked through my spear haft as he succumbed to his wound.

I stamped on his neck, breaking it, as I drew my sword. I yelled, "Ragnar's Spirit!" My helmet meant I could only look ahead but I swear I felt our whole line surge like a wave below my drekar as I gave my war cry. I blocked a spear with my shield and smashed my sword at the next warrior's head. He brought up his shield but it merely slowed down my sword. It bit into his mail and the blade that was touched by the gods severed links in his poorly made armour. A spear was thrust hard into my shield. Finni the Dreamer and Erik Ulfsson had their shields in my back and the head embedded itself into the wood as the three of us formed a solid block. I twisted my shield and, as the head sheared stabbed the warrior in his unprotected middle. I pulled my shield higher and punched at the next warrior who advanced towards me. He had no shield and the broken wooden haft of the spear rammed into his eye and skull. He fell instantly at my feet.

We now had momentum. The mailed warriors had slowed us up but their uncoordinated and disjointed attack had been doomed to failure from the outset. Now we had men with no mail. Even when their blows penetrated our defences our mail held. I had no doubt that, along the flanks, the many warriors in our clan who did not have mail would be suffering but our shields were better and we all had helmets. The arrow that was my wedge was driving deep into the heart of the enemy. I saw just twenty paces from me, the bodyguards of the King. I stared up at him, on his white horse with his falsely silvered mail.

I yelled to him, "Come and fight me!" I raised my sword as I did so and my men let out a roar. I do not think he understood my words but he understood the meaning and he said something to his standard-bearer and the warrior with the horn. It sounded four times and the banner was waved. He and his bodyguard turned and fled the field. He had decided that he would live to fight another day. His attack had failed. It was like a dam being breached. At first, it was a trickle and then a flood as his men realised they had been abandoned and they ran. Had we been mounted we could have pursued them. Cnut Cnutson led my men from Cyninges-tūn to pursue and slay those who had been tardy. They were not encumbered by mail and could run faster than we did. Ketil and his men followed. Asbjorn and his wedge wandered the field slaying those who lived.

I stood amidst my Ulfheonar. We had had the hardest fight and we had survived. There were now less than fifteen of us but we banged our shields and chanted, "Ulfheonar," over and over. As we finished Haaken One Eye began to howl like a wolf and we all joined in. It was eerie and somehow disquieting in the bright sunlit meadow but it felt good to be a pack and to join together in this celebration of victory and life.

Aiden, leading the boys and archers, arrived with the horses and ponies. "Aiden, take the archers into the stad. Ulf may need their help. Leif, take my banner there. Einar the Tall, join Ulf on the walls. Tell him we will follow 'ere long."

Asbjorn joined me. "They are wild men, Jarl."

"Did we lose many?"

"A few have wounds which will need Aiden's skill and six of mine went to Valhalla. I saw four of Cnut's men fail to rise but Ketil lost ten of his men."

I nodded, "He had the largest band. He led his own and the men from Windar's Mere." I pointed north. "He will exact his revenge. Fetch any treasure from the field and join me as quickly as you can in the stad. I fear that Ulf and his men will have need of us."

"Aye Jarl." He pointed, "Some of the men are some distance away. It will take time." He picked up a sword and bent it. "The weapons are poor but these barbarians like their torcs and their warrior bands."

"Come, Ulfheonar. Our work is not yet done."

The gates were opened for us as we approached. Ulf's men had put the bridge back over the ditch. It would need clearing of bodies and it would have to be done sooner rather than later. We would not want it to become pestilential.

Lars Siggison, one of the slingers, was waiting for us inside the gate, "Jarl, the galdramenn said you are needed on the walls."

"Come. We must hurry." We ascended the ladder to our left and ran around the upper rampart. On the opposite side, I saw that Einar the Tall had led his men to help Ulf on that side. It was our side, the west where the danger lay. I could see that the Hibernians had gained a foothold on the ramparts and a knot of men were hard-pressed. Beyond I could now see that they had landed in four of their tubby ships. Rollo Thin Skin and Rolf Horse Killer were the youngest of my warriors and they raced ahead. Snorri and Beorn were almost as fit as they were and they hurried after them. Both had their Saami bows.

Haaken chuckled, "We are getting too old for all this running. I prefer standing and letting our enemies come to us!"

Finni the Dreamer was with us too and he laughed, "Ulfheonar never get old! That is for ordinary warriors!"

Rollo and Rolf charged into the backs of the warriors who had claimed a foothold. Snorri and Beorn began loosing their arrows from a ridiculously close range. Their bows were so powerful that one of Snorri's arrows went through two men. I drew my sword and laid open the back of a warrior wearing leather breeks and with his limed hair raised into a point to resemble a helmet. Even though he was mortally wounded he still turned, like a wounded animal and tried to skewer me. I brought my sword backhand to take his head.

A head appeared over the wall from behind me and a wild warrior leapt to stab me in the back. Finni the Dreamer shouted, "No you don't. He swung the sword two handed and sliced through the man's body to almost sever him. The bloody corpse tumbled to the Hibernians below.

Olaf and his axe, racing ahead of us, did the most damage. His huge swings struck three men in succession. Although not all killed outright they were soon finished off by the defenders who eagerly fell on them. As the last of those who had made the ramparts died, I shouted, "Spread out and stop them ascending." We had stopped the flood and now we had to close the breach.

Ulf was a hundred paces from me and he raised his sword in acknowledgement. To his right stood Einar the Tall. We now had much better warriors ready to defend against the next attack. I saw how they had crossed the ditch. The ships which had scouted the land must have seen the ditch and they had brought rush mats that they had laid across. The stakes and spikes beneath the water had actually supported the mats. It explained their initial success. Below me, on the walkway between the two ramparts, I saw many bodies. Ulf and his men had done well.

It was not, however, over yet. They still had plenty of men on their ships and the mats were still in place. "Snorri, Beorn, organize the archers. I want their steering boards clearing of men." Although the range was two hundred paces or more we were elevated and my men had good bows. If we could kill those steering the ships then it might deter the others.

Some of the men we had slain had spears and javelins. I picked one up. The range to the ditch was too great for the spear and I waited. The next wave of attackers crossed the dead ground and then began to ascend the palisade. I waited until one was pulling himself over the top before I threw the spear. It entered his shoulder, close to his neck and then embedded itself in the wooden palisade. I picked up another and prepared to throw at the next man who tried to breach our first line of defence. When they came they did so together. They had no mail and were all fit young warriors who were both lithe and strong. Twenty of them suddenly clambered over the top. I threw my second spear and caught one in the leg and then they were at the palisade below our feet. I took a third and jabbed down with it. The Hibernian I struck had quick hands and he grabbed the shaft of the spear. Luckily I had the presence of mind to let go and draw my sword.

Until Asbjorn joined us we would be outnumbered. The man who had taken my spear held it up for protection as he started to pull himself up the wooden wall. I knocked the head away and then sliced down to sever his hand in two. He fell backwards and knocked another warrior back down to the ditch. I heard a cheer from my right and risked a glance. Asbjorn had joined us and led his men to help Einar the Tall sweep the enemy from their rampart.

Haaken said, "The arrows have done it, Jarl. See, one of the ships is drifting out of control. The crew is dead and it is a ship of ghosts."

Snorri and Beorn's marksmanship had paid off. A horn sounded from one of the other ships and the survivors fled back to their vessels. We had beaten off the attack. I took off my helmet and sheathed my sword. I walked along the fighting platform towards Ulf. I saw that he and his men had paid a price. Many of his warriors had been killed and in greater numbers than I had anticipated. The sudden attack from the sea had caught us out and almost undone my carefully laid plans.

"I am sorry we did not get here in time, Ulf. My plan went awry."

Before he could answer Haaken said, "No, Jarl, it did not. Nor was it the Norns. Their king was more cunning than we thought. He will not catch you out again so easily."

"You are right he will not. I will make sure that he does not wrest the initiative back from us. We will visit him back in his homeland and these men from across the sea. When their homes are burned ruins they will realise the futility of attacking us in the land of the Wolf.

It was almost dark when Ketil reached us. He and his men had pursued the enemy to the Esk. They had even captured some horsemen's mounts and they brought them back with them laden with mail and treasure taken from the dead. We left the enemy dead until the next day but our own were buried together beneath a turf mound with their weapons. We buried them beside the gates. The men would be remembered each time we entered or left our stad on the Eden. Then we slammed them shut and set a good watch. There might be individual survivors. We would not be caught unawares. We butchered the dead animals and ate those at a feast held in Ulf's hall.

Stories were told of individual bravery and great deeds done by the different war bands. Those who had died were remembered. I sat with my Ulfheonar and Ulf, who had been Ulfheonar. "They nearly caught us out this day, Ulf."

"Aye. Now I know why those ships came to spy out the land. How can we defeat them if they use mats, Jarl?"

Aiden answered for me. "That is simple. Enlarge the ditch so that it is part of the river. If you dig a couple of channels then, eventually, nature will do the job for you. It will also mean they cannot land their ships as closely as they did."

"And you need sharpened stakes for your walls. They will be harder to scale and if they fall from the higher rampart there is a good chance that they will impale themselves."

Snorri downed his beer, "But most of all you need archers, Ulf. The high walls aid you. If every warrior had used a bow then no one would have come close to the second fighting platform."

He shook his head, "There is much to learn when you are the Jarl."

Aiden spoke of the wild warriors from the west we had fought for he had studied the writings of the Romans and, indeed, had been born on the island of the Hibernians. "The clan is the Ulaid. They were once far more important than they have become. The Uí Néill leaders have taken much of their power. Their stronghold is Dún Lethglaise. It is close to the coast in the northeastern part of their land. I spoke with one of the wounded Hibernians before he was sent to the Otherworld. He said their chief was Donnachada mac Fiachnae. He did not come on the raid. He is an old chief. His son was slain today. He led the charge against you Jarl."

I nodded, "And King Dumnagual still has his stronghold at Alt Clut?"

"He does but we could not take that stronghold. Remember, Jarl, it is carved from rock."

"I remember, and it guards his river and his ships. Well, I have seen his ships and I know that ours are better and our warriors superior. The ones which fled today will be in that river and we shall sink them! He will pay a price for this attack."

The next day we collected the bodies of the enemy. The animals and birds had been at them and they had begun to stink. We made a pyre and set them alight. There were so many that the fire burned all day.

As we watched it burn I spoke to my jarls. "We will return to Cyninges-tūn and I will lead my ships against Alt Clut and Dún Lethglaise. If that does not deter this king then we shall ask our friends from Dyflin and Raven Wing Island to aid us in a great raid."

They nodded their agreement.

"Ulf I wish you to improve your defences. Your people suffered much. Ketil you lost many warriors. I will take just those from Windar's mere. They did well today."

"Aye Jarl and we now have more mail taken from the hearth-weru of the King of Strathclyde."

As I mounted my horse I said, "I urge you both to be vigilant. As we have seen we have enemies who are cunning and seek to make their thrones greater. They wish to remove us from this land. Have your scouts seek out strangers and let me know what you find. Ketil, have conference with Prince Athelstan. I deemed him honest and he may have more knowledge that could be useful to us. If we are allies then we should use that alliance."

"Aye Jarl."

And so we headed home, richer in treasure but poorer by warriors who would not be coming back to their hearths. The women who had said farewell to husbands and sons would now weep when we brought back their share of the treasure. Their spears and seaxes would be passed to their sons and brothers so that they, too, could go to war. It was our way.

Chapter 4

Even before I saw Brigid and my family I went to the women who had lost men. I gave them their share of the treasure and told them how they had died. It was important that they knew they had gone to Valhalla. None had broken their oath. The families knew that they would be cared for. Those who were now alone might go to the hall of the women. Kara used their skills in cheese and beer making, sewing, weaving, spinning and healing. They would be part of a community. The ones with families would be watched over by my warriors who were unmarried. We all understood the duty we owed the dead.

Brigid's smile told me that she was also relieved to see me. She smiled, "I know what you wish. I will not be long." She left the hall and went to the chamber we shared.

I then had to suffer the assault of questions from Ragnar and Gruffyd. They wished to know every moment of the battle in detail. I was saved by Elfrida.

"The jarl needs his rest. He will tell you the tale after we have eaten. If you are that eager to know then go and ask Haaken One Eye. He is sure to have a song ready and he has yet to leave for his home."

They raced out knowing that Haaken would gladly tell them all. "Thank you, Elfrida."

"I remember that Wolf Killer was always quiet after a battle. Like you, he remembered those who had died and would not be returning home." I nodded. "I was pleased to see that Einar the Tall and his men survived. I feared that they would have the death wish upon them."

"I think you are right but I spoke with them and asked them to be the hearth-weru of Ragnar. They accepted. It seemed right."

She beamed, "As ever, Jarl, you do exactly the right thing." She kissed me on the cheek. "It is what I would have done had I been a man. Now go and enjoy some time with Brigid. She has missed you."

The steam hut we had used had been burned down some time ago but I still enjoyed the ritual of the Water. Brigid returned with my clean kyrtle and drying blanket. I took them from her. She walked with me to the Water carrying the freshly made bar of chestnut soap. She linked my arm. "I am sorry that I was so upset when you left. I think that Wolf Killer's death affected me more than Elfrida."

"It did affect her but she learned to hide her feelings well. She was married to a man she hated when she was Egbert's wife. I do not doubt that she weeps at night but she can take comfort knowing that Wolf Killer is in Valhalla."

She shook her head, "But if she was a Christian then she would believe in heaven!"

"Valhalla is heaven... to a Viking."

We reached the water and I took off my clothes. She placed them on a rock for me and handed me the soap. She ran her hands over my scars. This was the only time she ever saw them. "Do they not hurt?"

"Not any longer but each one is a memory of a battle won and some of a friend or comrade lost. I would not trade any of them."

She sat on a rock as I immersed myself in the chill waters of Cyninges-tūn. I allowed myself to sink to the rocky bottom. It was still and it was peaceful. I kept my eyes opened and looked at the shifting waters. It was silent as the world above never was. I felt at peace and it was here that I felt the closest to my first wife, Erika. I closed my eyes and her face appeared before me. I found myself smiling and when she disappeared, I stood.

"You were down so long that I thought you were drowned!" She had a fearful look on her face.

I smiled. She did not enjoy bathing in the open. When she bathed she did so indoors. She had the slaves heat the water for her. "I thought you Christians were all baptised in water?"

"That is when we were young and we did so fully clothed not naked!"

I shook my head as I began to rub the soap on my body. "What is wrong with the human body? We are all, largely, the same."

She shook her head. "It is not seemly. The priests say so."

"Ah, the priests! Then it must be so!" I enjoyed teasing her about the priests. Kara and Aiden were the nearest thing we had to priests but they did not dictate the way we lived. They were a way to speak with the spirits. They were there to heal and interpret hidden messages. I could never understand why the Christians had to listen to priests who used a language no one could understand. These men, who lived apart, seemed to be constantly telling people what they could and could not do.

Bathed and clean I allowed Brigid to comb and oil my hair, beard and moustache. She then helped me to dry myself with the drying blanket. I donned my clean kyrtle. The blood from the battle was gone and I felt whole once more.

Brigid walked back to my hall with me holding my arm tightly. "I miss you when you are not here. The bed is empty without you sprawled all over it."

"As I miss you."

"We will have a fine feast tonight. One of the fishermen caught a pike and gave it to us as a gift. I will cook it slowly and use some of this season's onions and the beer I brewed yesterday." She suddenly looked at me with a worried expression on her face. "We will be alone this night?"

"Just Elfrida and the children will dine with us. Aiden was away too. I dare say Kara has missed him. "

She relaxed, "Good for we can have a meal without the talk of war!"

In that, she was mistaken but it was not my fault. Ragnar and Gruffyd had had all the details of the battle from Haaken One Eye before he returned to his farm and they told me all about it as though I had not been there. Once again it was Elfrida who saved us. When we had finished the meal, she whisked the children away with her, "Come, the Jarl needs some peace this night. I will tell you the tale of Beowulf."

Ragnar said, "But I know of Beowulf and Grendel already."

"Ah, but do you know of Beowulf and the dragon?" Her words silenced him and he shook his head. "Then come and I will tell the tale as it was told to me by my father the Eorledman."

After she had gone I said, "That was kind of her."

Brigid took my hand, "I asked her to do that. I told you I have missed you and it is time that Erika had another brother or sister." She led me to our bed and showed me just how much she had missed me.

I should have gone to our shipyard the next day but Brigid had been so attentive that I felt guilty. Instead, I sent Olaf Leather Neck to give instructions to prepare my drekar for sea. Riders were sent to fetch Sigtrygg Thrandson and to ask Raibeart to prepare his drekar for sea. My son's drekar would not be used. She was a reminder of his death. Hauled out of the water and laid on logs *'Wild Boar'* would be kept until Ragnar or another warrior gathered a crew and took her to sea. She had taken many warriors to war. It would be some time before we did so again.

I took Ragnar to the warrior hall. Einar the Tall and his six warriors were waiting for me. No one else was inside. I had dismissed them.

"Ragnar these were your father's oathsworn. They would now be yours. These men will be if you will have them, your hearth-weru."

He looked up at me, "Warriors to fight with me?"

"When you defeat Karl One Hand then yes. But first, you must decide if you wish to have them serve you. If you do not then they will seek another lord to follow."

He looked amazed that I had to ask the question, "But of course I wish them to be my hearth-weru. I have known them all my life."

"Then all seven of you must swear an oath and this will be a blood oath." I took out Ragnar's Spirit. "As you are of my blood we will use the sword which was touched by the gods. " I saw that all seven were both touched and impressed by the use of my sword. "Come, I have a place prepared." I handed a pair of broad-headed spears to Einar. I led them down to the Water. Rollo Thin Skin and Rolf Horse Killer kept everyone else well away from the place I had chosen. It was a natural small mound of grass-covered turf but it looked across the water to my first hall, now destroyed by fire. It also lay within view of the flower-covered barrow of my first wife, Erika.

I took my seax and made two long cuts along a piece of turf. I used the seax to lift the turf away from the soil. Einar and Günter placed the spear so that they held the turf, still attached to the ground, above the soil.

"Kneel around the hole." They did so. I had had the sword sharpened by Bjorn Bagsecgson and I could have shaved with it. I placed it beneath the sod. Einar and the others knew what to do but not Ragnar. I explained the ritual to him. "Take your right hand and when the others do so run the palm down the blade so that it is cut. Your blood will mingle in the earth. Do you understand?"

"Aye, Grandfather." He bit his lip. "I will do this." He suddenly looked up at me. "Do I have to say anything?"

Einar smiled and shook his head, "No, lord, for the earth will bind our blood together. We will be oathsworn. We will die for you and you will be our lord and protector." His face became serious. "We did this with your father before you were born. But this time we do it with a magical sword. The ceremony will be special for the sword has been touched by Odin."

"Grasp the blade and let the blood flow. Let the mother mix your blood and make you one. May this oath bind you unto death and if any is foresworn then they will never see Valhalla but serve Hel until the ending of time."

Ragnar winced as the blade bit but he made not a sound. I withdrew the sword and the spears. The turf fell and covered the bloodied soil.

"Stand upon the turf. It is time for the mingling." Ragnar looked confused. I said, quietly, "Hold up your right hand so that the hearth-weru can complete the ceremony."

First Einar and then the others held their right palms to Ragnar's. Each one nodded to Ragnar as they did so. Their eyes held. Günter was the last to do so. It was over. They were now blood sworn and his hearth-weru would serve him so long as they lived.

"That was well done, Ragnar. Your father would be proud of you. Now go with your oathsworn to the warrior hall. There is a firkin of beer there and the Ulfheonar await you."

Einar and the others waited until Ragnar moved and then followed him. The beer would be unwatered. Ragnar would drink and he would be ill. I had warned Elfrida and she understood. This was as much part of the ritual as the bloodletting. My Ulfheonar would tell Ragnar how his life would change and what he needed to do. This was the next part of Ragnar's journey to become a warrior.

He was ill and Brigid berated me for it. Elfrida was more understanding. "Next year my son will have seen thirteen summers. He will be a man. Today was the day he ceased to be a boy. He is changing and I must accept it."

I nodded, "My son would understand if you took another husband."

"I know but I have two. One was the best thing that ever happened to me and the other the worst. I am content with what I have had. When Ragnar leaves to go to the warrior hall I shall join Kara in her house of women. I would like to learn to become a healer and I can give something back to the people who gave so much to me."

I nodded, "Wolf Killer would approve. This is *wyrd*."

I left for my ship two days later. Olaf had said that my drekar would be ready by then and we would only await the arrival of Sigtrygg. We would take four drekar. Each oar would be manned but we would not be overloaded. We would bring back slaves, animals and treasure. Olaf Grimsson was there with my knarr, '**Weregeld**'. I had not seen him for some time and after I had inspected '**Heart of the Dragon**' I boarded his knarr.

"How are the seas these days, Olaf?"

"No more dangerous than they were but we have to stand out to sea more when we round the coast of Wessex. King Egbert's men are more aggressive than they used to be."

"And what of the markets?"

"Frisia and Dorestad are a little more open these days. Dyflin has become a bigger market since Gunnstein Berserk Killer took over from Hakon the Bald. Many merchants come from the north, east and south to trade there. All manner of goods can now be bought; at a price. But I fear that Neustria and Austrasia are both dangerous places to sail. Since our raid and those of Jarl Gunnar Thorfinnson, we are not welcome."

"Perhaps we need to find new markets."

"The lands of the Arabs are dangerous, Jarl. Their dhows are fast and almost the equal of a drekar."

He was right. We had met them ourselves. "Take care then, Olaf, better that you return home with small profits than risk greater ones and lose all. Besides we can raid those places where we are not welcome."

"I am lucky, Jarl Dragonheart, Raibeart ap Pasgen can sail his smaller knarr into places I cannot and he warns me of danger. I have a good crew and they can fight. My knarr is well made and lithe."

"Good. I do not see you often but I am glad I made you captain of my knarr."

"As am I."

We were a family. The whole clan was close and that pleased me. I stayed one night to ensure that all was well and then returned home. Summer had ended and soon would begin the wintery showers and longer nights. We had to leave soon or the journey to our enemies might take too long. As soon as I reached my hall I had the horn sound. It brought every man and boy to the open area before my home.

"Tomorrow I sail to punish the Hibernians and men of Strathclyde. I go to raid. I seek warriors who wish to go A-Viking. I take four drekar only!"

It would be up to my Ulfheonar and myself to select the men. As I was leaving Einar the Tall and Ragnar's hearth-weru in my settlement I could afford to take more of the better warriors. The hearth-weru would give steel to the old men who were my town watch. We still needed a balance of younger men who would gain experience but I limited that number to four for each drekar. We also took more extra ships' boys for each drekar. Some would only last one voyage but others might end up as Erik Short Toe had and become captains. Who knew? *Wyrd*.

Aiden asked, "Would you have me with you, Jarl?"

I shook my head, "It is time for Ragnar and Gruffyd to learn the ways of the spirit world and the ways of the written world. Show them how to read the Roman words. They will hate it as Wolf Killer did but it is necessary."

"Aye Jarl."

Brigid was still worried as I left but there were no tears. This time her eyes twinkled and she whispered, "Hurry back," as I left.

Once at the river, we would sail on the evening tide. Sigtrygg and Asbjorn were already there and just awaiting the extra men whom I would bring. I had time, as we loaded the drekar and allocated new men to their oars, to see my new warriors and how they fitted in with the older ones. My veterans were to be husbanded. I could not be reckless with them. They would always be the deciding factor in any battle whether at sea or on land. I saw Finni the Dreamer helping to put the new warriors at ease. He was a kinder warrior than Olaf Leather Neck. To Olaf, there were two ways of doing things, his way and the wrong way. Finni was more understanding.

Erik nodded, satisfied that Olaf had arranged the rowers to his satisfaction. "We are ready Jarl."

I stood next to Erik and said, "Take us to sea."

We would row for the first few hours even if the wind was with us. It helped to make us one again. He chose a chant the crew knew.

Through the stormy Saxon Seas
The Ulfheonar they sailed
Fresh from killing faithless Danes
Their glory was assured
Heart of Dragon
Gift of a king
Two fine drekar
Flying o'er foreign seas
Then Saxons came out of the night
An ambush by their Isle of Wight
Vikings fight they do not run
The Jarl turned away from the rising sun
Heart of Dragon
Gift of a king
Two fine drekar
Flying o'er foreign seas

The galdramenn burned Dragon Fire
And the seas they burned bright red
Aboard 'The Gift' Asbjorn the Strong
And the rock Eystein
Rallied their men to board their foes
And face them beard to beard
Heart of Dragon
Gift of a king
Two fine drekar
Flying o'er foreign seas
Against great odds and back to back
The heroes fought as one
Their swords were red with Saxon blood
And the decks with bodies slain
Surrounded on all sides was he
But Eystein faltered not
He slew first one and then another
But the last one did for him
Even though he fought as a walking dead
He killed right to the end
Heart of Dragon
Gift of a king
Two fine drekar
Flying o'er foreign seas

He had chosen a good one for it sang of a sea battle and it might come to that. We would head for Dún Lethglaise. It was closer than Alt Clut and we could strike at dawn. That was our preferred time to raid. We knew that it was *wyrd* when the wind sprang from the south and east. The Norns were guiding us to the Hibernians!

Aiden had made a map of the area and we knew that we had a large lough in which we could shelter. A lough was what we called a mere or a water. This one was so big that Aiden said Windar's Mere would fit inside it many times. We would have to travel for two Roman miles from the lough to get to the stronghold for the river, although deep enough was too narrow for our vessels. We did not want our drekar to be trapped. We were able to stop rowing and prepare our war faces as we cleared the coast and headed into the dark and empty water which separated us from the island of Hibernia. We already wore our mail and our swords were sharp but some men liked the ritual of plaiting their hair or donning colours to make their faces look fierce. My preparations were simpler. I smeared red cochineal around my eyes. When I donned my helmet it made my eyes look red. Some said I looked like a wolf, especially wearing my wolf skin but Brigid had told me that those of the White Christ thought that I was the one they called the Devil. He was the enemy of their White Christ. From what I could gather he was like Loki but without the smile. I had often wondered if the priests of the White Christ had stolen the Allfather and Loki from us. It mattered not if they thought me the Devil or a wolf just so long as they hesitated when they fought me. I was older now and any advantage I could wrest from my foes was something I would take.

The first danger we had, as we headed west, was the island of Man which lay directly between us and Hibernia. It was a patch of the sea that we knew well. I always looked to the island when we passed by its northern edge for that was where my mother had died when we had been raided. The Hibernians who had slain her had lived further south than those we now sought but they had paid the price. The island was a reminder that we could not relax our vigilance. It made me think of my home and hearth. I hoped the Ulf and Ketil had their scouts out and that Karl One Hand kept a good watch. I needed my home to be safe.

My men sat on their chests as the four drekar ploughed west through the rolling seas. It was not a flat calm and that helped us. I doubted the Hibernians had watchers at night but if they did then the rolling seas would help to hide us. I stood with Haaken and Olaf at the steering board close by Erik. "Do we know if there is a stronghold, Jarl?"

"There will be, Olaf Leather Neck, but if it is well-defended we will just ravage the land of King Dumnagual. That will be punishment enough. Our main purpose is to destroy their ships. They will take time to rebuild. The time it takes will help them to reflect on their folly. They will still hire out their swords but I want them to think twice before doing so against us again."

Erik had been listening, "If you find the ships in the Lough and destroy them then that will warn the Hibernians that we are in their land."

I shook my head, "I am hoping that they will think that we are still in the land of the wolf. Aiden told me that the other chiefs around here vie with each other and make raids on one another's lands. The Uí Néill are not their only enemies. Other lesser chiefs seek their riches. The fact that their chief is getting older may embolden some of his rivals. I hope that they will think the burning of their ships is the work of a rival clan and they will sortie forth to punish them."

"Leaving their stronghold undefended." Haaken nodded. "A clever plan, Jarl Dragonheart."

"And it came from Kara and Aiden."

"Did they dream it?"

"No. It came from their knowledge of the minds of men. That is where much of their magic lies, Haaken One Eye. They see into men."

"So Jarl, we sail in and sink their ships?"

"Not quite, Olaf. There are some islands in the Lough. We will use those to hide our approach and Erik will land the Ulfheonar. They will travel across the land and slay any sentries that await us and then we can sail close to their ships without fear of alarm."

Erik now had his sons as ship's boys. Arne had lost two fingers in our last battle and was now Arne Three Fingers. He and Guthrum Arneson were at the bows while Knut Eriksson stood by his father. The new ships' boys were standing ready to take in the sail. It was Arne who raced down to hiss, "Land ahead."

Erik nodded, "Reef the sail. Haaken, oars. Knut, signal the others."

We had, below the sheerstrake, a lit candle in a pot. Aiden had marked it so that we could tell the hours in the night. We also used it to signal. Knut carefully reached in to take it from its pot and, sheltering it from the wind, raised it above the sheerstrake. He moved his hand away three times and then returned it to the pot. The ship's boys on Asbjorn's drekar would see it and know what we did. They would repeat it for the others. Even so, we saw the figurehead of Asbjorn's drekar loom up out of the dark. He had been sailing close and the time it took to receive the message had brought him closer to our stern.

We would now sail closer together with just a ship's length between us. With the sail reefed our progress was slower. The men faced us at their oars which were still raised. The reefed sail helped us to see ahead and I saw the black smudge which was the land. I often wondered how Erik always made such good landfalls. I think it was a mixture of Aiden's maps and those skills that good captains seem to be born possessing. Without waiting for more news from his ships' boys he hissed, "Take in the sail. Haaken slow and steady."

He put the steering board over to take us parallel with the coast. He would now be reliant on the eyes of his son and Guthrum at the bows. They would watch for the breakers which would tell us that there were rocks ahead. We could sail through quite shallow water but sharp rocks could rip out our keel. Arne ran halfway down and signalled that we were too close and Erik edged the steering board over another touch. With our sail furled, we would be harder to see. That was the danger of a dragon ship; we could become invisible and silent when we chose. Erik saw the gap almost at the same moment that Guthrum signalled. It was the entrance to the huge sea lough. Knut helped his father to put the steering board over. Once we had passed the headland the sea became calmer. Erik followed the coast around to our left. The other three drekar followed us in turn. We sailed north and the entrance to the main lough narrowed. However, even at its narrowest, it was still six hundred paces wide.

As soon as we passed the narrows it widened to an inland sea and Erik headed south. There were tiny islands and Erik took us between the islands and the mainland. Knut had Aiden's chart open and it lay next to the pot with the candle. By its light, Erik was able to see where he was heading. We were seeking the large island which looked to be closest to the anchorage where we hoped we would find their ships. The fishing boats we had seen on our way north had been drawn up on the beach. I did not think we would be so lucky with the ships of our enemies. They would be anchored in the lough and guarded.

Arne ran down the drekar and said, "There!" he pointed to a larger island than we had hitherto seen.

Erik nodded, "In oars! Knut, signal the others. We anchor." He turned the steering board so that we approached the mainland where we would be hidden from the lough by the island.

Guthrum was ready at the bows and we heard a splash as he leapt ashore followed by a second one as Arne joined him. They would not be tying us up but holding the drekar to allow the Ulfheonar to land. It was pitch dark and we could see little but if Aiden was right then there would be guards at the river leading to their stronghold at Dún Lethglaise. They said nothing as they slipped ashore. From the map, it was less than a Roman mile to the river and they could be there quickly but we had to allow them time to negotiate any obstacles and eliminate any sentries. We waited in the dark with the waters of the lough lapping around our keel. When I judged the time right I nodded and, with only half a crew we rowed out of the shelter of the island towards what we hoped would be the anchorage of the enemy ships.

As we edged into the bay beyond the island I craned my neck to see if I could spy the ships. I could not. Erik glanced up at the masthead. Leif Leifsson, a young boy on his first voyage, pointed ahead and to steerboard. Erik nodded and said, "Knut, signal the others to go to steerboard."

We kept on our course. Our job was to prevent any from leaving the ships and making it to shore. We had allowed enough time for my men to get into position and slay any sentries. I saw the ships then. There were seven of them and they were identical to the ones we had seen off the stad on the Eden. The other three drekar, fully crewed, slid like sharks from the sea. Inevitably they were seen. As Erik hissed, "In oars!" there was a cry as the three drekar were spotted. My crew manned the side with bows ready to slay any that they saw. I heard the clash of metal on metal and cries of pain and screams. There was even a splash and then silence.

Asbjorn came to the bows of the ship nearest us. "The watch is slain."

"Take the ropes and sails from all of them and then use axes to hack through their mast and their hulls."

"We do not burn them?"

"We do not need to and this way we can reach their stronghold by dawn when they open the gates." He nodded. "We will wait for you at the beach."

"Out oars!"

We rowed to the beach and we clambered over the side. "You know what to do?"

"Aye Jarl. We will be here when you are done."

When I reached my men I saw that Snorri and Beorn were missing. Haaken pointed inland, "They left to scout the road. We found six warriors. They had a fire." He pointed to the bodies of the dead sentries.

It did not take long for my jarls to destroy and sink the ships. Even if they could be salvaged the work needed to make them whole would take as long as to build one. The loss of ropes, tackle and sails would also be a severe loss. They would not sail abroad for some time. As we prepared to leave I wondered if I had set off a series of events. Was I the stone in the pond? Perhaps others would see the loss of ships as a weakness and attack them. Was I creating a new enemy for myself or others? Would Jarl Gunnstein Berserk Killer suffer as a result? I had begun now and I could not alter events.

We moved off down the greenway which led to the distant stronghold. Now that I was ashore I could smell smoke. It signified a settlement. Dawn was breaking to the east as I followed Olaf and Rolf. We had travelled barely a thousand paces when Snorri loomed up out of the dark. "Their walls are just over a Roman mile ahead. They have a ditch and a wall. There are ramparts but only one wooden palisade. The gate is wooden and guarded."

"Can we hide close by?"

"The river has trees running alongside it and the wood rises to within forty paces of the ditch. We can hide."

Such mistakes cost men lives. Ulf, Ketil and I all had a killing ground of two hundred paces around our walls. That was the comfortable range of our bows. "Then lead us there and we will wait for dawn."

He led us down by the river and along a narrow trail just wide enough for one man. While it slowed down our approach it enabled us to reach the wood below the walls without being seen. Beorn awaited us. We went to the river where the noise of the water would mask any words we whispered. "They have four men at the bridge over the ditch. I saw three others on the fighting platform on the gate. The bridge over the ditch is fixed."

That told me all that I needed to know. "Then as soon as the gate is opened Olaf Leather Neck and Rolf Horse Killer will lead the Ulfheonar to the gate. We will take it and hold it until the rest can enter."

"There are two more gates, Jarl. One to the southwest and one to the northeast. I guess it guards the main road. This is not the main gate."

I shrugged, "If some escape then so be it. We have achieved what I set out to achieve already. They have no ships. Whatever we take from this stronghold and whatever damage we do is an extra reward." They nodded. "Snorri and Beorn I rely on your arrows to clear the gatehouse."

"Aye Jarl."

I led the jarls and my Ulfheonar back to the woods to await dawn which was imminent. I silently slid my sword from its fleece line scabbard and swung my shield around to the front. Time was Haaken and I would have led the charge but the two axes of Olaf and Rolf would do more damage. Soon Olaf would be too old to lead the charge and someone like Rollo or Olvir would take over. I watched the men on sentry duty. They were coming to the end of their watch. Two of them went to the ditch to make water while a third emptied the ale skin. The fourth shouted something to the men in the gatehouse. I did not hear the reply.

The sun peered over the walls of the stronghold. It was just a greying at first but as the sun rose, powerfully in the east, it became brighter. Finally, the gates began to slowly creak open. We would use no words. Olaf did not need a command to judge the time right. As the gates opened and the four sentries turned their backs on us to walk through the gates he leapt like a deer towards them. Even Rolf struggled to keep up with him. We rushed after them.

The men were in the centre of the gate when they heard his feet on the bridge. His scything axe swept across the middle of two of them and he eviscerated both of them. Rolf brought his axe down across the neck of a third. Two of those in the gatehouse fell to my archer's arrows but the third shouted something as did the last of the watch who ran through the with Olaf and Rolf in close pursuit. Once my Ulfheonar and I were through the gate we halted to allow the other warriors to reach us. Cnut Cnutson had been charged with leaving men to guard and protect the gate. We needed to be able to get out as quickly as we had entered.

We had caught them unawares but they reacted quickly. The buildings into which we had emerged were the poorer quarters. They belonged to those who toiled by the river. Even so, men grabbed weapons and others grabbed farming implements to beat us off. We needed to get to the warrior hall quickly and leave these for the more lightly armed bondi who were with us.

"Olaf, carve us a route to the hall."

"Aye Jarl."

With two scything axes in their hands, Olaf and Rolf quickly cleared our path; men were slain or they fled and we ran through the rude, crude huts towards the distant church and hall. In the time it took us to reach the better halls and homes the Hibernians had organised their defence. A line of warriors stood before King Dumnagual's hall. One in three had some mail and about half had helmets and shields. Had they stood and faced us then they might have had a chance but they broke ranks to get at us. Haaken and I quickly joined Olaf and Rolf. I easily fended off the strike from the sword held by the mailed warrior. He came at me so quickly that his momentum carried his face next to mine. To allow myself to swing I pulled my head back and butted him in the face. His open helmet gave him no protection and he fell backwards, unconscious.

With the freedom to swing, I brought Ragnar's Spirit over my shoulder and across the middle of the warrior whose shield was too small to block my blow. My sword cut his shoulder open and grated on his ribs. I punched with my shield to force him back and then brought my sword over for a second strike. His wound meant he could not raise his shield as high and I cut his body through to his back. My Ulfheonar were in their element now. They fought like heroes. I saw Finni the Dreamer take on two warriors. He ducked below the swinging sword of one warrior as he hacked the leg of a second. He spun so quickly that he was able to slice his sword into the back of the neck of the first warrior before ending the life of the warrior he had maimed.

Karl Karlsson and Einar Hammer Arm ran together towards four warriors at the right side of the King's line. They did not hesitate but threw themselves at the four who stood before them. Three were hurt in six quick blows and then the two of them ended the life of the fourth.

With more of my men joining us, we were almost within the hall. I realised that I could no longer see the king. Suddenly I heard the drumming of hooves and I saw a white horse protected by four warriors on ponies gallop from the building to the right of the hall. The King was escaping. His bodyguards had done their job, however. We still had six to slay before we could follow him and by then he would be beyond our reach and through his gate.

When the last one had been sent to the otherworld I led my Ulfheonar into his hall. Two warriors rushed from the darkened interior and almost caught us unawares. Einar Hammer Arm and Finni the Dreamer had fast reactions and their swords darted in to kill the last of the bodyguards. In the far corner were an older woman and two younger ones. The two younger nursed babes. From the torc around the older woman's neck, I took her to be the Queen.

"Finni, find four men from our village and escort these prisoners to my drekar. We will take them."

"As slaves, Jarl?"

"No, we will ransom them."

The women screamed as Finni drove them from us. They did, however, obey. In the fire-lit hall, we looked terrifying.

"Search the hall for anything of value. Look beneath the floor for chests."

Haaken grinned, his face lit by the fire, "We need Aiden here with us. His nose can sniff out treasure."

"Snorri, Beorn, come with me."

Outside seemed like chaos. Women and children screamed and men cried out as they were slain. "Ketil, fetch some men to the church!"

"Aye Jarl." I hurried to the church. The door was shut and, when we tried to open it, appeared to be barred. One of Ketil's men ran up with an axe. We had done this before. There would be a bar across the middle and Ketil's man hacked at the middle plank of the door. In four strikes he had made a hole and his sixth broke the bar in two. He put his shoulder to it and we burst in to the candlelit church. A priest ran up and shouted something. He held a cross before him. Cnut's warrior had blood in his nostrils and he brought the axe down on the priest's head. The other four tried to run but the men from my settlement, who did not wear mail, caught them and before I could stop them, slew them. It was a pity. They were valuable in the slave markets of Dyflin and Frisia.

"Take the treasure to the drekar. Snorri and Beorn search beneath the altar."

They kicked over the alter. There was an oblong stone below it. I could not read the writing which lay on it but it mattered not. They picked up and threw the stone to the ground where it broke. They took out the three small chests. They would not contain gold, I knew that they would contain some relics. They could be bone or even wood. I did not understand their purpose. When I returned home I would ask my wife what they meant.

"Take them to the drekar. Tell Erik we will be ready shortly."

Once outside the combat was over. Haaken came to me. "We have much treasure and animals. How many slaves do we need?"

"As many as we can carry. The prisoners for ransom are the most important but we can sell these others in Dyflin."

"I will choose the most valuable."

I waved over Sigtrygg. "Burn this down. Burn everything! Let us leave a memorial for King Dumnagual!" While half of my men collected treasure the other half began to fire wooden buildings. Soon the flames took hold and a pall of smoke rose in the sky. The people of Dumnagual would know that an enemy was loose in their land.

It did not take us long to return to the drekar. Loading took longer. We had no jetty and we had to improvise a bridge to get the two cows and three horses we had captured. I saw the smoke in the distance and knew that Sigtrygg had done as I had asked. He had destroyed the stronghold. We had the drekar loaded and there were forty slaves we could not take. I could have slain them but, instead, I left a message.

I spoke but a few words of their language. I pointed to the royal prisoners who were held at the mast of my ship. "I am Jarl Dragonheart of Cyninges-tūn. I take those. Your king pays gold and he can have them back. He pays no gold then they die." I looked at an old man and woman who were closest to me. "Understand?"They nodded vigorously. I pointed to the boxes, "I take these too." If King Dumnagual wanted them back then he could pay for them but I suspected he would want his family back first.

I climbed aboard my drekar and we pushed off. The boats were heavily laden but we had not far to go. We would take them to the stad on the Eden. As we sailed through the lough we saw that there were many fishing boats upon it. They fled when they spied us. I could see that the sides of the lough were filled with many small villages. However, we saw no strongholds. It would be a land ripe for raiding if we needed slaves. Horsemen spied us on the northern shore and shadowed us until we reached the open sea. Who they were I had no idea but horses could never catch our drekar. We left the land of the Hibernians and crossed the seas to the stad on the Eden.

Chapter 5

We had to row home for the winds which had taken us west now slowed us down and with overloaded drekar, we were anxious to be across the sea as quickly as possible. The song we sang was one of our favourites.

The Saxon King had a mighty home
Protected by rock, sea and foam
Safe he thought from all his foes
But the Dragonheart would bring new woes
Ulfheonar never forget
Ulfheonar never forgive
Ulfheonar fight to the death
The snake had fled and was hiding there
Safe he thought in the Saxon lair
With heart of dragon and veins of ice
Dragonheart knew nine would suffice
Ulfheonar never forget
Ulfheonar never forgive
Ulfheonar fight to the death
Below the sand they sought the cave
The rumour from the wizard brave
Beneath the sea without a light
The nine all waited through the night
Ulfheonar never forget
Ulfheonar never forgive
Ulfheonar fight to the death
When night fell they climbed the stair
Invisible to the Saxons there
In the tower the traitors lurked
Dragonheart had a plan which worked
Ulfheonar never forget
Ulfheonar never forgive
Ulfheonar fight to the death
With Odin's blade the legend fought

Magnus' tricks they came to nought
With sword held high and a mighty thrust
Dragonheart sent Magnus to an end that was just
Ulfheonar never forget
Ulfheonar never forgive
Ulfheonar fight to the death
Ulfheonar never forget
Ulfheonar never forgive
Ulfheonar fight to the death

Our crew always rowed better when they sang the song of our attack on Din Guardi. Erik laughed, "We should teach the other crews that song, Jarl. They are slipping astern!"

I pointed to the smudge on the horizon. "Ulf's home is not far away. Let them catch us."

It was easier landing our slaves, animals and treasures than it had been loading. We were close to the stad and Ulf's men helped us to unload. "We will have to build a slave pen, Jarl."

"Use the slaves to do so." I pointed to the boxes we had taken from the church. "Have your men take those and the royal prisoners to Cyninges-tūn. Aiden can determine their worth. As for the slaves, keep whatever you need and the rest we will sell in Dyflin. We will go there when we have raided Alt Clut."

Once we were all inside his walls the gates were shut and barred. The four drekar rode at anchor in the river, protected by our archers on the walls. As we ate that night Ulf asked, "You still intend to go to Alt Clut then?"

"Aye. We will destroy his ships and see what else we may pick up."

"I have four young warriors who wish to go with you. Their father, Egil, was slain by the men of Strathclyde on the walls. They seek vengeance."

"We have berths. Do they know the dangers?"

"They are handy lads, Jarl. The eldest has seen sixteen summers and the youngest eleven." He smiled, "Haaken told me that you went to war when you had seen ten summers."

I nodded and laughed, "They were different times. Have they weapons and mail?"

Shaking his head he said, "They have helmet, shield and spear only. The eldest and second eldest have swords. They hope to pick some up against the men of Strathclyde."

"If they do not come forth to fight us then that might be a vain hope. I am not going to try the walls of Alt Clut. That would be suicide." I had been there once before, with Aiden and I had seen firsthand how they had built the castle into the solid rock of the cliff. It was a stronghold made by the gods themselves.

We did not leave on the morning tide. Erik and the other drekar captains shared out the ropes and sails we had captured. They were placed in the holds of our ships. Not only would they be useful at sea they would also help to give the drekar a better balance. We set sail on the later tide and headed north. We used the winds which had veered around to the south to take us north. We would lay up overnight by the island of Hersey. There were Norse settlements there but not many of them. I suspected that, as at Ljoðhús, King Dumnagual would be trying to rid his land of Vikings. But even if we were spotted we would not be in danger. This was still the land of the Vikings even if they had been weakened. So confident were we that we did not wear mail as we sailed north. It was a most pleasant voyage save that we knew we would have a battle at the end of it.

Haaken sought me out. I was at the prow enjoying the sea breeze blowing through my hair. "Have you a plan, Jarl Dragonheart, or do we just sail in and hope for the best?"

"You think I should have brought Aiden?"

"It might have helped but I know that there is a plan inside your head but you have yet to share it with us."

"You are right. As we discovered at the Eden we can make plans and then our enemies or the Norns themselves do something which makes us change our plans. I know what I hope to do: we find their ships and destroy them. We land close to Alt Clut and we take slaves and animals. If any warriors come we fight them. Then we sail home. There, is that a plan?"

He laughed, "It is and it sounds so simple and yet I know that it cannot be that simple. And you are right, in the end, it will come to our warriors in a shield wall fighting their warriors. It is just the place we do not know."

"Not quite true. When I was searching Aiden's map I found a village a couple of miles from Alt Clut. It is called Càrdainn Ros. On the map, Aiden marked it with a cross which means that there is a church. He has marked it as flat and there is no sign of a castle. When we have destroyed his ships we make our base there and tempt our enemies to us. The followers of the White Christ do not like it when their churches are threatened."

He stood and stretched, "It is good to know that you do have a plan then! I shall sleep now for tomorrow I shall win enough coin to give my eldest daughter a good dowry so that she can marry a fine farmer who does not go to war and keeps me in ale when I grow old!"

I laughed, "You and I will never grow old, Haaken. We will fall together in battle. Sadly that will mean someone else will have to sing of our end."

He suddenly became serious, "And that would be a fitting end. We fought our first battle together and have been at each other's side since first I lost my eye and you became the Dragonheart. That would be a story worth telling. Sadly, I know not who could do it justice for I would be already dead!"

Even when he tried to be serious he could not be and his vanity always ended with a comment about himself.

We reached the island in the middle of the afternoon. The seas and the winds had been both kind and favourable. We went ashore on a deserted beach and collected shellfish to cook. Experienced warriors rested while they could. The younger ones, like Egil's boys, spoke of the glories they would win in the coming raid. They spent the coin they had yet to collect and they dreamed of fabulous weapons they would take. I lay on the beach as the sunset before me and enjoyed the warmth before the chill of winter began. Haustmánuður was the last month of summer and I enjoyed the sun.

Olaf woke me, "It is time Jarl. Everyone else is aboard."

I looked up and saw that it was a dark night. Someone had covered me in my wolf skin. "You should have woken me."

"There was no need. We knew what we were about."

Once aboard I began to don my mail. My men had put on theirs while I had been sleeping. The rest had been a good one. I felt refreshed and my mind was clear. Any doubts about our action were gone. We had gained great rewards from the Hibernians. Perhaps the men of Strathclyde would provide as much again.

We had to row for we were heading upstream. They had no watchtowers but as it was pitch black and we had sails furled we would be hard to see. With our low freeboard and sleek lines, we cut through the dark waters. Once again we were reliant on the skills of our ships' boys. The difference was that this time *'Red Snake'* was on our steerboard side. The river was wide enough for the two of us. In addition, Raibeart ap Pasgen was as good a captain as Erik and had a nose for the sea. We knew that Alt Clut lay above the river where it narrowed sharply. It was still wide but the stronghold could control those heading upstream. What I did not know was if his ships would be anchored in the river or tied up to a quay. The only sound which could be heard was the sound of oars slicing through the black waters. There were no lights. Those on land were behind shut doors and would not venture forth. Inside their barred doors, they were safe. Or so they thought.

Knut came running down the centre of the drekar. He pointed to the left. "Father, there are boats tied up along a quay. There are ten of them. Some are as big as this. I have seen the stronghold. There is a light on the walls."

I nodded, "You have done well."

Erik put the steering board over. Raibeart would mirror our actions and the other two would follow us. Ten ships that were tied up to a quay were an easier prospect than ships at anchor. However, we would not have the luxury of stripping them of sails and ropes.

I walked to Haaken and Olaf who rowed along with Cnut Cnutson. "We will use fire. We will tie alongside the furthest ship. Arne, signal *'Red Snake'* to attack the ones downstream." The ship's boys had worked out a series of signals using the candle. Arne went to the steerboard side and began to uncover and cover the candle. When he saw a light flash in response he knew that they understood. The other two would, naturally fill in the gap. Erik would pass the end ship and then turn to allow my men to pull in their oars. We would let the current and Erik's skill take us next to the enemy.

We passed the last ship and as we turned Haaken hissed, "In oars." The sound rippled up the drekar.

I strode to the steerboard side and drew my sword. The ship's boys would secure us to the end ships but they would need protection. I stood next to Arne Eriksson. As we neared the first ship we were seen. One of the sleeping night watch had risen to make water and he stared at us from no more than thirty paces. He managed a squeaked shout before Snorri's arrow blossomed from his chest. The damage was done and they knew we were there. His shout aroused the watch on all the ships and that, in turn, caused a shout from the lofty stronghold. I knew that we had to work quickly before the garrison descended upon us.

As we bumped next to the sterns of the last two vessels Arne and I leapt together. A sentry with a small axe rushed at Arne. Erik's son was not distracted from his task. He wrapped his rope around the steering board of the ship. Even as the axe sliced down towards Erik's son I lunged forward. The warrior impaled himself on my sword and he fell in a bloody heap. I ran down the vessel. Haaken and Olaf were behind me. I saw a spear coming at me and I blocked it with my shield but did not slow up. I was mailed and heavier than the sentry who was knocked over the side when I hit him and he fell between the vessels. As they rubbed together he was crushed. The last of the watch was slain by Haaken. We had taken one of the ships.

We clambered over the side. I saw that some of the men from Cyninges-tūn were climbing over the side. I pointed to the ropes holding the ships to the land. "Cut their lines! Then get back aboard. Make fires!"

I saw that all of the ships had my men swarming all over them. I turned to my Ulfheonar. "Shield wall!"

We stood together at the end of the track which led from the stronghold. I saw, in the darkness, shadows moving. They were sending men to investigate the cries. We did not need to hold them long for as soon as the ships were untied we could board our drekar and fire the ships in the middle of their river. We heard hooves. They had sent horsemen and they would be here quicker than we had anticipated.

"Lock shields! Horsemen!"

As the shields were interlocked I glanced over and saw that they were ponies rather than horses. A horse might try to jump a shield wall. A pony would not. That became obvious when the fifteen or so riders began to slow when they saw the wall awaiting them. A couple had spears and they hurled them at us. As one, our shields came up and blocked them. They had reached us but their leader did not seem to know what to do.

It was my turn to surprise the enemy, "At them!"

We broke the shield wall and hurtled the twenty paces towards them. They were riding bareback and had no mail. Rolf Horse Killer lived up to his name as his axe smashed into the skull of a pony. Olaf's axe almost took the mane of a pony as he hacked into the middle of a warrior. I brought my sword around to slice through the leg of a rider. The rest of the Ulfheonar, in terrible black wolf cloaks and with fierce red eyes, fell upon the riders like real wolves. The six at the back turned and fled in fear.

"Jarl Dragonheart! We have the ships! The river takes us!" Erik's urgent voice meant we had to return to the ships.

"Back to the drekar!"

We backed to the ships and climbed aboard. Ships' boys held the ropes which had held the ships to the land. As Beorn boarded Arne Eriksson was the last to leap aboard. Cnut Cnutson's men had kindling laid at the mast. Bergil Leifsson grinned as I passed. "Best hurry Jarl soon this will be a fire fit for a funeral. These warriors will have a hot journey to the Otherworld."

We clambered over the side of *'Heart of the Dragon'*. Ahead I could see that most of the other ships we had captured were well away from the bank. Flames licked up the masts of two of them. As our men leapt aboard Erik shouted, "Let go!" He put the steering board hard over to take us to the middle of the river. Bergil had been correct, the burning ships did make fine funeral ships. The timbers were dry for winter had not yet begun and our kindling accelerated the work of the fire. Each mast flared and burned like a beacon. By their light, I saw armed men gathering at the quay. The survivors of our attack had summoned help but it was too late. King Dumnagual's fleet was burning. It would be some time before he attacked Vikings by sea.

We did not have far to sail. Erik put the steering board over and we headed to the small wooden quay at Càrdainn Ros. The fire and noise from upriver had alerted those in the houses and, as we approached we saw them flee.

"Cnut, take your men and see if you can catch any villagers and then find out what the land is like."

"Aye Jarl."

Soon it would be dawn. We had achieved the first part of our plan. Could I make the second part work? Could I draw the King of Strathclyde from his stronghold to face us in the field? I took off my helmet and felt the cool night air. It refreshed me. Sigtrygg and Asbjorn joined me. "My men are searching the land further afield. Sigtrygg, have your men watch the road from the east. Asbjorn, see if your men can find any food. We will have the rest of the men eat. When daylight dawns I would have them raid to the west of us. See what we can gather."

As they turned to obey Haaken and my Ulfheonar took off their own helmets and cloaks. We laid them by the river. "Snorri, you and Beorn rest. I want you to head back to Alt Clut when daylight is here to give us warning of the enemy."

"Aye Jarl."

Haaken was in good spirits. "To the church then eh Jarl? It looks poor to me but who knows what we may find."

"Aye. I doubt that the village will hold much for us but its purpose was to draw their king here."

"Rollo Thin Skin was one of my younger warriors. He had not sailed with me as much as some of the others. "Will he not just follow our ships anyway?"

Haaken One Eye snorted, "No, for he saw us sail away. You cannot catch a dragon ship. He will have thought our intent was to sink his ships. He knows not who we are. We could be from Hersey or Ljoðhús. Perhaps we are from Orkneyjar. When the people from the village reach him he will know we have not left. When he came south he gathered men from his kingdom. This is the time of the cutting of the corn. Most of his men will have returned to their farms. He does not keep a standing army. Does he fight us or let us raid his land? Jarl Dragonheart is clever, Rollo. Whatever the King does, we win."

I shook my head, "You tempt the Norns, Haaken. With the help of the Allfather, we might win."

"They follow the White Christ. That makes them weaker."

I shook my head. Sometimes Haaken's vanity and overconfidence worried me. Just because we had been successful before now did not mean our luck would continue. I would make a Blót. The church was disappointing. The candlesticks were base metal. There were no holy books and it was only the white cloth on the altar which was of value. There were no relics hidden beneath the wooden altar.

"Burn it!"

The church would confirm to the king what the survivors told him, that Vikings were still in his land. As we headed back to the centre of the settlement the sun began to rise. The smell of the burning ships and occasional clouds of smoke drifted down the river. Cnut and his men returned. "We did not catch any, Jarl. Six of their men tried to hold us off. They were brave but they died." He turned and pointed. I saw that his men led a cow and two pigs. "We found a farm. The farmer and his family had fled but they left these as offerings for us."

"Good, get them butchered and jointed. They will cook quicker that way. Feed your men first. I would have them raid in the morning."

I walked to the river and took off my mail and kyrtle. I laid them and my sword on my shield and cloak and jumped into the chilly river. I would not rest and the best way to awaken myself was to let Icaunus give me strength. I sank to the muddy bottom and pushed up. My head broke the surface and I saw that the river had taken me downstream. I stroked my way back to the bank and pulled myself from the water. I had no drying blanket and I stood, watching the rising sun to allow myself to dry. I could see, in the distance, the ramparts of Alt Clut. Now that it was daylight they would see us. The smoke from the burning church rose in a black plume. It was a challenge to the King. It would be seen from miles around. What would his people think?

I dressed and returned to the centre of the small settlement. I waved over Asbjorn. "Have some of your men relieve Cnut Cnutson and his men. I want us all fed and rested by noon."

I saw that there was a grindstone outside an open hut. It looked to be a weapon maker's hut but the fire was out. I went over and put an edge on Ragnar's Spirit. My Ulfheonar joined me and they did the same. Finni the Dreamer pointed to the rest of the warriors. They were laughing and joking as though we had won a victory. "That is the difference between us, Jarl. We think of the next battle. They think of the last."

Olaf said, "And that is why we are Ulfheonar, Finni the Dreamer. Would you change places with them?"

"Of course not."

"Then do not criticise them because they are not us."

Thus chastened Finni sharpened his own weapons. I saw food being taken to Sigtrygg's men. They were the smaller cuts. Already the smell of roasting pig was making me hungry. Once Cnut Cnutson's band had been fed he came over to me. "How far west should we raid?"

"As far as you need. If the enemy comes this should be enough and if there are too many then we will board our drekar and wait in the river for you. Tomorrow I will send Asbjorn to the north. This will be our last raid of the year. Let us make it a profitable one."

Snorri and Beorn returned before dark. "We waited until it was obvious they were not setting forth this day. They have sent many riders to the north and the east. We saw them from our vantage point and since afternoon people have been flooding into the stronghold."

"Thank you, Snorri. I will send other scouts on the morrow. Rest, you have done well."

Cnut returned as darkness was falling. They came from the setting sun. They had half a dozen women and children and were driving a great number of animals. My men looked happy. "We found no warriors and little treasure but the animals were plentiful." He pointed to the four ponies his men led. "We slaughtered some chickens and geese. It was easier than driving them. There are some weapons from the men who fought us."

"Is it worth heading west tomorrow?"

He shook his head, "No Jarl. They are fishing villages and they will just take to sea in their boats. We came upon one such village and that is what they did."

"Churches?"

"Even meaner than this one."

"Then rest. Tomorrow your men shall stay in camp while Asbjorn and Sigtrygg raid north. We shall make it a wasteland."

After three days of raiding, there was nothing of value to be had and I called my jarls together. "We have achieved what we wanted to. The fleet is destroyed. We have hurt the men of Strathclyde and the weather worsens each day. We will leave on the morning tide."

Asbjorn nodded his agreement. "We have lost no men and gained a great number of animals. I have never eaten as well on a raid!"

"When we return to the Eden I will send for Siggi and Olaf Grimsson. We can use them to take our trade goods to Dyflin."

The Norns were listening as we made our plans. I had not been foolish enough to remove my scouts and in the middle of the night, they returned. "Jarl Dragonheart. There is a warband heading from the east. They must have gathered on the far side of the stronghold. They will be here by dawn. I think they mean to surprise us."

Their arrival had aroused my men. "Load the drekar. King Dumnagual, it seems, has come to punish us. Erik when the drekar are loaded stand off from the bank. We will fight before we leave."

My men were more than happy for a battle. It would not do to flee without giving battle. The enemy would see it as a sign of weakness. When we had chosen this village it had been because it was flat and there was an area between the village and the river which we could defend. While my drekar were loaded we formed ranks. My Ulfheonar formed the centre of the line. Asbjorn and Sigtrygg with their hearth-weru formed the front rank. Forty warriors wide it was made up of our best warriors all of whom wore mail. Cnut Cnutson had the second rank filled with the other warriors while Snorri and Beorn had those with bows, all thirty of them, in the rear rank. Although we had had little time to prepare my men had been waiting since we had landed for the chance to fight the enemy. We were Vikings, it was what we did.

Erik and the drekar stood off and it was the ships' boys, high in the masts and armed with bows, who heralded the arrival of the men of Strathclyde. Guthrum Arneson whistled and pointed upstream.

"They come. Lock shields!" We had spears this time and we, in the front rank, held ours above our shields. Cnut's men, behind us, had theirs resting on our shoulders. It was a reassuring weight. Snorri in the third rank would loose over our heads. We saw nothing, but a large army makes a noise and we heard the leather creaking, the metal jangling and the sound of men moving through the undergrowth. They appeared suddenly from the trees. Their king had been clever for he had timed his attack to coincide with the sun's first rays. Shining from the west he hoped it would be in our eyes. It was simple enough to look down where the brows of our helmets shaded our eyes from the worst of it.

The enemy halted to form lines. They had fought with us once and knew the dangers of a piecemeal attack. If they thought they knew us from one battle then they were wrong. As they banged their shields and then stepped forward Snorri and his archers let fly. The men of Strathclyde still had much smaller shields than ours and even though some men had both mail and helmets, a large number did not. The archers, although but thirty strong, were able to keep up a withering shower of arrows. Then the ships' boys, perched in the masts used their slings and bows. Their elevation gave them greater range and soon there was the sound of clattering as lead balls hit helmets and shields. They also made a crack and a snap as they struck flesh and bone. Some arrows found flesh too. Men died.

I could see that the King had raised his levy. Men with pitchforks, bill hooks and hunting bows massed around the rear of his lines of warriors. They posed no threat. It was those at the front who did and we were ready for them. The arrows and stones had thinned their front ranks but the deaths appeared to have enraged them. They hurled themselves at us. I yelled, "Spears! Now!"

As one we punched forward. Inevitably some of us hit air but many found shields or flesh. It was mainly flesh. The clatter of metal on wood, as they stuck our shields, showed that they had not all been injured or slain. My spearhead was bloody. A mailed warrior brought back his arm to strike a blow at my head. I lifted my left arm and brought it up to eye level. I stabbed with my spear as I did so. As his sword clattered off the edge of my shield the tip rang off my helmet. My ears rang but the head of my spear penetrated the shoulder of the warrior. I pushed and twisted. Harald Fair Hair, in the second rank, stabbed forward with his spear and it tore into the warrior's nose and skull. He must have struck something vital for the warrior fell backwards. I saw that a number of their men in the front rank had fallen.

"Warriors! Push!"

I pulled back my right arm and stepped forward with my right leg as did the rest of the front rank and those in the second rank. My spear struck a warrior's shield as the enemy advanced. The weight of my blow and the advancing line of spears made him stumble. I quickly raised my hand and stabbed down into his neck as he sprawled beneath my feet. We kept advancing. My men would do so until I told them to halt or until I fell.

I heard a horn. It had to be the enemy and it signalled something. I glanced up, beyond the warriors who were immediately before us, and saw that the King was bringing forward his levy to bolster his weakening line. The arrows and stones were doing far more damage now for they were striking flesh rather than mail. Even as I watched a stone struck the side of a farmer's head. He had no helmet and I watched the life leave his eyes as his skull was cracked. Our arrows were doing terrible damage. The enemy did not know if they should use their small shields against the arrows and stones or our spears.

One of King Dumnagual's hearth-weru suddenly ran from the side of the king. He had mail and he had a long curved sword. He barged his way through the half-armed levy and the warriors. He was coming for me. Leif and his banner were in the third rank and marked my position. Arrows and stones struck him but still, he came on. We were still moving and the two of us were on a collision course. I used my longer spear to stab forward. His sword came around and chopped it in two. Without breaking stride, I drew my sword. Harald Fair Hair jabbed forward with his spear. It bought me the time to pull Ragnar's Spirit from its scabbard as the hearth-weru pulled up his shield to protect his head. I did not tell my men to halt. I would deal with this act of desperation and my men would continue their advance.

Instead of swinging my sword, I jabbed, blindly at his middle. His shield still protected his face. The sword rasped and grated against his mail and I heard a crack as something gave. He swung his sword in a wide swing to take my head. My shield absorbed the blow but it was a mighty one and my arm was numbed. I had planned on using my shield to strike him but that was out of the question. The front two ranks of my men had moved on and only Leif the Banner remained behind me.

The warrior swore at me. I recognised '*Viking*' and *'son of a whore'*. The rest of the words were meaningless. I did not waste my breath on such insults. I looked for weakness in this warrior who was half my age and was built like an oak. He swung his long sword at me a second time. I warily raised my numbed arm and it felt as though I had been struck by an iron bar. I feinted at his head with a quick jab. His hand instinctively came up and I stabbed again at his middle. This time it was not blindly. I had seen, when he swung, the severed links of his byrnie. This time I put the whole weight of my body into it. I saw his face contort and he grunted. My sword came away red. He was wounded. It enraged him much as a wild boar is enraged by a spear that does not kill it. He smashed his sword towards my head and even though I raised my shield to block it the blow drove me to my right knee. As he triumphantly raised his sword to end it I stabbed upwards under his byrnie and drove my sword through his groin and deep into his body. My hand felt flesh and I saw the tip of my sword sticking out of his side. I must have pierced his heart for his eyes were dead. I used my shield to push him from my sword as I stood.

My men were forcing the enemy back and my archers joined me. Leif said, "He was a hard man to kill Jarl."

"Aye, and my left arm knows it." I saw that my men were in danger of advancing beyond the protection of the village and there the enemy would outnumber us. I yelled, "Halt!" Turning to Snorri I said, "See if you can hit the king. Keep the pressure on their flanks. Force them onto the swords of the Ulfheonar. Leif, let us show them that we live still!" We hurried forward as my men locked shields. I found Harald Fine Hair to my left. He had joined the front rank. Our sudden halt had caused the enemy to halt too and I heard a horn sound. "

"Harald, step back. Thank you for your spear thrust."

As he stepped back he said, "It was an honour, Jarl."

Leif and Harald guarded my back. I looked down the line and saw that all of my Ulfheonar and jarls lived. There were gaps for men without mail now stood in the front rank. I turned to Haaken. "They will come at us again. Snorri will use his arrows to drive them to us. We are the rock and we hold!"

He nodded and began beating his shield, "Ulfheonar! Ulfheonar!" The chant was taken up by the whole front rank and then Haaken changed it to a chant.

> *Ulfheonar never forget*
> *Ulfheonar never forgive*
> *Ulfheonar fight to the death*
> *Ulfheonar never forget*
> *Ulfheonar never forgive*
> *Ulfheonar fight to the death*

On the last word in each line, my men all banged their shields with their swords or their spears. It was like a crack of thunder. I saw the enemy recoil. Even when they came forward they would be beaten. I saw it in their eyes.

I stepped from the line and opened my chest, "Come, you cowards! We are waiting for you!"

They did not understand the words but they did the gesture and they surged forward as I had hoped. I stepped back and shouted, "Lock shields." Swords and spears were presented and the men who charged were met by a wall of steel. My sword stabbed forward and a half-naked warrior impaled himself upon it. Harald Fine Hair's spear took a second. Olaf's axe killed one and wounded a second in one mighty blow. Then we were amongst the levy and they could not face us. When the first dozen or so were slain without laying a blow on us and arrows fell amongst those behind they turned and they fled. There was no attempt to retreat. This was a rout. Once again the King and his hearth-weru joined the stampede for Alt Clut. If I had wanted to stop my men I could not. The blood lust was upon them and they chased the enemy.

Only the Ulfheonar, my jarls and their hearth-weru halted when I raised my sword. "Leif, signal Erik to close with the shore. We had best get our dead aboard. We will not bury them here where their bodies will be despoiled we will take them to the stad on the Eden and there we can do them honour."

Part Two

The Avenging of Wolf Killer

Chapter 6

It was late afternoon when the last of my men finally returned. Many had trophies of war; torcs, bracelets, swords, and rings. The men of Strathclyde went to war showing their finery. The dead warriors were stripped of their mail and helmets. We took them back for our smiths. The sea of enemy dead we left where they fell while our own lay in the bows of our drekar and were covered with cloaks. We had their shields and their weapons. They would be buried as warriors. As we sailed past Hersey and into the sunset Haaken said, "We did what you set out to do. We return with slaves, treasure and animals. I have a great song to sing of the fight between you and that mountain of a man. You must be satisfied."

I spoke quietly as one can with your oldest friend, "You would think so but there is an empty place in my heart still."

"Wolf Killer?"

I nodded, "We slew the Danes and Norse who killed him but there were two other hands in that murder. Grimbould of Neustria and Egbert of Wessex."

"They are both mighty prizes. They have armies to guard them. They have strongholds that are the equal of Alt Clut. Do you think we are strong enough to face and take them?"

I nodded, "We managed to enter Din Guardi and slay murderers did we not?"

"We did but for that, we needed a galdramenn and we used but a few warriors."

"Then perhaps that is what we will do." I rubbed my left arm. It had taken some time for the feeling to return to it after the blows of the King's bodyguard. "I have the winter to think and to heal. I have long months of darkness to speak with Aiden and I have time to speak with the spirits and seek their guidance." I smiled. "But already I feel better. Speaking with you has focussed my mind. I know what I must do."

We sailed all night. We did not row hard but we did row. Halfway through the morning we saw the estuaries of the rivers and headed for the Eden. Haustmánuður was half over and soon it would be Samhain. I wished to be home. We unloaded our cargo. I sent Cnut Cnutson and half of his men to drive the animals down to Cyninges-tūn. The slaves and the treasure we took with us. All of my jarls received their fair share and were happy. Before we left we buried our dead with those who had fallen in the earlier battles. Each had his own stone-lined grave and was buried with all the accoutrements of a warrior. We laid those who had fought together close by so that they would have friends on their journey to Valhalla. We covered them with wood and then stones. Finally, the turf was laid on the mounds and the seeds of wildflowers were thrown over them. We would remember and we would honour our dead.

My four drekar, with much-reduced crews, sailed around our coast back to Úlfarrston. Since my talk with Haaken, I felt much happier. I had made poor decisions before but just lately I had not. Perhaps my visit to the Old Man had been preordained. When we reached Úlfarrston we left the slaves who would be sold at the Dyflin slave market with Coen ap Pasgen. We had enough slaves and they would fetch a reasonable price in Dyflin. The other goods which we had captured in Hibernia had been sorted by Aiden and some were ready to be traded in Dyflin. I noticed that the relics in their boxes were amongst them. That was interesting for we would normally sell those in Lundenwic or Dorestad. Aiden did nothing without thinking matters through.

Raibeart had not returned yet from his voyage and I asked Coen to send him to us as soon as he arrived. He told me that a letter had arrived for me from the old king in Hibernia. He had sent it to Aiden. I was anxious for news from the north. We marched through the forests to our home. We were seen by the fishermen who sailed up the Water to our home to warn our families of our imminent arrival. We had buried some of the men on the Eden and I would have to tell them of their deaths.

Half way to Cyninges-tūn Ragnar and Gruffyd rode up. They were accompanied by Einar the Tall and the rest of Ragnar's hearth-weru. Gruffyd threw himself from his still-moving pony and rushed to me. "You have had great victories! We had the word. You have defeated the Hibernians and those from north of the wall! Can we come next time?"

I smiled, "And have you defeated Karl One Hand yet?"

"Ragnar almost did."

"Then he can almost come. Is that good enough Ragnar?"

I saw his hearth-weru smiling. Ragnar nodded, "It is fair and besides we have winter coming. No one will be raiding in the cold time. I will improve during the winter. Einar is helping me."

Einar shook his head, "Do not forget, master, that Karl One Hand is Ulfheonar. That is why the Jarl set this task. Any who can defeat an Ulfheonar will be a mighty warrior."

As we made our way north we were bombarded with questions. Those warriors who lived south of our village left us before we reached Cyninges-tūn and we arrived at the same time as Cnut Cnutson who had driven our animals from the Eden. The word had spread of our arrival and we were greeted as heroes. Haaken would be disappointed to have missed the adulation. For myself, I did not need it. I had done what I had done for the clan. Ragnar and his hearth-weru left us to practise while the light held.

Brigid greeted me warmly, "I have invited Kara and Aiden this night. I know you will have much to say and now that Winter is almost here I shall have you all to myself with no war or raid to distract you."

I put my finger on her lips, "I know you do not believe in them but such statements make the Weird Sisters come up with plots and plans to make our lives difficult."

I saw that I had made her think. She did not believe in the Norns but she had her own superstitions. I smiled as her hand went to the cross she wore about her neck. Uhtric was waiting for me with my drying blanket and clean kyrtle but Brigid was too busy with the food to accompany me. After bathing, refreshed, clean and dressed I returned to my hall. Each time I came back from a raid there was nothing I liked more than sitting before the fire in my hall in the chair that Uhtric had made for me. I would enjoy a horn of freshly brewed ale and enjoy rye bread and cheese. Brigid called it my throne but it was just a well-made chair with furs laid upon it. Of late I had found myself falling asleep in it. That would not happen after this meal for I had much to ask Aiden.

It was Gruffyd who brought me a horn of ale and sat on the floor by my side. "Leif the Banner told me that you fought with a champion of King Dumnagual."

"He was not a champion. He was a warrior who wanted glory and sought to gain it at my expense."

"And Leif said he was much younger and bigger than you are."

I would have to speak with Leif and ask him not to be so honest with my son. "Size and youth do not guarantee victory."

He nodded, "Even so he could have beaten you but he did not. Why?"

Many men had asked me that for I was not the biggest of warriors and others were as skilful with a sword as I was. Olaf Leather Neck could and did kill more men in combat but I survived each time someone tried to defeat me in single combat. I could not lie to my son. I had promised myself that I would be completely honest with this son. "I think it is the sword." I had hung it on the wall and the fire made the blue stones sparkle.

"Because it is touched by the gods?"

"Do you want me to tell the story or would you like to guess what I am going to say?"

"Sorry."

"The sword was touched by the gods but when Bjorn Bagsecgson made it for me there was part of the spirit of Old Ragnar in it as well as my blood. The lightning which struck it made it harder but that does not mean it gives me extra power or strength. Rather it means that when I use it the blade is guided by the spirits. Old Ragnar lives in the sword." I shrugged, "I trust the blade and when it is in my hand I feel at one with it. A sword, any sword, is special and the warrior who thinks not so will die sooner rather than later."

He looked disappointed and was silent.

"What is in your heart, my son?" He looked up at me. "I want honesty. There will be no mistrust between us."

"I thought that I would have your sword when I became a warrior."

I stared into the fire. "If I die in battle it will be buried with me if my men can claim my body. If I grow old and incapable of fighting then it will be yours but that does not mean you will be a great warrior."

"No?"

"No. When you are a warrior we will pay Bjorn Bagsecgson to make you a sword. He will speak with you and he will spend many weeks thinking about what is the best for you. He will make it carefully. It will be like a baby being born. It will take months for you will want it to be perfect. When it is ready to be tempered for the last time then we will shed some of your blood. Your mother will not like that. And the blood will join you and the blade together."

"And then it will be ready?"

"No for then the blade will be engraved, the guard and pommel fitted and the handle made. When it is sharpened it will almost be ready but then you will have to make your own scabbard. Finally, we will visit with Aiden and he will use his magic so that it can only be used by you."

"How do you mean?"

"When you and your sword are together you will be greater than you and the sword apart. If another steals your sword or takes it from you in battle it will avail him nothing."

He too stared into the fire. "Then I need to grow as quickly as I can for I need a sword to fight alongside you. I am not far behind Ragnar and I will be going to war next year. I can feel it."

I leaned over and whispered, "Then let that be a secret between us. Do not let your mother know or both our lives will be made a misery!"

The moment when we were alone was soon broken as the servants and slaves began to bring in the food. Brigid said, "Gruffyd, tell Ragnar we are eating. He will be with those warriors of his in the warrior hall." As he raced out she said, "Your son has missed you. Ragnar spends less time with him. He was close to Garth."

I nodded, "I will be here for most of the winter. It will be fine."

She gave me a sharp look, "Most?"

I was saved from answering by the arrival of Kara, Aiden and Ylva. I knew I had not escaped an interrogation it was merely postponed!

One of the joys of being at home was the food. Brigid and Elfrida were both excellent and inventive cooks. The riches we enjoyed also included spices and ingredients from further afield. When we raided we ate either salted meat or fish or hunks of horsemeat cooked over a fire. When we were home we also had wine. I liked beer but as I grew older I found that I needed to make water more often when I drank beer. Both food and drink were plentiful and the mood was happy.

I sat with Aiden and we spoke of our raids, "Why did you send the relics back to Dyflin? I would have thought they would have fetched a better price in Lundenwic."

"And normally they would but these were relics of St. Brigit, St. Columba and St. Patrick. These are saints who are revered by the Hibernians. Two of them contained bones. Believe me, they will have a higher price in Dyflin. I will accompany Olaf Grimsson when he travels to Dyflin. I will set the price."

"And the prisoners? You had a letter."

"It was addressed to you but I knew what it was about. Donnachada mac Fiachnae is keen to have his family back. The price he offers is satisfactory. I waited until you returned to confirm that we would accept." I nodded. "His ship returns soon. I will go with the prisoners to Úlfarrston. When we have exchanged I will take my family and the relics. We will travel to Dyflin."

I looked up, surprised, "Kara will leave here?" Since she had been duped into going to Ynys Môn she had rarely wished to travel.

"It is Ylva. She wishes to visit the land of her father's birth. She is a deep one. She says the rocks and the earth will speak to her."

"She has the power then?"

"She has far more than either Kara or myself."

I was aware that both Ragnar and Gruffyd were hanging on our every word. That was natural. They learned how to fight with Karl and Einar. By listening to Aiden and to me speaking they learned how to think.

"And you, Jarl Dragonheart, have the two raids settled your fiery heart and eased the pain of your loss?"

Smiling I said, "You know that it has not which is why you asked the question, galdramenn."

He nodded, "Wessex and King Egbert are too big a mouthful for you, Jarl. It would not be like going to Din Guardi." I stared at him. I was used to him knowing me but how did he know that had been in my mind? He smiled, "It is no trick. I spoke with Olaf. He said you had spoken of Din Guardi. Had we tried to kill the king in his castle it would have been hard. We sought renegades who would not be missed. Did you think we would have escaped the wrath of the Saxons if we had killed their king? If you wish vengeance upon Egbert then it will be on the field of battle. Are we ready to face his armies?"

I turned and looked at the eager faces of Ragnar and Gruffyd, "Not until my son and grandson can stand in the shield wall." That pleased them and seemed to satisfy Aiden.

"That is wise. I heard from our knarr captains that Mercia is on the brink of defeat. When you defeated King Coenwulf you aided King Egbert. His sons were not the king their father had been. When Wessex controls Mercia then there will only be the kingdoms of the East Angles and Northumbrians which are outside his control. He is close to being the High King of the Saxons. He will have armies beyond number then."

I emptied my horn and held it for Uhtric to fill. He used a cloth to wipe the surplus from the silver rim of the cow's horn. "Then perhaps we need to have an army to match that of the Saxons."

I knew by his silence that I had surprised Aiden. His silence was evidence that he was thinking of my words.

"Could we do that grandfather? Where would we get the warriors?"

"We did it on a smaller scale when I gathered our allies. When your father was alive we had jarls like Gunnstein Berserk Killer and Gunnar Thorfinnson who brought their drekar to sail with us. Although some, like Thorfinn Blue Scar, are gone there are others. The islands to the north of us are filled with small communities. Alone they can only raid villages. If we all sailed together then we could take Lundewic!"

I saw that I had excited my son and grandson. Aiden poured cold water on the moment, "But you will not."

I shook my head, "You read my mind, Aiden, no I will not. Not yet." The disappointment was written all over the faces of my two young heirs. "But Neustria is a different proposition."

Aiden nodded, "It is far from here and it is winter. Your enemy will think you have forgotten him and that he is safe. That would need careful planning. You would need information such as we had when we attacked Din Guardi."

I nodded, "I did not expect to go soon."

Ragnar asked, "Neustria? Have we enemies there?"

"Grimbould of Neustria paid for the killers who came for your father. We raided his lands and he was using others to do his work for him. He is a Frank and has no honour."

Gruffyd asked, "Where is Neustria?"

"It is part of the Empire of the Franks. Grimbould had power and was second only to the King and Emperor, Lothair. Your father's raid lost him his power and his title. He still rules part of Neustria."

"Where?"

Aiden shook his head, "It is in the north of the kingdom close to the border with Austrasia. It is said his wife is a Frisian noblewoman. From what Raibeart discovered on his last voyage to Dorestad Grimbould has aspirations to be king. He seeks a throne. He paid the gold to the assassins because he had lost power. He thinks you have forgotten him."

"Then he is wrong. We would need charts and maps as well as information as to his whereabouts."

"All that we know is that he has his home on an island on the River Somme. I think it is near to an abbey."

I smiled, "Then it seems your visit to Dyflin is *wyrd*. We may be cut off from news but Gunnstein Berserk Killer has many visitors. He may know more. When you return, we will talk again of this."

I was suddenly aware that Brigid and the others had stopped talking and were listening to us. "Talk more about what? Return from where?"

Kara knew my mind as well as any. She smiled, "Ylva wishes to visit Dyflin. We will be travelling hence with the royal prisoners."

Brigid seemed mollified, "But what information do you wish?"

Aiden said, easily, "Charts, maps, writing. The more we know about our enemies the better we are prepared." He stood, "Let us drink to Jarl Dragonheart. He is a wise leader and successful leader. What we have we owe to him. Dragonheart!"

All stood and toasted me. Brigid and my son had pride in their eyes. I saw in Elfrida's face, gratitude while Kara, Aiden and Ylva had a look of satisfaction. The three of them had become one and that one could read my mind and my actions as easily as an ancient book.

As we lay in bed that night Brigid cuddled in to me. "What is going on in that mind of yours, my husband?"

"Nothing. I enjoyed this evening and the food was well cooked."

"What is cooking, my warrior is something which involves the wizard and you. I am not a fool and I saw your heads close together. When you and Aiden are thus then it means something is afoot."

I could not lie to my wife but I would not worry her either. "Aiden is finding information which may lead to a raid in Neustria."

She pulled away from me. "But we have all that we need! We are told not to be greedy!

"Your White Christ says that. We are pagans are we not? There is no such thing as enough. Besides is it not better to raid far from home rather than risk the enmity of our neighbours? We have quelled our enemies close to home. The King of Wessex is our enemy. He will come for us one day. We have bloodied his nose too many times for it not to be so. We do not have a large number of warriors so when he comes we need the best-armed warriors we can manage and that requires treasure. You would have our son and daughter be safe would you not?" She nodded. "Elfrida deserves to be protected from the husband she left?" Again she nodded. I saw a tear trickle down her cheek. "Then I must do what I do. I must prepare for war and hope for peace."

She kissed me, "And that marks you as different from the others like Haaken and Olaf. They hope for war."

It was my turn to nod, "And the difference between us is my mother. She is from the old people and is part of this land. She guided me to

Hibernia and Strathclyde. That turned out well. You must trust me, my love."

"And I do. But do not chide me for worrying about you too!"

Aiden and Kara left for Úlfarrston with Ylva three days later. Before she left Kara said, enigmatically, "The spirits will reward you soon, father."

Before I could say anything more she was gone along with the royal prisoners. Karl One Hand was happy to see them go. He had to provide guards and servants for them. He was a warrior and did not enjoy being a gaoler! Despite the fact that the winds had turned to come from the north bringing rain and sleet he seemed as happy as I had ever seen him as he worked with Ragnar and Gruffyd as well as the other young warriors. The addition of the hearth-weru had helped for they did not stand idly by when help was needed. We had another fifteen boys to train as warriors. Most were mainly younger than Ragnar although Erik Larsson and his family had only arrived in the summer and, at thirteen summers had less training than even Gruffyd.

"How goes it, Karl?"

"Better since I got rid of those Hibernians. Do they never wash?"

"And my son and grandson?"

"Since you gave them your decision they have improved each day. Ragnar continues his training with Einar and the others when he has finished here. Einar is almost exhausted by him. By Gói he will be ready."

"Good."

"But Jarl, you need to look no further than the others for your next crew. Having Einar and his men has helped. I shall be sad when Ragnar leaves me for he will take with him six warriors who know their business. They are not Ulfheonar but they have skills. The ones you see here will be ready by this time next year to go to war."

I pointed to Ulf Bergilsson who was but eight summers old, "Even young Ulf there and my son Gruffyd?"

"Ulf? Yes for his archery is good and while he cannot pull a war bow yet, he can use a sling. His sword and spear skills are improving. It is only his size which would stop him."

"But his father is a big warrior."

"Aye. Sometimes the young get a spurt. Perhaps he might benefit from a little longer but his skills will be of the standard you desire. As would Gruffyd but I do not think that Gruffyd will defeat me yet. He has the eye and he has the mind but he does not have the strength." He hesitated, "Will you take them on the wolf hunt this year?"

"Perhaps."

"Ragnar mentioned it and Gruffyd seemed keen. They know the story of how you were Ragnar's age when you killed your first wolf and all know the story of Wolf Killer."

Once more Haaken and his tales came back to haunt me. "It depends if we have any who would be Ulfheonar."

"I have only heard of two. Cnut Cnutson wishes to be as his father was, oathsworn and Ulfheonar. The other is Erik Bjornson. He too would be as his father."

"They are ready?"

"I would ask Snorri but they have all the skills you need. I know not if they could hunt the wolf. Even I found that hard."

"Then we will go hunting the wolf. Even if Ragnar and Gruffyd do not take part, watching others would give them an idea of what it takes to be a warrior."

I watched them spar for a while and then when I saw Gruffyd begin to try to hurt Ulf Bergilsson I left. He was showing off to impress his father. My departure would send a message to him. I would not humiliate him by telling him off. That was not my way. When I left I went to Bjorn Bagsecgson. He was hard at work at one of his fires. His sons and grandsons were all employed by this master weaponsmith.

"How goes it, son of Thor?"

He laughed, "Aye it sometimes feels like I have taken on the weight of the gods. Business is brisk and we all profit. My family are happy. All that I have left, at any rate."

The departure of Bjorn's favourite son had upset him. "You know that your son, Bagsecg, had to leave. He could not live in your shadow. It was why Wolf Killer left me."

"Aye Jarl and that is what makes me ache inside. He lives far across the ocean. I know that Jarl Gunnar is a good leader but it is a small clan. I have more grandchildren I will never see. It saddens my wife too. Each day she dies a little."

"As we all do. I can offer you no comfort Bjorn Bagsecg for I, at least, have my grandson and my son's wife to remind me of what I lost." I waved a hand at the strong young smiths who toiled away. "Perhaps this should give you satisfaction. Your family who remain."

"You are right and it does no good to bemoan our fate. The Norns weave their webs and we must endure." He brightened a little as he touched Thor's hammer hanging from his neck. "And what can I do for you this morning?"

I told him of my conversation with Gruffyd. "And I daresay I will need a sword for Ragnar."

"They are both some way off. Ragnar grows day by day. Einar the Tall and his hearth-weru are helping to make him into a strong warrior but he still has some way to go until he grows into his father. I would say this time next year for his sword. As for Gruffyd...?"

"I thought to bring them to you so that they can tell you what they wish for the blade that they will use. If Ragnar will be ready in a year then you will begin it soon after the winter moon."

"Aye, that would be the best. Bring them along then. I will find a good blank."

I shook my head. "When you forged my sword you began from pieces of iron which you carefully chose. I would have that for my grandson. I owe his father as much."

"Then you are right. We will need to begin that soon. I will choose the metal. The mines have been processing a rich vein of late. The last batch was amongst the purest I have seen." Nodding he said, "This is *wyrd.*"

"And they will both need mail. Karl thinks that Ragnar will be ready for war soon and Gruffyd will not be long after."

"Will they be in the front rank?"

I laughed, "They will be watching the horses or guarding the archers. I doubt that the mail will need to take a blow but it will harden them if they wear it."

"I have some from Strathclyde. They wear shorter byrnies. I do not mind making one to fit but it takes time and if it will not need to take a blow then I would rather re-use one we already have."

I nodded, "As I recall the first mail I had I took from a dead Saxon and it was both too big and badly made. I survived."

I knew that Aiden would not hurry back. He would have to wait in Úlfarrston for the ransom and then sail to Dyflin. Once there he would try to get the best price he could for the slaves and the relics. Good trading took time. There were not markets every day and Aiden would wish for a good price. In addition, he would need to wait for the church to hear of the relics.

The ransom arrived two days after Aiden had left. Raibeart Ap Pasgen himself escorted it. Donnachada mac Fiachnae had kept his word and we were richly rewarded. I gave Raibeart his share and put Ketil's and Sigtrygg's to one side. There was no rush to send it to them and both jarls would visit me around Yule and the winter moon. Asbjorn was pleased to see his share. He had his eye on the daughter of a hill farmer and wanted to buy slaves for her. Then he would marry her. We had been capturing slaves since our time on Man and now we had children born whose parents were slaves. That was one reason why we did not need to break in new slaves. The ones we had were born to it and were more compliant. Asbjorn's marriage was another sign that my men were ageing. Soon some would fall in battle or hang up their swords. Even as the thought came into my head I dismissed it. My Ulfheonar would all die with a sword in their hand.

Chapter 7

Aiden did not return until Samhain. However, before then my wife gave me news. It was news my daughter had hinted at but it still took me by surprise. "I am with child, husband." She patted her tummy. "I have felt him move."

"Are you certain? Kara is not here."

"Your daughter is not the only woman in the settlement. Elfrida has skills and she has confirmed it. The signs are all there but most important of all, I know."

I hugged her and then said, cheekily, "That does not sound very Christian to me! Feelings sound pagan!"

She cuffed me about the ear, "You never change!"

"And would you wish me to? I think not. You say he, how do you know?"

She blushed and shook her head, "I know not! It is just a feeling." Her head came up and she glared at me, "Not a word from you! It would serve you right if it were a girl!"

I picked her up and kissed her, "I care not if it is boy or girl so long as the bairn has the right number of toes, fingers, eyes and a nose!"

I was in a good mood when Aiden and his family returned. I now understood Kara's parting message. He came back with carts full of goods they had bought. As they were unpacked I saw that there were many fine pots. I knew that they had come from Frankia and would be expensive. Bolts of fine cloth were also unloaded as well as the spices and herbs we could not grow ourselves.

Aiden saw my look and took out a chest, "I did not spend all our gold, Dragonheart. I sold the relics to three different churchmen. They were keen for them all and they spent heavily to get them. I made a note of where their churches lie for if they have that much gold to spend how much more will they have hidden?"

I took his arm and led him to the Water, "And most important of all what news did you glean?"

"Jarl Gunnar's brother, Gunnstein, was lost on the Liger. He and his whole crew died. He has taken it badly."

"Then he has suffered a loss as hard as mine."

He nodded. "The Hibernians we defeated are now in danger of being swallowed up by their High King. Gunnstein Berserk Killer was worried that there would be an alliance of local kings under the High King. It could threaten Dyflin."

"And Strathclyde?"

"No one had any news. Their ships have not traded since the raid." I nodded. That was to be expected. "Mercia is now beleaguered by Wessex. It is a matter of time before he is defeated. Kent and Essex are kings who pay homage to Wessex. He is almost High King. They have kings but they are kings in name only. Of the East Angles, I have heard little save that they are biting chunks out of Mercia. That kingdom is being devoured by its neighbours."

"And we will need to wait until Ketil visits before we will know of Northumbria."

I stared across my Water. Things had changed so much since first we had come here. Then Northumbria was our biggest enemy and now it was Wessex.

I turned back and saw a smug smile on Aiden's face. "And the maps and charts?"

"I have them and more. By chance or perhaps it was the Norns I know not but there was a small vessel from Dorestad in port. Frisia, it seems is under attack by raiders such as us. The Emperor has hired Danes to protect it."

"That is like inviting the wolf to be your sheepdog."

"Aye, I know. He will learn. However, this has upset Grimbould of Neustria. His wife's family have suffered at the hands of these sea raiders and Grimbould has petitioned the Emperor to be Mayor of Frisia. It was rejected. It was felt that as he could not stop us in Neustria then he would have little chance against more numerous enemies. The sea captain suggested that Grimbould had made many enemies. He has few friends and only the men he hires."

"That is good and I believe that this is the work of the Norns. The Weird Sisters have been quiet overlong! You have good maps and charts?"

"I paid a good price to the Frisian. I will make copies for you over the winter." He hesitated, "You have not mentioned this to Brigid?"

"No, and she is with child so I will wait a while longer."

"But you will be going over winter?"

"Aye, but how did you know?"

"The enemy will not expect it. One ship sailing alone could hide and a good crew could pull this off. It is like Din Guardi."

"Would you come with us?"

"Of course. Ylva now has great powers. They do not need me and there is an abbey close to Grimbould's island and the remnants of a Roman fort. I cannot resist such a treasure. They mean little to you but to me, they are more valuable than gold."

"Good, my men will be much happier knowing that you are with us."

We butchered the old animals and after taking the bones which could be used we burned the rest to spread on the ground for better crops. The pigs were let loose in the fields of barley, rye and oats to feed on the stalks and to lay their dung on the land. The meat from the dead animals was salted, smoked or brined. We packed them into barrels that were buried beneath the ground. Drying fish littered the side of the Water. The harvests were sorted into that which could be stored and that which would spoil. Some was fed to the animals but others were mixed with the spices which Aiden had brought back and the last of the previous year's stored meat and then soaked in beer and honey. We would eat the pudding at Yule. It was a treat we all enjoyed. As we were not at war everyone, warriors too, joined in the race against time to preserve what we could while we could.

Aiden had barely made it back before the first snows closed off our valley. Ketil did not manage to reach us before the snow came. We struggled to have riders reach Windar's Mere and Ulla's Water was also cut off. I had planned on visiting Harland Windarsson to see how his improvements progressed. We found ourselves restricted to our hall and our walls. We had had a good year and our granaries were full. Most of the animals had been brought down from the fells and the high ground before winter. A few hardy farmers struggled up with their dogs to bring them back down. Even though it was winter there was no time for idle hands. We had cut logs before we went raiding but we would need more. Men and their sons went up the slopes to trim the trees of their lower branches. Ragnar and Gruffyd went with them to strengthen their arms and backs. We left the longer ones for our drekar and knarr. Women were busy spinning and weaving. The cloth which Kara had bought was carefully sewn into new garments. They were finer than that spun in the homes of our women. As such, they were prized, not by the men, but by their wives.

And all the time Bjorn and his smiths turned out metal; most were weapons but there were implements for farming and weaving. The iron still came from the mountains. We could still mine, even in winter and Bjorn's furnaces were fed the charcoal we made in the forests. Our wars and raids had depleted our stocks of arrows and spearheads as well as lead balls for the boys. The day we ran low would be the day that men began to die.

Kara confirmed what we all knew. Brigid would have another child. The gods had sent me another child to replace Wolf Killer. Elfrida was happier than any. Since the death of my son, she had grown closer to Kara and my daughter had begun to develop her skills. She had something of the volva in her. She was Saxon born but the Saxons, too, had witches. Since the coming of the new religion of the White Christ, they had been shunned and Elfrida had hidden her ability for years. In the house of women, it was harnessed. She was spending an increasing amount of time there.

I was wrapped in my wolf cloak walking along the shore of my Water and she, also wrapped in furs, joined me. "What brings you out here, Elfrida? I thought it was just mad old warriors who did such things."

"I enjoy the fresh air and the sharpness of the cold. It makes me realise the power that is nature as well as the warmth of our hall."

"Good, for I shall enjoy the company." I knew there was more to her presence but I was happy to be alone with her. I had liked her since before she had first chosen my son over King Egbert.

We walked in silence and then she said, "I cannot lie nor deceive you, Jarl. I came out here to speak with you."

I nodded and said nothing. She slipped her arm through mine and I put my cloak over her shoulders. I was warm. My sealskin boots kept out the cold and my woollen kyrtle was well made. I had spent my youth in the high mountains of Norway. This was not cold. I waited. She would speak when she was ready.

"When your child is born that will be the time that Ragnar becomes a man and goes to war."

"Perhaps. Just because he has hearth-weru does not mean he will defeat Karl."

"Einar has spoken with me. He believes that he will. I am not unhappy. His father wanted him to be a warrior but I know that I will be losing him. All mothers lose their sons. It is hard but we must bear it for it is *wyrd*."

"You are wise Elfrida. I fear Brigid will not be so understanding when Gruffyd goes to war."

"She will have to learn." She stopped so that she could face me. "When that happens and your child is born I shall leave your home and join Kara's house of women."

For some reason that saddened me even though the two halls were close together and I would still see her every day. "You need not leave because your son goes."

"I know but this is something I wish. Your daughter and I are close. We are closer than Brigid and me. It is not your wife's fault. She is a good woman but she frowns upon our beliefs and I would not offend her by staying. Besides I can be of more use in the house of women. I have skills. With Ragnar a man grown and not mine to care for I can harness all of my powers. The clan needs the power we have. We can heal and we can use our connection to the Mother to increase the yield and bounty of the land. You know it is no accident that we have a fine harvest every year and our animals produce many young."

"Aye, you are right. Windar's Mere and Ulla's Water do not produce as much as we do." I squeezed her shoulder. "I shall be sad to see you go."

"And I shall be as sad. I could not have hoped for a better father. Even when Wolf Killer behaved badly you did not abandon him nor me and his children. You are a true leader, Dragonheart. I had heard of you before I met you but I was afraid of you. The man I imagined and the man I met are as different as night and day." She stood on tiptoes to kiss my cheek. "And I am not leaving you. I am giving you space. That is all."

We turned to walk back. "Will you tell Brigid?"

"Let us leave that until she has had the child. She is a little more fragile than I was."

"Aye, she is that but you are right, she is a good woman and I am happy that she came into my life."

Yule came and went and the snow did not abate. If anything they increased in ferocity. I began to wonder if we would be able to hunt the wolf. Mörsugur would soon be upon us. The wolves were howling and, no doubt, hunting but would we be able to venture forth and hunt them? I sought the advice of Aiden and Kara. They seemed to be expecting me and they had the news I wished to hear, "It will be cold but no more snow will fall in the first week of Mörsugur. The wolves can be hunted."

"My father is right, Jarl Dragonheart but there will be danger when you hunt the wolf. I fear for my cousins."

I turned to face Ylva. "How do you know they will be on the hunt? I have not decided if I will take them or not yet."

She smiled enigmatically, "But you will take them will you not?"

I shook my head, "I should have known that a child made by you two would not behave like a child." I picked her up and cuddled her. "You are a woman in a child's body. I shall embrace the child and fear the woman."

She kissed me and, as I placed her back on the floor, she said, "I will always be your grandchild but I carry on the work of my parents when they are in the Otherworld. I will ensure the safety of the clan."

"Good and you can trust me to protect your two cousins. I have been hunting the wolf since I was a little older than you. I do not take risks and I respect the wolf."

"Good." She hesitated, "Then give them a wolf token. If the smith makes one I will put a spell upon it."

I looked at Kara who smiled, "She has great powers, father. This is good."

And so we prepared for the hunt. I had two metal wolves made for Ragnar and Gruffyd. They were identical to the ones I gave my Ulfheonar. The difference was that these were not made of gold. Golden wolves were given to Ulfheonar. Cnut Cnutson and Erik Beornsson were asked if they were ready to hunt the wolf and they said that they were. With Beorn the Scout and Snorri, we would make a party of seven who would hunt the wolf. Einar was unhappy that he could not come but when we pointed out the magic number and told him that Wolf Killer had done this at the same age he was a little happier. It mattered not for it was my decision.

The hard one to persuade was Brigid. There were tears. That was not unusual. Elfrida was right she was more fragile than my daughter or herself. It was Elfrida who persuaded Brigid that this would turn out well. How she did that I have no idea but when they returned to the hall Brigid was resigned to the expedition.

Our preparations were made for the hunt. Snorri and Beorn left, while it was still snowing, and they scouted for wolf tracks. They needed fresh snow to confirm the position of the pack. Their howling told us roughly where they were but we needed the site of their lair. When they returned they told us that the wolves were back in Lang's Dale. Lang had been a farmer who had lived in this land before we came and he and his family had been taken by wolves. It was imperative that we rid that dale of wolves. Snorri told me that they had found one farmstead where the wolves had taken the farmer and his family. They were a family who was new to my valley and I had not even met them. The wolves would have to die.

My daughter's predictions were perfect. The night before we were to hunt the snow stopped and the night was clear and cold. The land froze once more. That was the perfect time to hunt for the wolves could not smell as well in the cold. We left before dawn when our breath froze before our faces. We rode ponies and we had four spares with us. We wore no mail for the metal attracted the cold. We were well wrapped in layers and three of us wore our wolf cloaks. Snorri and Beorn carried bows as did Ragnar and Gruffyd. My two Ulfheonar candidates and I carried boar spears. I had Ragnar's Spirit around my waist. We rode in silence for while the wolves sense of smell might be impaired, they still had excellent hearing. I rode behind my two heirs. Cnut and Erik would concentrate on hunting the wolf while Snorri and Beorn would have to find them.

As we neared the dale I realised that Snorri was not taking us to the place the wolves had lived before. They had moved. It showed the intelligence of this deadly predator. We dropped down the dale into a tangle of rocks and scrubby bushes. Snorri held up his hand and dismounted. He hobbled his pony and then tied it to a tree. We emulated him and prepared to go on foot. This would be hard for the boys. On a pony, you felt safer. Here, on the ground, everything seemed a threat. I had taken them both hunting but that had been with many more men and for deer. This was a killer we hunted. He would be hunting us. I pointed to Cnut's footprints and mimed for the boys to put their feet in the same place.

The wolf pack had chosen a good den. The narrow jumble of rocks would be easy for a wolf to navigate but it was hard for hunters. It ascended and twisted through stunted trees and scrubby bushes. The frozen snow made them even more treacherous. To one side a mountain beck tumbled and spluttered. I began to worry about my two charges. This was a dangerous country. I tapped them on the shoulder and motioned for them to get behind me.

The task for Snorri and Beorn the Scout was to get the two warriors close enough to the wolves to hunt them. As soon as Snorri stopped and waved them forward then I knew we were close even though I saw and smelled nothing. Erik and Cnut had discussed their strategy. They would work together. It was safer that way and in the spirit of the Ulfheonar. They both dropped their cloaks as they began to ascend the last hundred paces to the triangle of rocks above a black hole- the lair of the wolf pack.

Ragnar and Gruffyd had their bows about their shoulders. I tugged at the bows and they nodded. They took them and pulled an arrow from their quiver. I held my spear in two hands. If the wolves attacked then it would take both hands and a good thrust to kill one. As soon as they had an arrow readied I stared to the sides of the two hunters as they climbed. The two hunters would watch the front but I knew that wolves could attack from the side. On either side of the two Snorri and Beorn were ready with barbed arrows. These were specially made by Bjorn Bagsecg and were perfect for hunting wolves.

I no longer felt the cold. The tension was too great. Each step took the two warriors closer to an unknown number of wolves. It could be just a family but it was more likely to be a pack. Snorri and Beorn would only release an arrow if the lives of Cnut and Erik were in danger. If that happened then they would have failed the test.

I saw Snorri looking around and listening. He sensed that something was wrong. I instinctively moved closer to my son and grandson. I too listened and I smelled the air. Erik and Cnut continued their painstaking way to the mouth of the lair. I was aware that Ragnar and Gruffyd were pressing against me and willing me to move. Then I heard it. A noise to our left where there should have been silence. The tumbling beck to our right made a noise but that was not what made me swivel my head to the left. I stared into the snow. The undergrowth was thicker there. I kept my eyes fixed on a bush and looked at the shadows. Perhaps it had been my imagination. The sound had gone. As I looked I was drawn to a leaf without snow. The snow was hard and frozen. We had not passed by the bush which was thirty paces from our left. I looked at the shadows. I had started to think that I had made a mistake when I saw breath becoming a cloud. When I saw the breath I saw the eyes. It was a wolf.

I clicked my tongue as I turned to my left. I moved my spear to point and as Snorri turned his head and saw the spear Beorn yelled, "Wolf! Left!"

Everything happened really quickly. Howls rang out around us as the pack gave their challenge. The large male which I had spotted leapt from cover. At the same time, four adolescent wolves jumped up at Snorri and Beorn. Erik and Cnut made the mistake of turning and two big female wolves erupted from the den with younger ones behind them. There was no time to think of the others. I had Ragnar and Gruffyd to protect. My warriors were men and they would have to deal with their wolves themselves. I braced the spear against my right foot and held it steady. The wolf would go for my head and throat. This would be a test of nerve. Most men ran when a wolf attacked. Therein lay death. You had to face your foe and trust in your weapons. You faced your foe as though he was a warrior and hoped that you were better.

Two arrows sped from behind me. Ragnar and Gruffyd were defending me. One caught the wolf a glancing blow and the other embedded itself in its shoulder. They did not even slow it up. He was a big one. My wolf cloak came from a large wolf but it was not as big as this chief who came to kill me.

I yelled over my shoulder, "Take out your swords!"

The arrows my son and grandson had would not hurt the wolf. The two boys' only chance lay in their short swords. If they could find a vital spot then they could kill the wolf should it succeed in slaying me. I concentrated on its head. When it leapt I would have one chance to kill it. Its mouth opened as it sprang. It jumped higher than any wolf I had ever seen before. It must have used the hard ground. As it came up I braced myself and adjusted the head of the spear. I wanted the wolf to impale itself on my spear but to do that I risked his teeth near my throat. Not for the first time I was glad that I had a wolf and a dragon around my neck. If I had not had my foot braced against the spear and a rock I would have been knocked from my feet but the spear drove deep into the wolf's chest. Its mouth bared wide showing savage teeth. They came towards me. It is not easy to kill a wolf. I lifted my left arm. It was well wrapped in layers. I rammed it across the mouth of the wolf. The teeth closed upon my arm and even through layers, I felt the pain of his powerful bite. I had struck a fatal blow but the beast was not dead. I used my left arm to throw the wolf to one side. The movement broke the spear. As we fell I drew my seax and, keeping my left arm in the wolf's mouth, I ripped the seax across its throat as we tumbled to the ground.

I looked up and saw that Cnut and Erik were beset by more wolves. I drew Ragnar's Spirit and yelling, "Ulfheonar!" I ran towards them. Beorn lay on the ground, a dead wolf at his feet. Snorri was just finishing off the wolf which had attacked him but the two hunters were surrounded by adolescent males. I brought my sword across the back of one young male. It severed its spine and almost cut it in two. I cursed myself for the blade stuck. I drew it out and plunged it into the side of a second young male. It turned its head to snap at me. Stepping back I pulled out my sword and slashed it sideways. The sword took the snout from the wolf.

"Dragonheart!" I heard the cry from my son and grandson as they ran up the slope with their short swords in their hands. They were coming to defend me once more.

It was a small thing but it proved pivotal. With a howl, the largest young male left alive turned and led the pack away. There were just six left. From their size, I guessed that there were four females and a male. They ran west. They would need to be hunted before they bred again. They had battled humans and wolves were clever; if they survived then they learned.

Cnut and Erik had both been bitten and were bleeding but I saw that they had both killed their females. "Ragnar and Gruffyd come and bind the wounds of these two new Ulfheonar."

I saw the look of pride in their eyes. I turned and ran down to Beorn. It was fortunate that I kept my sword out for, as Snorri bent over Beorn and I neared the unconscious scout, the wolf which had lain at his feet suddenly leapt at Snorri. I put all my strength into that one swing of my sword. Snorri had no weapon in his hand for he cradled his friend's head. Ragnar's Spirit did not let me down. It bit into the neck of the wolf and tore through the powerful muscles and then severed its bones and its head.

Snorri looked up, "Thank you Jarl. I owe you a life."

"How is he?" I sheathed my sword and seax.

"It looks like his head collided with the wolf even as he stabbed it. He is unconscious but she bit his arm." I looked at the left arm. The wolf's teeth had ripped through his layers of clothes and I could see the bone and chewed flesh.

"We need fire and we need shelter. Go into the cave and see if they are all fled." As he did so I grabbed a handful of the snow and packed it around the wound. Aiden had told me that snow slowed the bleeding. I then took off Beorn's belt and used it to tighten around his upper arm. That done I picked him up and laid him over my shoulders. I plodded my way up through the snow. Cnut and Erik had been tended to by Ragnar and Gruffyd.

"Cnut, go with Snorri and clear the den. Erik, go with the boys and fetch the ponies. I do not want the survivors of our attack to take them."

"Aye Jarl. Come boys and keep a good watch. We are not out of danger yet."

It was a short time since Erik Bjornson had killed his wolf but already there was a change in him. He had a more authoritative manner. He was Ulfheonar. I had to lay Beorn down outside the cave for I could not climb inside with him on my shoulder.

Snorri appeared. "There are none alive but we have found the bones of the farmer and his family." Over his shoulder, I saw a glow. He had the fire going.

"Then perhaps we will keep Beorn out here. I have sent for the ponies. If we can burn the wound we can get back to Cyninges-tūn and Aiden can heal him. I am not worried about his arm but remember when Haaken had the head wound?"

"Aye, and we have not the skill to go into his skull no matter how thick it is!" He meant well for he and Beorn were old friends and had shared many dangers together.

Cnut Cnutson emerged, "The fire is going well. I used the bedding the wolves had gathered and their fur," he looked back towards the cave, "and the bones. It seemed fitting."

"Aye Cnut, that was well done. You had best begin to prepare the wolves. We have six to gut. You both did well!"

He smiled, "It was a shock when they attacked from the side."

"The hunt is good preparation for a battle. You know not what the enemy will do."

"How did you know Jarl?"

"I did not but Snorri's ears alerted me."

Snorri said, "I heard something but could see nothing. It just did not feel right. Wolves keep sentries watching and you and Erik were so close that you should have been attacked. The leader was a cunning one."

I heard a whinny as the ponies smelled the foxes that had been attracted by the blood. I heard Erik singing to them to calm them. "Cnut, skin Beorn's wolf. We will use its skin to keep him warm. Snorri, go and get a brand hot enough to sear."

They both left and I used my seax to cut open the remaining garments on Beorn's arm. I loosened and then tightened the belt. As the blood flowed I looked within it for anything which should not be there. The last thing we needed was an embedded tooth in his arm. As the flow stopped

I looked at the bone. The teeth had scored it but it was not broken. Beorn would have an arm that would now ache in the cold weather but at least he would have an arm.

Ragnar and Gruffyd joined me. Now that the battle was over I could see its effect. They were both shaking and it was not with the cold. It was often that way when men fought for the first time or had been close to death. They needed to be kept occupied. "Go and help Cnut skin the wolf. When he has done so then go and gut and skin my wolf."

"Truly! You will let us do that?"

"You did not falter and stood by your jarl. It was your sudden attack that drove away the wolves; of course, you can. Just do not make a mess of it. That will make a fine new cloak and I can retire this old one!" As they hurried to help Cnut I reflected that I did not mind if they butchered the cloak. Their survival was more important to me than a new cloak.

Beorn appeared to be breathing easily enough. I took some snow and, opening his mouth, forced some inside. It would melt. Kara had told me that water or beer helped to heal. I did not know how but I trusted my daughter. Snorri shouted from inside the cave, "The brand is almost hot enough, Jarl."

"Then bring it out. The sooner he has the wound sealed the better."

The fact that Beorn was unconscious helped. Snorri handed me the brand and, as he held down his friend's shoulders, I applied the fire to the flesh. There was a hiss and Beorn's body jerked a little. Then the air was filled with the smell of burning hair, flesh and cloth. I had to apply the brand in three places to make sure that the bleeding had stopped.

"Untie his belt and let us see if we have sealed it."

As Snorri did so I saw a small rivulet of blood appear from the seared and scorched flesh. I put the brand next to it and counted to two in my head. When I pulled it away it appeared to have stopped.

I looked up at the sky. It was just after noon. "We must leave now. We have a long way to go." Cnut appeared with the skin from Beorn's wolf. It had been a young male. "Wrap him in the cloak and tie him across his pony. It is not dignified but it will be safe. Erik, tie the carcasses to the ponies."

Ragnar and Gruffyd ran up with the skin of my wolf. They had done a good job. The skull was still attached. I had to smile to myself. Taking a skull out was not an easy task. Wisely they had left that task for me. Ragnar pointed to a long scar in the wolf's side. "We did not do that, grandfather."

"I know. It is an old wound. This was a mighty wolf, you have done well. Now help Erik and Cnut tie the wolves onto the ponies' backs and be gentle with the ponies. The smell of the wolves will make them afraid. Do as Erik did and sing to them."

The thought of having to spend a night in the open spurred us all and we soon had the animals packed. They were all heavily laden. We would have to leave some of them at the farm by the bridge at Skelwith. We headed down the slope and then picked our way back along the trail. Beorn began to move when we were just a mile or so from the bridge. We stopped and Snorri went to him.

"Good to see your eyes open, my old friend."

"Why am I strapped to a horse like a piece of meat?"

"Because you nearly were a corpse but your hard head helped you." Snorri untied him and we helped Beorn onto the back of his pony.

He looked at the wolves. "We defeated them?"

Snorri nodded, "We did but I think we will let others lead the hunt next time. We are getting too slow. If it had not been for the Jarl then the wolves might have feasted on our flesh."

It was a sobering thought that the oldest warrior had had the sharpest senses or perhaps it was the spirits. My work was not yet done.

Chapter 8

The weather began to warm at the start of Þorri. Beorn had healed and the two new Ulfheonar had been accepted into the ranks of my elite warriors. The hunters had been so impressed by Ragnar and Gruffyd that they had insisted that two of the young males' skins be given to them as cloaks. Gruffyd had said quietly to me, "Does this mean we are Ulfheonar?"

I laughed, "No it just means you will be warmer in winter. You did not kill them but you saw how hard it was to do so." My son had nodded. He learned quickly

The warming of the weather merely turned the snow into a muddy morass. Brigid complained about the mess we brought in each time we went out. Part of that was the child. She was much larger and our child was kicking more. My son and grandson spent every waking moment working on their skills. The wolf hunt had not diminished their desire to be warriors. It had, instead, shown them how hard it would be.

Gói was approaching and Einar the Tall had told Ragnar that he would be ready for Karl by then. I felt sorry for my son. He was younger but he so wanted to be able to be a warrior. I saw the envy in his eyes each time Ragnar was praised by his hearth-weru. I could do nothing about it. This was a lesson to be learned; the lesson was patience and would stand him in good stead when he did become a warrior.

The warming of the weather did bring Ketil. He stayed overnight and we feasted. After he had received his share of the treasure and we had eaten well he told us his news. "I have spoken with Prince Athelstan. His father appreciates our efforts against the King of Strathclyde. It has curbed their advances into Northumbria. In return, he told us of events in his land. The Danes have been driven from Eoforwic."

"There was a battle?"

"No. They just made life difficult for them. Some went to Frisia where they were employed to keep raiders from their shores. Others went to the land of the East Angles. There they are used as mercenaries too but some just disappeared into the quiet places. The Prince told me that they had set themselves up across Northumbria as warlords and petty chiefs.

They find somewhere they can defend and they extort from the Saxons. He and his horsemen will scour the land for them when the weather allows."

"And he is worried that they may come to our land?"

"We both are. I have been gathering wild horses and schooling them. We have enough now for me to send patrols deep into the high places when the snow has gone and the passes passable. I will be vigilant." He looked over at Ragnar, "It is good to see Wolf Killer's son with the cloak of the wolf skin. He is growing."

"Aye, Karl One Hand will test him when the ground dries out a little. He is eager."

"And then you raid?" I shrugged. "If you do then I am happy to come with you."

"When I sail I take but one drekar. I have an unfinished task I must complete and I would prefer you to watch your land. If there are Vikings on the loose then we, of all people, should recognise the danger. A Viking enemy is the most dangerous of enemies. When I return then we will think about a raid."

Brigid had sharp ears. "Return? Where are you going?"

There was little point in delaying the inevitable. The sooner she discovered my plan the sooner we could have the upset and then return to normality. "We will sail to Neustria. There is something I must do."

Her eyes filled with tears, "You raid?"

"Grimbould of Neustria lives yet."

Elfrida put her hand on Brigid's. "You need not do this for me, Jarl. I would prefer that men did not die on my behalf."

"It has nothing to do with you. My son needs vengeance. I want my enemies to know that if you hurt me I will come for you even if you live on the other side of the world. Even Egbert has learned that. We have discovered that Grimbould is more isolated now than he ever was. This is our opportunity."

Elfrida nodded as Brigid wept. "And Ragnar will go with you?"

"Ragnar and Gruffyd will be aboard the drekar. I know not if Ragnar will come ashore. He knows how to make that happen."

Ragnar nodded.

Brigid ran from the table. Elfrida said, "I will go to her. She will calm but I wish that you would not go."

"Do you see death?"

She shook her head, "I see no deaths but I know that there will be."

After the women had left us Ragnar asked, "We will be coming then?"

"You will." I smiled, "You might not be ready to fight but rowing will help."

"Rowing?"

"Your father did it. I did it. Ketil and all my Ulfheonar row. It helps you become part of the clan and it makes you into a rock. You cannot lead if you have not followed. Besides it is the best way to make a warrior have strong arms and a broad back."

"And me?"

"And you, my son, will come too although you will be used as a ships' boy. We shall only use you at the oars if we are desperate."

His jaw jutted as he said, "I can row!"

Ketil laughed, "That is the spirit but when your hands are red raw and blistered with salt; when your back aches then you might hope for the joys of racing up to the masthead!"

Although it was still unpleasant the road to Úlfarrston was passable and I went with Ragnar and Gruffyd to visit with Erik. When we were not at sea Erik and Bolli our shipwright worked on my drekar. I paid Bolli each time we raided. It was coin well spent.

They stopped what they were doing when I approached. "Jarl, this is unexpected."

"I wish to sail at the beginning of Gói."

"Where do we sail?"

"Neustria. I have the charts and Aiden will be coming with us but that information is for us only. We tell the rest of the world that we sail to Wessex."

Bolli, who was no warrior, asked, "Why Jarl Dragonheart?"

"I trust all of my people but other ships put into Úlfarrston and if word reached Neustria then the man I seek might flee. Besides, it does no harm to have King Egbert hearing of this and watching his borders. It might slow down his conquest of Mercia."

Erik shook his head, "From what we learned this winter Mercia's defeat is imminent."

"Then all the more reason for our deceit. We will take a minimal crew. I will be using the Ulfheonar. We travel light and, hopefully, return laden with treasure."

We left them and headed to meet with Coen Ap Pasgen the headman at Úlfarrston. When we were alone, with his brother Raibeart, I told them of my mission and my deceit. "But you can trust my people!"

"I know, Coen, but what of the ships of Jarl Gunnstein Berserk Killer? I trust him but do I know all of his men and sailors? A careless word can cost men their lives. The prey I seek is slippery. He is hiding from all and he will bolt if he knows I come for him. I will have to use cunning to catch him. I pray that you tell all that we are in Wessex."

"Even Jarl Gunnar Thorfinnson?"

"Even our friends. He lives close to Neustria. He might try to help me and in aiding me would hinder me. I mean no disrespect to our friends and allies but I know my mind. I wish to cloak myself in darkness. When we appear it will be as though we are wraiths from beyond the grave and my vengeance will be terrible to behold."

"I understand."

"Raibeart I would have you take the *'King's Gift'* and raid the south and west of Hibernia and Ynys Môn. It will give your young crew experience and if you leave after me then it might draw attention to you."

"I will and gladly. I like not this idleness. Since we returned from Strathclyde and Hibernia laden with treasure I have many young warriors who wish to serve. The *'King's Gift'* is a bigger drekar and I will enjoy the experience."

As we headed back to our home, hurrying to be back before darkness fell, Ragnar said, "There is more to being a leader than just fighting is there not grandfather?"

I nodded, "There is a game we must teach you. It came from the east. Aiden knows it well. The warriors of Miklagård call it the war game and some call it chess. It is hard to learn but it teaches you how to plan for war. When you learn the two of you can play against each other. It is a battle of the mind and not the arm. You should be equally matched."

"I look forward to that! It will be another skill for me. And do I take the hearth-weru with me when you raid?"

"You do. They can row and I will not have to worry when I leave the two of you aboard my drekar and seek Grimbould!"

Although Aiden was busy preparing charts he did not mind teaching the boys how to play the game of war. It gave me the chance, over the next few days to assemble my crew. With two more Ulfheonar and the six hearth-weru, I only needed six more men to man the oars. My Ulfheonar suggested some and I had others in mind. It took a week to finalise the preparations but we were ready. The ground had dried and the snow disappeared save from the top of the Úlfarrberg and the other high peaks. Ragnar came for me.

"We are ready to try to be warriors."

I looked at Gruffyd. "Both of you?" He nodded. "Then prepare and I will fetch Karl." I turned to Einar the Tall. "Bring the weapons we will use." We had swords that had no tips and blunted edges. If you were struck they could still break bones but they would not kill. I doubted that Gruffyd would even be able to lift his sword let alone use it but I admired him for trying. Hitherto they had used smaller swords. This would be the real thing.

Ragnar went first. That was good. He could have let Gruffyd go first and tire out old Karl but he did not and that showed character. Both Karl and Ragnar wore mail and had a helmet as they faced each other. Ragnar's shield looked slightly too big for him but it was the same size as the one he would take with us to Neustria. Snorri and Olaf Leather Neck sat with me and we would be the judges. It might be that the bout had to be ended and that would be our decision. We would be fair for if we were not then others might die because of our generosity. If Ragnar won it would be because he deserved it.

Karl had used many swords over the years and he soon had the feel of the training sword but this was the first time Ragnar had used a heavier sword. Einar had let him down a little. He should have used a heavier sword in practice. I hoped that the tree felling which Ragnar and Gruffyd had done had strengthened his arms.

Karl gestured with his sword, "Come on then, son of the Wolf Killer, my bad leg makes me stay in one spot. Let us see if you can dance around me."

It was, of course, a ploy. Karl's lame leg just slowed him a little. It did not affect his mobility. I was pleased that Ragnar ignored the jibe. He was moving around to get the feel of the sword and the ground beneath his feet. The speed of the youth would tell; the question was did he know how to use that quickness of feet and hands?

He answered us by suddenly darting in and feinting towards Karl's left. Karl brought his shield up and that temporarily blocked his view of Ragnar. Ragnar spun around to his right so that when the sword of Karl One Hand came down it struck fresh air. Even worse for Karl, Ragnar's sword was slicing around towards the old warrior's back. He had to shuffle around and bring his sword to block Ragnar's but it unbalanced him and Ragnar was not finished. He continued his spin and as Karl tried to turn to face him he lost his balance. Even as he was falling over Ragnar was leaping across the space between them and with his foot on Karl's sword he had his own at Karl's throat.

He grinned as he took off his helmet. "Yes Karl One Hand, I can dance around you! Thank you for the advice." He held out his hand to pull Karl to his feet, "And thank you for the training. I would not have beaten you had you not spent hours working with me."

Karl had the good grace to clasp Ragnar's arm. "And you are a worthy warrior. Your father would be proud of you."

Karl could not have paid him a better compliment and Ragnar nodded. He was too full of emotion to speak. Karl turned to Gruffyd, "Come on then. Let us see if you are as quick as your cousin."

Ragnar was full of encouragement for his cousin. "You can do this Gruffyd, you have quick hands too and Karl is slow."

It was the wrong thing to say. Karl had been beaten once. He would not be beaten a second time. Gruffyd's shield was slightly smaller than Ragnar's had been but he had the same size sword. He looked at me and I smiled and nodded. He turned to Karl and raised his shield. This time Karl did not give Gruffyd the opportunity to feint. He brought his sword over to strike at my son. Gruffyd did not seem to move and I wondered if the sword would render him unconscious when it struck. At the last moment, he took a step to the side and allowed the sword to slide down the shield. Instead of hitting at Karl's shield, he made a scything blow at Karl's bad leg. Karl hopped backwards.

Next to me, Olaf chuckled, "He is a warrior, Jarl. That was the blow of someone who wants to win." To Karl, he shouted, "He nearly had you there!"

Gruffyd began to hop from foot to foot. I had seen him do this when sparring with Ragnar. It was effective because he could leap at his opponent from either foot. Karl was not watching his feet but Gruffyd's face. Even so, my son almost caught him out when he darted in and punched with his smaller shield at Karl's hand. He caught Karl's knuckles cleanly.

Olaf said quietly, "Now, son, go for the kill."

My son did not have the confidence and the moment passed. Karl did not choose subtlety. He brought his sword over his head and this time Gruffyd could not get completely out of the way. It was a full blow and I heard a cry as the sword struck the shield and my son's arm. Karl stepped forward and used his own shield to smash Gruffyd in the face. There was an eruption of blood and he fell backwards. Stunned he lay there like a stranded fish and Karl's sword was at his throat.

Ragnar ran to his cousin, "That was bravely done cuz! You nearly had him. You should have struck with your sword when his hand was hit. You would have won."

The blow to his nose had made his eyes stream. I went to him and pinched him above the nose. "You did well Gruffyd. I am proud of you."

Karl came over rubbing his right hand. "Your father is right, you nearly had me there. When you have used a practice sword more then I fear you will have me."

"Thank you Karl One Hand. I am not ready yet. But I will be. This has made me even more determined."

"Ragnar take him to Aiden. I fear his nose may be broken. Aiden can fix it."

Olaf and Snorri patted Karl on the back. "Not bad for an old man with only one good leg!"

Karl shook his head, "No Olaf. I can see now that I am only fit to command the watch and train young warriors. I would be a liability on a raid but I am happy to serve. When Ragnar goes to fight he will take the skills I gave him. That is no bad thing eh, Jarl?"

"No Karl it is not! Olaf, I think this calls for some beer!"

"Aye! Uhtric! Beer for thirsty men!"

Of course, Brigid was unhappy when her son came in with a bloodied face. I dreaded what she would think when his eyes became black and blue in the next couple of days. "What were you thinking about letting that old man hurt our son?"

"He is a Viking and he will be a warrior. Enemies do not care how old you are. Our son did well."

She went to Gruffyd and fussed over him. "Mother, I am fine and I will be fighting Karl again when I am bigger and stronger! The difference is I will defeat him next time!"

"The men in this house are all as mad as fish! I am glad I have Erika!"

Her humour did not improve over the next few days as we prepared for our raid. Gruffyd's face grew worse before it became better and each time she saw him she glared at me. I had Uhtric gather the clothes we would need and put them in our chests to avoid having to go into the hall too many times. The wolf skins we had given to Ragnar and Gruffyd had been cured and made into cloaks. We have removed the heads for they were not Ulfheonar. The cloaks were there to hide them in the night and to keep them warm. They both understood. Both boys were desperate to leave but we had to wait until all of my Ulfheonar arrived and then we headed down the Water. It was a relief to leave for Brigid had been unbearable for the last three days.

Kara put her arm around my wife. "Do not worry Jarl, you watch over my husband and I shall watch over your wife."

Haaken One Eye found the whole thing highly amusing. "And I thought I had it bad in a house full of women. You have but one and she drives you hence!"

My drekar bobbed about in the estuary. As we arrived Erik used the wind to bring her to the wooden quay. He shouted, "I hope you are all ready to row for the winds are against us!"

Olaf Leather Neck ruffled Ragnar's hair. "We have seen you fight! Let us see if the two cubs can row!"

While our chests were taken aboard I spoke with Coen and Raibeart. "My people think that you raid Wessex and my brother will sail with you to further confuse the enemy." Coen pointed to the sea, "There have been strange ships in the bay. They drew close and then disappeared. We could not determine whose they were but someone is taking an interest in what we do."

"Thank you both. You are true friends. Do not risk your men, Raibeart. Raid easy targets and come back with profits."

"Aye Jarl."

I was the last to board. I saw that Ragnar and Gruffyd had been given the two small oars at the bow. They each shared their oar with one of Ragnar's hearth-weru. Both looked more afraid of that than fighting Karl One Hand.

"Ready?"

The Ulfheonar shouted, as one, "Aye ready!"

"Haaken, a good song to help us on our way!"

We had new men on board and Haaken honoured them all with our favourite song.

The storm was wild and the gods did roam
The enemy closed on the Prince's home
Two warriors stood on a lonely tower
Watching, waiting for hour on hour.
The storm came hard and Odin spoke
With a lightning bolt the sword he smote

Ragnar's Spirit burned hot that night
It glowed, a beacon shiny and bright
The two they stood against the foe
They were alone, nowhere to go
They fought in blood on a darkened hill
Dragon Heart and Cnut will save us still
Dragon Heart, Cnut and the Ulfheonar
Dragon Heart, Cnut and the Ulfheonar
The storm was wild and the Gods did roam
The enemy closed on the Prince's home
Two warriors stood on a lonely tower
Watching, waiting for hour on hour.
The storm came hard and Odin spoke
With a lightning bolt the sword he smote
Ragnar's Spirit burned hot that night
It glowed, a beacon shiny and bright
The two they stood against the foe
They were alone, nowhere to go
They fought in blood on a darkened hill
Dragon Heart and Cnut will save us still
Dragon Heart, Cnut and the Ulfheonar
Dragon Heart, Cnut and the Ulfheonar
'Ulfheonar, warriors strong
Ulfheonar, warriors brave
Ulfheonar, fierce as the wolf
Ulfheonar, hides in plain sight
Ulfheonar, Dragon Heart's wolves
Ulfheonar, serving the sword

Cnut Cnutson sang lustily for this was not just a song about me and my sword but his father; a true oathsworn.

Erik was right, it was a hard slog against the wind. He took us to the east of Man to find some relief from the southwest wind and relentless rain. It helped. I wondered if my decision to come with the smallest crew could have been a wise one. Aiden and I wrapped our cloaks around us as we huddled around the steering board. "I think we have little choice, Jarl, we have to go around Ynys Môn. The straits are too dangerous into the wind."

"You are right but it takes us close to Hibernia. Their ships are poor but even they might stand a chance with the wind behind them and we alone."

Aiden smiled, "Then we trust to Erik's skill and put our faith in the gods." I nodded and Erik put the steering board over to take us due west where we were able to make a little headway. We would hold our course until we saw Hibernia and then loose the sail and take advantage of wind from our quarter. Our drekar could fly if the winds allowed it.

I saw the men flagging. We had long ago stopped singing. "Come Aiden, let us take a turn with them. Let us join my son and grandson."

We made our way to the prow and sat next to Ragnar and Gruffyd. Gruffyd's hands were bleeding and he looked distressed. "I will take over now, son."

He shook his head. I think if he had spoken it would have been too much. He had a determined look on his face. Siggi Blue Eye shook his head, "I told him the same, Jarl. He has courage this one but he is hurting himself."

"Then let us see if an old warrior like me can add a little power eh, my son."

I pulled on the oar. It had been some time but you never forgot. I began to talk of my early days when I had been Gruffyd's age. I spoke of Old Olaf and Prince Butar. I told them of Cnut and Haaken when they had been younger. I spoke of raids along the fjords. Soon Ragnar and Gruffyd forgot their pain as they listened to tales of warriors long dead and deeds forgotten until I gave them utterance. There were no songs and sagas for these stories. We had fought to survive. It was as simple as that. I had almost finished when Erik shouted, "In oars, we are turning! Let fly the sail!"

We all gave a weak cheer as we pulled the oars inboard and then carried them to lay them in the centre of the drekar. Aiden took the two boys with him and led them to the stern. He took out a pot. There was a salve he and Kara had made. It smelled foul and contained seal oil as well as ground chestnuts and some herbs. He coated their hands with it. I saw them wince for it stung but they did not utter a sound. They nodded their thanks.

"Have some beer and then cover yourselves with your cloaks and try to sleep. We may have to row again before too long." They looked appalled. "This is the life of a Viking. We do not spend all our time fighting and feasting. This is your lot."

Ragnar nodded, "Come Gruffyd. We cannot complain. We asked for this although how I am to wield a sword I do not know!"

Haaken joined me. "They did well and it is not just they who are exhausted. That was hard for us all."

"Erik, we will lay up at Ynys Enlli. It is safe there and we can find plenty of food."

"Aye Jarl."

I looked at the masthead. "The Norns, it seems, are not making life easy for us."

"If they did Jarl, where would be the challenge?"

Haaken laughed, "Only a wizard and part-time rower could make such a statement."

"The gods gave me a brain and gave you a sword. We both fight in our own way. Is it my fault that my way is easier?"

"You will never defeat a wizard, Haaken, not with words anyway."

It was with some relief that we tied up in the lee of Ynys Enlli. Snorri went ashore with the new men from Cyninges-tūn to hunt while we set up camp on the beach. The rain had stopped and this might give us the chance to dry out a little. Having Aiden with us meant we managed a fire quicker than we would have done without him. There was plenty of driftwood on the beach. The island was in the main current and wood came here from beyond the far seas. Aiden often speculated about the origin of some of the strange and twisted timber.

While the birds the hunters had collected were being cooked Aiden applied more salve to the hands of Ragnar and Gruffyd. "Do not worry. Your hands will harden. It will help you when you wield a sword and the rowing will broaden your shoulders."

They nodded. Einar the Tall said, "This is not what you expected, is it?"

Ragnar shook his head, "When my father came home it was with tales of how many enemies he had slain, the treasure he had taken and the places he had seen."

"And he did, Ragnar Arturusson, but we often had to sail great distances. Sometimes even a short journey took longer than you thought."

"Einar is right. The Liger and the Issicauna are long rivers with many twists and turns. It takes a long time to navigate them. That often means rowing rather than sailing."

"And this river we sail, father, is that a long one?"

Aiden had finished with the salve and as he put the top back on the jar he said, "It is, but the place we seek is but twenty Roman miles from the sea and perhaps there will not be too many twists and turns."

Haaken and Olaf walked over from the fire, each with a wooden bowl of food for Aiden and me. Einar said to Ragnar, "I will get you some."

"No Einar, you are his hearth-weru and not his servant. They have legs and they can get their own food!" To their credit, the two of them rose and headed to the fire.

Haaken and Olaf sat next to us. "Do we have a plan for this raid?" Olaf was a blunt speaker.

I nodded, "I will take Aiden and the Ulfheonar to the island where Grimbould hides. We will try to gain entry quietly."

"No offence, wizard, but can you remain hidden as an Ulfheonar?"

"None taken Olaf Leather Neck. Aye, I can. Besides I have been reading some of the writings about Myrddyn. When he and the Warlord travelled the land they often went alone and the wizard managed to get into difficult places... without the need to smash down the doors with axes!"

Olaf was not put out, "It works!"

"It does, old friend, but the wizard is right. It is noisy!"

I wiped the bowl with the last of the damp, salty bread. We would have no more until we raided. From now on it would be salted meat and fish. "I do not think this will be an Alt Clut or Din Guardi. It is on an island and that affords, they think, protection enough. It is close to an abbey across the river. They think they are safe and we are far from their thoughts. Grimbould dreams of the crown. He thinks we have forgotten him. He is a Frank and does not know the Viking mind."

"So the plan is just to land and kill him?"

The boys had returned and both listened as they ate.

I shook my head. "Not quite. If we were taking our men from Cyninges-tūn then we would send Snorri and Beorn to scout. We only bring Ulfheonar. Einar and our men from Cyninges-tūn can guard and sail the drekar. We are Ulfheonar and are all capable of scouting. We need speed. I want us in and out in one night. I would have us as wraiths or spirits. These are Christians but the pagan is not far below the surface. They have not met the wolves of the north." I drank some of the beer. "This will be a tale like the death of Magnus the Foresworn in Din Guardi. Men will wonder how we did what we did."

Olaf nodded, "And the Abbey?"

"We will raid that after Grimbould has been eliminated." I nodded to Einar. "That is where you and your men will prove their value, Einar. You will have to guard our way home."

Ragnar answered for him, "Do not worry, grandfather. By the time we reach the land of the Franks my cousin and I will have toughened up and we will stand a watch too. We will not be passengers. We will be warriors."

Haaken laughed, "Aye, you will. I can see Wolf Killer in your eyes and hear his words in your voice. This is *wyrd*!"

Chapter 9

Perhaps the Norns took pity on us after our difficult beginning for the wind veered a little and we did not need to row for a whole day. We laid up off Corn Walum as Erik and Aiden were loath to risk the Syllingar Insula at night. Nor did we wish to risk the land. Although we had defeated and cowed the men of Corn Walum there was little to be gained from any combat with them. They had little treasure and the weapons were only fit to be melted down for ploughshares and hoes.

Every oar was manned as we negotiated the treacherous rocks and islands that marked the edge of the land the Romans had called Britannia. I do not think that Ragnar and Gruffyd truly understood the apprehension and fear in my men's hearts as we rowed south and east. Even Einar and the hearth-weru were surprised at the silence of the Ulfheonar. There were no songs and no banter. It was not until we were in open water that they sang again.

The dragon sails from west to east
They look for men on which to feast
With Leather Neck and old One Eye
They row and make the dragon fly
Ulfheonar never forget
Ulfheonar never forgive
Ulfheonar fight to the death
No stronghold's walls can keep them out
They fear no warrior nor sentry's shout
They walk unseen in strange new lands
They fight and kill all warrior bands
Ulfheonar never forget
Ulfheonar never forgive
Ulfheonar fight to the death
Ulfheonar never forget
Ulfheonar never forgive
Ulfheonar fight to the death

It was a song Haaken had written for just such an occasion. When Erik shouted, "Oars in!" there were smiles once more.

I saw Ragnar talking to his hearth-weru. Then he walked to me, "Grandfather why were the Ulfheonar afraid of those islands?"

It was Erik Short Toe who answered, "There is a witch who lives on those islands. We have often been becalmed or half wrecked on her island. It happens when she wishes to speak with Aiden or your grandfather."

Haaken said, "And once Hrolf, the Frankish slave."

"Aye. I had forgotten him. And no matter how fierce the storm we have little damage but that does not make us happy for the Jarl descends into the bowels of the earth. Sometimes he and Aiden disappear for a whole day and night. We never know if they will return."

"We always return!"

"You are a wizard and you are comfortable in the company of such witches. We would all prefer that the witch ignore us and do as she has done this day and let us by."

Aiden looked astern, "And I am always sad when she does not speak with us for each time she does I have more knowledge and more power. Perhaps she will call us on our return."

Erik and the Ulfheonar each grabbed their tokens to ward off evil, "Aiden do not speak thus! You may not fear her but we do. Do not risk her wrath."

Aiden laughed. "The hammers and wolves around your necks will not stop the witch if she wishes to speak with us. Do you not know yet who she is?" I had guessed but my men had not. They shook their heads. He had the attention of every Ulfheonar, "She is one of the Norns. She is Verðandi, one of the Weird Sisters."

I was suddenly aware that the only sound I could hear was the creak of the ropes and the rigging and the snap of the canvas. It seemed that all had stopped breathing. My Ulfheonar now realised that they had been as close to the Otherworld as any warrior alive. The fact that they had survived those encounters was good but all knew how close to death they had been.

Aiden broke the spell, "You need not fear her unless she is with her sisters, Urðr and Skuld." He seemed quite calm about the whole matter.

Haaken forced a smile upon his lips, "That is all right then!"

It was a sombre crew who watched the islands recede into the west. The prospect of a fight against Neustrians suddenly seemed more appealing and less dangerous than the voyage back through the islands. The winds helped us as we headed east but we did not travel fast. Ragnar and Gruffyd, under Aiden's critical eye, played the game of war. Gruffyd was the better of the two. He won two games out of three. I could see Ragnar trying to come to terms with the fact that while he could best his younger cousin with a weapon he could not outwit him on the board.

I studied the maps and charts with Erik. None of us had ever been to this river before. We were in the hands of the Frisian who had sold them to Aiden. I took comfort from the fact that no sailor would deliberately upset a wizard. The pagan was never far below the skin of all sailors even those who wore the cross of the White Christ.

I waved Aiden over, "This is your chart. Come and explain it to us."

"What do you need to know?"

"How far from the sea to the island? On your map, it does not look far."

"It is not. Ten Roman miles that is all."

"But?"

"But with the twists and turns in the river, it will be more like fifteen. The island is not high and is protected by the Somme and a smaller river. The Frisian did not mark its name. He did not say so but I think that the land around it will be swamp and marsh."

"Why do you say that?"

"The river is slow and sluggish. That is why there are so many twists and turns. It helps you for it means it is unlikely that there will be ramparts. If this is an old Roman fort which has been converted then there will be a ditch around it and the buildings will be stone."

Erik nodded and I said, "Then we should have brought ladders."

"They are easy to make and besides they will not be expecting an attack, Jarl. Their enemies are their own people. Their eyes will not be to the sea but to the east and Paris."

Erik pointed to a small stream, "Is there a port here or a village?"

Aiden looked at the map, "No. The river is deep enough and wide enough but the Frisian said there is neither harbour nor village here."

"Then we will lay up there. It is not far to the Somme."

"Good."

It took another day and night to reach the uninhabited river. We knew it was called the Tella but that was all. The Frisian captain had been right and it made me hopeful that the rest of his information was accurate. We reached it just after dawn and Erik was able to anchor in deep water after he had landed men who would seek out wood to make ladders. Einar the Tall and his men went with Snorri and the wood hunters. I think he wanted to feel as though they were doing their share. As far as I was concerned his work was protecting my son and grandson but I understood the warrior in him.

It was noon when they signalled that they were ready to be picked up. We headed inshore. They had made four ladders and had hunted game. While the ladders were brought on board the game was cooked, along with some fish we had caught, on the beach. Erik sent his sons and the ship's boys to refill the water barrels from the river. We gathered supplies when we could. Who knew when we might run out?

In the late afternoon, we were ready to move north. We made no attempt to hide the remains of our fire. Snorri and his scouts had seen little sign of Franks. There were no strongholds. The river, he reported, was too narrow for boats and was very shallow in places. It explained much. As we headed north, along the coast, I knew that we would be seen from the shore. The afternoon sun was beginning to dip in the west and we would be seen as a silhouette. However, we saw only rude huts along the shore. If they saw us they could do little about it and I began to see why Jarl Gunnar Thorfinnson and his Raven Wing clan had chosen to live so close to this land. The rivers were navigable for great distances and there appeared to be few strongholds. The Saxons had their burghs but here they had nothing, save the rivers, to protect them.

We prepared our war faces. There would be just twenty of us going ashore leaving twelve warriors to guard and row the drekar should that prove necessary. Ragnar and Gruffyd were becoming excited as they saw us readying ourselves. Envy was written all over their faces. We would take no spears. They would get in the way. Our swords, axes and seaxes had been sharpened by Bjorn and would need no attention. Snorri and Beorn the Scout had their bows and they would be the ones to eliminate any sentries. It was when I applied the cochineal to my eyes and forehead that I felt I was close to being prepared. With the new wolf cloak about my shoulders and the head on my helmet, I was ready.

We reached the estuary just as the last light of day shone like a beacon to direct us to the wide river mouth. Erik Short Toe was taking no chances and he had his two sons in the bows with the other ships' boys in a relay down the centre of the drekar to warn us of danger. We had our sail furled and twelve men rowed us up the sluggish river. If this had been the Liger, Tamese or the Dunum then they would not have been able to move us; they were three powerful rivers. As it was our slow speed helped for we did not know what obstacles lay beneath the dark water. The Frisian captain had been vague about the river bottom. Aiden was confident. His reading of old Roman books had given him the idea that the river was deep enough. He told me later that he knew there was a Roman fort close by and Romans liked to supply their forts by water when they could. He wore a helmet and carried a seax but that was all. About his shoulder, he had no shield but a leather satchel with what he needed to heal those who might be hurt. I took heart from my wizard's confidence.

The relay of boys passed regular messages down to us and Erik corrected the steering board with each one. Not far into the estuary, we passed a settlement on the south bank. A bell tolled which told us that there was a church but we saw nothing else.

I was standing with Haaken and Erik when Aiden came to me and said quietly. "The Frisian captain said he thought there was a village at the mouth of the river but he did not know."

Haaken nodded. "Perhaps we might visit on our way home."

"Let us deal with Grimbould first. We will take nothing for granted."

After we passed the tolling bell we saw nothing. Arne Eriksson came down the drekar, "The river is very narrow. How far do we go, Jarl?"

He looked at me but his words were for his father. "We will risk a little further. We are riding higher than normal. Let us save the legs of the Ulfheonar. They are getting old!" Olaf Leather Neck gave a derisory snort.

We managed another two miles or so before there was the slightest of judders as we touched the bottom and then moved off. I took the decision for Erik. "We will stop here and my men will walk. It cannot be far. Turn the drekar around and be ready to sail when you see us."

"Aye Jarl."

Snorri and Beorn slipped over the side first and then the warriors with the ladders. We would not be bringing them back. We went ashore on the north bank. It happened to be the closest and also the one which was easiest to climb. As events turned out our feet were guided there by others who had come this way. There was a greenway. I had wondered if there might be a Roman Road but there was none. We made good time. Snorri and Beorn had long since disappeared. Rolf Horse Killer and Rollo Thin Skin led us. They had sharp eyes and ears. In the darkness, they were almost invisible in their black wolf cloaks.

I almost ran in to the back of Rolf as they both suddenly stopped. Beorn the Scout's face appeared from behind a bush. "We have found it,

Jarl. There is a guarded bridge ahead and there is an old fort but they have built a hall next to the wall and extended a ditch around it. We found the church. It is a thousand paces from the river and the bridge. It is on a ridge."

"Where is Snorri?"

"He watches the men on the bridge."

It was just four hours since sunset. The watch would not be set. We might have to wait until they changed the watch on the bridge. We hurried down the greenway. The Franks had been lazy. They had only cleared the land for forty paces from the bridge. Beorn led us to Snorri who crouched in the trees and bushes. He pointed to the sentries on the bridge. There were four of them. He put his head close to my ear and said, "They changed the watch not long before you came."

I nodded. I saw that the bridge was a wooden one. There was a second bridge over the ditch and then the rebuilt walls of the Roman Fort. It was not a well-made gatehouse but I could see men moving on it. I waved Finni the Dreamer and Olvir Grey Eye over. I pointed to the sentries and then drew my hand across my throat. They nodded and I pointed to Snorri's bow. All four nodded. My two scouts would wait until the two Ulfheonar were close and then slay two of the sentries. Olvir and Finni would kill the other two.

Even though I watched the two of them as they slipped down the road I found it hard to see them as they ghosted up the bank of the river. The four sentries were standing around a brazier and chatting. They had become complacent because nothing had happened before. They were in for a fatal shock. It was only when I saw Snorri and Beorn draw back their bows that I knew the two men were in position. The only sound I heard was the twang of their strings. Two of the sentries looked up as they heard it. For one it was the last thing he heard as Snorri's arrow knocked him backwards. Beorn's arrow took a second and even as the other two sentries stared at their dead friends Olvir and Finni had risen and drawn their knives across their throats.

By the time we reached them, they had taken all of value from the bodies and lowered them silently into the water. They would journey to the sea. We had to move quickly before the men on the gatehouse saw that their four sentries had disappeared.

Snorri and Beorn kept their arrows aimed at the shadows on the fighting platform. I could hear voices and knew that the sentries chatted. They would probably be gambling. We hurried across the bridge and the four ladders were laid against the walls. The man who placed them managed to do so silently. Times gone by I would have led the men up the ladders but there were younger warriors who could climb faster. Cnut Cnutson and Erik Beornsson were new Ulfheonar and keen to show their new brothers their skills. The other two who leapt up the ladders were Rollo Thin Skin and Rolf Horse Killer. By the time I reached the top, the four sentries lay dead in widening pools of blood. Cnut and Rolf ran down the steps and opened the gate. I followed Olaf and Snorri who ran to the east gate which led to the hall of Grimbould.

Once in the centre of the fort I swung my shield around and drew my sword as I did so. I saw that Aiden was the last to enter the fort. I would not worry about my wizard. He knew his own business better than I did. Snorri and Beorn halted and loosed two arrows. The two sentries on the inner wall fell to the ground with a crunch. The noise would be heard. I hoped that it would be dismissed. I knew that there would be armed men within the old Roman fort but I guessed that the majority of warriors who might give us trouble would be close to Grimbould. My men opened this second gate. Just at that moment, there was a shout from behind. There were sentries on the south gate. Snorri and Beorn sent arrows to silence them but the alarm had been given.

"Rolf Horse Killer, keep four warriors here and deal with any trouble."

"Aye Jarl."

Haaken and Olaf had not waited for me but run through the gate into the heart of Grimbould's home. Already warriors raced towards my men. They had not been asleep but they were not prepared for the wolves who raced through the night. We were a nightmare come to life. The first four warriors fell not knowing who had slain them for we were almost invisible in the dark. The hall was a well-made building similar to my own hall but it was not built for defence. Two men stood in the doorway with swords and shields. Olaf and Einar Hammer Arm put their shields together and ran through the two men. They simply bowled them over. Already trampled by the two heaviest warriors in my clan their lives were ended by Haaken and Finni the Dreamer who followed them.

As we burst into the hall there were screams and shouts. The screams were frightened women and the shouts were of alarm from the men within. Some had been sleeping and had had a rude awakening. Grimbould himself would be defended by bodyguards. They would be well paid, well armoured and the best of warriors. We would not underestimate them. He would also have the best of quarters.

I headed towards the fire which was in the centre of the hall. Snorri and Haaken were at my side. I saw mailed men advancing towards us. They had no helmets but they held shields and spears. They had to be hired warriors. They were not as good as I had expected. They did not sleep in their mail nor did they have a plan for an attack such as ours. They had taken the Frank's money and not given him the protection he needed.

Even though there were six of them we did not hesitate. I knew that more of my men would be following. The shields of the Franks were smaller and narrower than ours. I brought my sword over my shoulder towards the heads of two of them. Although one managed to block the blow with his shield the other did not and Ragnar's Spirit took the top of his skull. A woman screamed. As my eyes became accustomed to the fire-lit hall I saw that there were two women and they were sheltering behind a large, overweight man. That had to be Grimbould.

A sword thudded into my shield and I jabbed forward with my sword. Although the Frank managed to bring his shield up it merely deflected the tip into his eye. I pushed hard. It entered his skull and I twisted. When his lifeless body fell at my feet then I knew that my sword had pierced his skull. Haaken was fighting two warriors. I hacked at their swords and my blade found flesh. Haaken took advantage and his sword removed the head of one of them. As the other hesitated between his two opponents I smashed my shield into his face before Haaken plunged his sword into his throat. We fought hard and fast and we were ruthlessly efficient. These bodyguards had not encountered Vikings before and we were too much for their skills.

All around us, my men were fighting with the bodyguards of the man who had been Mayor of Neustria. He held a sword before him. I shouted, "Take the women!" If one was a noblewoman from Frisia then she would be valuable. Her relatives might ransom her. The two women screamed as my men took them. Grimbould shouted something at me. I did not understand his words. I doubted that he would understand me but I felt honour bound to speak them. "I am Jarl Dragonheart of Cyninges-tūn. You paid for killers to come to my land and they took my son's life. Tonight I claim the weregeld for that death. You will die!"

In that moment he knew his fate. He decided to go out fighting. He lunged at me and I easily deflected his blade. I brought Ragnar's Spirit around in a wide sweep and took his head. I sheathed my sword and picked the skull up by the hair. As his remaining bodyguards realised that they had failed they tried to flee. My men showed no mercy to the mercenaries. They were butchered where they stood.

"Olaf, search for anything of value and then fire the hall." I found a spear and jammed the grisly trophy upon it. Aiden appeared. I held up the spear. "I need a message for the Franks."

Aiden picked up a piece of charcoal and looked around. A white-robed priest lay dead. Aiden tore a piece of material from his robe and began to make marks upon it. I could read a little but I did not know what it said. "What have you written?"

"Here is the head of Grimbould. He was executed by Jarl Dragonheart. Do not make an enemy of a Viking!"

"That will do. Give it here and then help Olaf search for anything of value."

When I stepped outside it seemed a world of calm for there was no fighting. I strode to the fort. Alf Jansson followed me, his sword drawn. Inside the fort were the bodies of those who had fought against my men. Cnut pointed, "Many fled through the gate. Rolf Horse Killer took the women prisoners to the bridge."

"Search for anything of value and then fire the fort. Let us leave a blackened scar here to remind the Franks of the folly of incurring my wrath!" I strode to the gate. The women cowered beneath Rolf's glare. When they saw Grimbould's head they screamed. I put the cloth with the message on the ground and then rammed the head of the spear into it, pinning it to the ground. The two women read it and then grabbed each other.

Rolf pointed to the north. I guessed it was the church because a bell was tolling. It called not to prayers but sounded the alarm. "The ones who escaped fled there. Had we more men..."

"This was enough. We did what I set out to do. We will wait for our men." I saw the sudden flare of a flame as the hall was set alight. It would not be long now. When there were more flames from inside the fort I knew that my men would soon appear. Aiden led a horse pulling a small cart. Cnut Cnutson and Rollo Thin Skin tugged at four horses laden with treasures.

"Snorri, take us back to the drekar."

"The church?"

"We can always return. Let us take what we have and rejoin the drekar. Finni you and Alf watch the rear."

The alarm had been given and silence was no longer necessary. We hurried back. It was the two women who slowed us up. However, when I closed with them they ran. The sight of my face was enough. It was still dark when we found the drekar. It did not take long to load but the extra weight made us lower in the water. We let the horses go and then Erik lowered the sail.

"It is a shame about that church."

I nodded, "There is another at the mouth of the estuary. Perhaps we can give Einar and the men who rowed the chance to use their swords and spill some blood."

"They will like that Jarl."

"Is the man who paid for my father's assassins dead, Jarl Dragonheart?"

"He is. I left his head with a message for others. Your father is almost avenged."

"Almost?"

"There is still King Egbert who must pay weregeld!"

"Perhaps I shall avenge my father's death by killing him."

Olaf Leather Neck nodded, "I admire your ambition, Ragnar! I will help you to become a warrior who can face this wily King of Wessex."

"Did we collect much of value, Aiden?"

"We did. The Frank had chests of gold and silver. I think he had been holding on to taxes. It may be as well that we ended his life for I think the Emperor might not have been happy with him. I also found parchments. I will read them when time allows."

"And we took many fine weapons and mail. It is different from our own but for those without any it will make them better warriors."

Dawn began to break. The ship's boys had done a fine job of signalling to Erik and we made good time to the mouth of the estuary. Erik ordered the sail to be furled as we approached the south bank. There was a small wooden quay with a ferry tied to it. We would be secure when we landed.

As we neared the shore I heard a bell begin to ring. It was the steady ringing of danger. Snorri pointed, "They have spied us, Jarl. See, they have barred their gate and the bell signals the alarm."

I heard Olaf chuckle. It sounded more threatening than a growl from someone else, "Then my axe will make kindling of their gate!"

I could see that they had a stone wall that surrounded their abbey. I guessed that the village had been emptied and that they would man the walls. I doubted that they would have a fighting platform; this was a church but they would use everything they had to protect their priests. It was the way of the followers of the White Christ.

Ragnar looked at me expectantly. I nodded. "Einar, watch Ragnar!"

He smiled, "Of course, Jarl."

Ragnar had his helmet already. As Gruffyd reached for his, I shook my head, "You have yet to defeat Karl and your mother would make soup from my bones if anything happened to you. You will stay with Leif the Banner, Erik Short Toe and the ship's boys. You will help to guard the prisoners. They are worth much money."

He nodded. He was my son and he accepted my decision. It was a sign he was growing wiser. None of us had taken off our mail and we were ready. My sword was not as sharp as I would have liked but we would be fighting fishermen and priests!

We had the luxury of tying the drekar to a quay and marching, rather than racing through the village towards the abbey. Olaf and Rolf led the way with their axes. The six young warriors from Cyninges-tūn had their shields ready to protect them from missiles. We might have been fighting a weak enemy but we took no chances and our shields were held to our front as the two Ulfheonar began to hack at the door. When Snorri and Beorn slew, with the bows, the three men who tried to hurl stones from the walls the shower of stones ceased. I glanced over and saw that Einar had been as good as his word. A ring of six mailed warriors surrounded my grandson.

As the doors were ripped asunder I saw that they had all fled inside the Abbey Church. It had a stone tower but the rest was made of wood. Haaken said, "Do we burn it down?"

I shook my head, "No, for we might be destroying treasure and we need to leave someone alive who will deliver our ransom demand!" I turned to Leif Sorenson who now led the men of Cyninges-tūn. "Take your men and search the village. Look beneath the floors for that is where they bury their valuables and then burn the village. When it is alight return here." He hesitated. "You will not miss anything. The fire will encourage them to either surrender or fight."

"Aye Jarl."

"Ragnar take your hearth-weru. There will be a rear door to the church. Make sure that none leave."

It was the safest task I could give.

"Cnut, search the other buildings and ransack them for anything of value, including food. When that is done then burn the buildings."

Aiden had joined me, "What is in your mind, Jarl?"

"There is little honour in killing priests and villagers and we may be missing profit. I want them to think they have no hope. When despair takes over I will offer them a glimmer of light."

I waved Olaf, Snorri, Beorn and Haaken to the main door. It was solid. There were metal studs and bars. It would not give way as easily as the gate we had destroyed. I took off my helmet. The cool air was pleasant. I had already swung my shield around to my back and I sheathed my sword. I had a feeling that I would not need it.

I waited until the smoke began to drift up from the village before I said, "Olaf, knock on the door and let them know we are here."

"With pleasure, Jarl."

He did not use the blade for the metal studs would blunt it. Instead, he used the back of the axe like a hammer. The door shook as his axe made a sound like thunder. He hit it seven times and then stopped. The smell of smoke was stronger now and as Cnut and my Ulfheonar set fire to the other buildings we heard the sound of singing from within the church.

I looked at Aiden and he shrugged, "They chant to their White Christ to save them."

"Good, then our strategy works."

When they stopped singing, sometime later, I said, "Olaf, knock three times and then Aiden, tell them I wish to speak with their holy man!"

Aiden used his Latin to speak with the priests. At first, there was no reply. "Tell them that if they do not speak then I will burn down the church with everyone inside."

This time they did speak. "He says what do we want? We are barbarians and we will rot in hell."

Haaken smiled, "He thinks we do not know who we are? I thought these priests were supposed to be clever!"

"Tell him that if they surrender they can live."

When the priest answered he shouted. "He does not trust us, Jarl."

Just then I heard a commotion from the rear of the church. "Snorri go and see if Ragnar and his hearth-weru need help." He ran. "Einar Hammer Arm, fetch kindling. If they will not listen they will die. Ask him again, Aiden, and tell him that I am losing patience."

After an exchange of words, Aiden shrugged, "The man is a fool. He says he does not trust us and if we burn them it will be the will of God."

Olaf shook his head, "I cannot understand these followers of the White Christ. If we were in the same position we would come out fighting with whatever we had! Teeth and claws if necessary! If we died then we would take some with us. This religion weakens them. The Saxons were powerful warriors until they followed this cross and now they are like women."

Snorri came back with a priest. The priest was bleeding from a head wound. Snorri was smiling, "Your grandson takes his instructions seriously. He slew one priest who ran and was about to send this one to his god when I stopped him."

"Perhaps we can use this to our advantage. Aiden, tell this priest that he has my word that they will live and not be enslaved if they come out but tell him that the fire is ready to be lit." Einar and my men returned with kindling and burning brands from the other buildings.

Aiden spoke to the priest. This time he seemed to be making progress. The priest asked him questions and Aiden answered. Then Aiden said, "He knows who you are Jarl and he says that if you swear on your sword then he will believe you and try to persuade the abbot."

Olaf said, "You are not going to swear are you Jarl?"

"I will not be foresworn. I said I would give my word and I will." I took out the sword and said, "I swear that if they surrender they will live."

The priest nodded and spoke, not in Latin but in Frankish. I trusted this young priest. I knew not why but I did. The debate was heated but eventually, the priest said. "They will come out."

"You speak our language?"

He nodded, "I was born a Dane and became a Christian. I heard what you said to the giant and knew that I could trust you." He hesitated, "I can trust you?"

"If you know my name then you know the answer to that."

The door opened and the abbot came out. He glared at me.

I turned to the Danish priest, "What is your name, Priest?"

"I am Brother James." He smiled, "It was the name I was given when I was baptised."

"Then, Brother James, tell the abbot that they can have their lives but their rings and jewels they cannot have!" I turned to Haaken, "Search them and take anything of value."

The sight of our swords, wolf skins and our aggressive manner made them submit. "Cnut, fetch my grandson. He is no longer needed at the back door. Aiden, go and search the church." I turned to the priest, "Brother James bring the abbot, I have someone I wish you to see."

I led them to my drekar. As I approached I shouted, "Leif, Gruffyd, fetch the prisoners."

I stopped the priests thirty paces from my drekar. When the women saw the abbot they called out to him.

"I have captured these. I will take them back to the Land of the Wolf. If their family or the church wish them to be returned home, then they send a thousand pieces of silver to Dyflin. You have until midsummer day to make your decision. After that, they will be sold as slaves."

Brother James translated and the abbot shouted. Brother James said, "The abbot thinks you gave your word to let them all go free."

"You are free. These are not." My men brought the holy books from the abbey. "And if he wants these holy books back then it will be ten gold pieces for each book." Einar Hammer Arm walked down with a large relic box. The Abbot became animated. "And the box, Brother James, I take it this contains some relics?"

He nodded, "They are the bones of Saint Valery. This is his abbey."

"Then if he wants them back it will cost a hundred gold pieces for the relics."

When he translated the Abbot's shoulders sank and he nodded. Brother James said, "Are you a new kind of Viking, lord? You show mercy and yet know, to the coin, the value of holy books and relics."

I smiled, "Let us say that I have been doing this for a long time. I can kill and I do kill but I chose my enemies."

We left before dark leaving the survivors wondering if they had been lucky. I suspect that the Abbot would say that God had saved them by making me merciful. They could believe what they wished. I had achieved what I set out to achieve. We headed home.

Chapter 10

We headed out to sea and I took Ragnar to one side. "You did well Ragnar but the priest was unarmed. You could have cuffed him."

"I saw someone running and I did not know if he had a weapon."

"That was my fault, Jarl. Our attention was not on the door."

"No harm was done, Einar, and we will make much profit from this."

Erik called out, "Haaken, have the oars manned!"

I turned to Erik, "Is there a problem?"

"It is the wind Jarl. It is coming from the west. The tide is turning. I do not wish us to end up on the rocks. Better that we row south and then use the wind later."

The men took to their oars. They were tired but the sea was a cruel mistress. Haaken used a long song which we had not used for some time. It seemed to fit the mood. When time allowed he would sing Grimbould's End but the death of Magnus the Foresworn would do as well.

The Saxon King had a mighty home
Protected by rock, sea and foam
Safe he thought from all his foes
But the Dragonheart would bring new woes
Ulfheonar never forget
Ulfheonar never forgive
Ulfheonar fight to the death
The snake had fled and was hiding there
Safe he thought in the Saxon lair
With heart of dragon and veins of ice
Dragonheart knew nine would suffice
Ulfheonar never forget
Ulfheonar never forgive
Ulfheonar fight to the death
Below the sand they sought the cave
The rumour from the wizard brave
Beneath the sea without a light
The nine all waited through the night

Ulfheonar never forget
Ulfheonar never forgive
Ulfheonar fight to the death
When night fell they climbed the stair
Invisible to the Saxons there
In the tower the traitors lurked
Dragonheart had a plan which worked
Ulfheonar never forget
Ulfheonar never forgive
Ulfheonar fight to the death
With Odin's blade the legend fought
Magnus' tricks they came to nought
With sword held high and a mighty thrust
Dragonheart sent Magnus to an end that was just
Ulfheonar never forget
Ulfheonar never forgive
Ulfheonar fight to the death
Ulfheonar never forget
Ulfheonar never forgive
Ulfheonar fight to the death

The song helped the crew to row until we were well away from the shore. When Erik shouted, "Oars in," my men breathed a collective sigh of relief. He took us west on the breeze which saved our arms. We took off mail and finished off the last of the beer. We had taken two barrels of wine from the Frankish hall but they would not help us row. We would drink water and save the wine for Cyninges-tūn.

I laid my wolf cloak out and lay down upon it. Ragnar and Gruffyd took their own and joined me. "You did not do what your men expected, grandfather. Why?"

"I do not know but I realised that the only way into the church would be to destroy it and we might have lost valuable goods. There was no honour to be gained from slaughtering priests and farmers. We did not need the slaves..." I shrugged. "Sometimes our heart tells us to do things that our mind does not understand."

Gruffyd said, "But it turned out well. It is like a game of war. There are many ways to win. A good leader chooses the right one."

Olaf Leather Neck took his cloak and walked further down the boat then he chuckled, "A clever strategy, Jarl Dragonheart. Time will pass. They will gain more treasure and we can return again!"

That had not been in my head but he was right. Until they built a burgh to defend the church they could not stop us. Their prayers to their White Christ would not save them from having their fleeces taken.

We sailed all night. It was a slow journey for the winds were light and from the wrong direction. I would have had the men row but they had had little sleep and there was no rush. Aiden and I helped Erik to steer. I was on watch as dawn broke but it was a grey, heavily overcast day. Rain began early. I woke Erik and he took over. He and Aiden checked our position. "We have travelled far to the south. We need to turn north and west. It means turning into the wind. We must row again, Jarl."

I nodded. "Haaken, to your oars."

Surprisingly he and the men seemed quite happy to row. It kept them warmer in the damp morning air and it gave Haaken the opportunity to compose a new chant.

The land of the Franks is filled with gold
Wanting to be taken by a warrior bold
Upon an island hidden from sight
Grimbould the coward cowered in the night
Roman forts were high with ditches deep
Warriors brave climbed the walls so steep
Ulfheonar never forget
Ulfheonar never forgive
Ulfheonar fight to the death
Like wolves, they rushed and slaughter all
Seeking the Frank hiding in his hall
His hearth-weru fought and died around their lord
Jarl Dragonheart slew them with his mighty sword
The coward begged as his men they fled
The Dragonheart took the faithless head
Ulfheonar never forget
Ulfheonar never forgive
Ulfheonar fight to the death

When he had finished Olaf said, "It is coming along but this is not quite finished eh Haaken?"

Snorri laughed, "No he has yet to give himself some glory!"

The Ulfheonar all laughed. Haaken was known for his vanity. Their laughter would not prick his opinion of himself. We rowed and then stopped to give the rowers a rest. When we stopped rowing Erik took us south again to take advantage of the wind. So we crabbed our way west. All the time, though we were heading further south and west than we would have liked. As the sky darkened and night fell Erik took the steering board. He pointed to the dark sky framing the setting sun. "I like not the sunset, Jarl Dragonheart and the wind is dropping."

I looked to Aiden, "Is there aught we can do? Should I make a blót?"

He shook his head, "I agree with Erik that the sky is looking threatening but I sense no danger. We are not close to the edge of the world yet. We will see what morning brings."

I lay down between my son and grandson. My old wounds began to ache. That was a sure sign of damp weather approaching. I took an old piece of canvas we kept by the steering board and laid it on the three of us. It would keep off the worst of the wet if it came on to rain.

I had a troubled sleep. I think that I dreamed but I remembered nothing save that I was trying to run through the sea but was dragged down beneath the black waters. I was woken by Aiden shaking me. I opened my eyes and I could barely see him, "Jarl, a fog has descended and there is no wind."

I stood and saw that he was right. It was as thick a fog as I had seen since I had lived along the Dunum. I wrapped my cloak around my shoulders for the damp air chilled to the bone. I went to the steering board. Erik said, "I am sorry, Jarl. I would have woken you sooner but the fog just came down suddenly."

"It cannot be helped. I will wake the crew." Turning I shouted, "Wake and take to the oars! It is time to row!"

Aiden said, "We will have to tread carefully Jarl. This kind of fog occurs near land and not in the middle of the ocean. The fog is so thick that we will need sharp-eyed ships' boys to watch for rocks."

"And yet you saw no danger."

"I sensed no danger. There is a difference. I still sense no danger although I can see it."

Erik said, "You talk in riddles, Aiden. Danger is danger and this fog could kill us all! Ships' boys take your positions."

Ragnar and Gruffyd stood, "You two go to the prow and watch from there. Call out if you see rocks."

Eager to be of use the two of them ran down the deck to the bow. I shook my head. Neither had taken their wolf cloaks. They would soon be frozen!

Erik shouted, "Haaken, take it steady and no song. We need to hear the ships' boys if they see danger. We will sail due north. I would rather risk the coast of Corn Walum than the edge of the world."

And so we rowed. I thought that the fog would abate but, if anything, it grew thicker. You felt as though you could cut it with a blade. The only consolation was the silence from the lookouts. The water remained dark without the flecks of white water which hinted at rocks. The oars barely moved us for the water appeared to be like a thick soup.

I was just going to walk to the bows myself when I heard a shout from my son, "Rocks to the steerboard side! We are almost upon them!"

Erik shouted, "Steerboard back oars!" He pushed the steering board over and the drekar lurched alarmingly to our left.

It was hard to keep my feet as Erik turned the drekar skilfully away from the rocks. Then there was a splash and a heartbeat later Ragnar's voice carried down the drekar, "Gruffyd has fallen overboard!"

Haaken shouted, "Up oars!"

I ran down to the steerboard side of the prow. Ragnar was looking over the side. He pointed to the water. "I cannot see him but he fell there!" Every man and boy on my ship stared along the sides of my drekar looking for a sign of him.

Ragnar and others began to shout his name. Aiden said, "Silence! We listen for him! He is in the water. If he tries to shout then he may drown! Listen for his splashes. If he lives he will try to swim."

I did not like the word 'if' but I had hope for both Gruffyd and Ragnar could swim. It was a skill that they had learned in the Water at Cyninges-tūn This was the sea and my heart sank into my sealskin boots. The Water of Cyninges-tūn was gentle compared with this. We listened but all we heard was the creak of the drekar and the slap of water against her hull. Both sides as well as the prow and the stern were manned but no one saw anything through the murk and fog.

Ragnar approached me, "Shall I swim around the ship and see if I can see him?"

I shook my head, "I have lost one of you. I will not lose another." I turned to Aiden. "Is he dead?"

Aiden frowned, "Perhaps I am losing my powers. I sensed no danger and I did not dream his death. He is in the water but I do not feel that he is dead." He looked apologetically at me, "Perhaps Ylva now has my powers."

Erik said, "You should shout for him Jarl. He may have drifted away. The fog is a treacherous thing. It is easy to become lost quickly."

I nodded and shouted, "Gruffyd!" The words seemed to be eaten by the fog and I called again louder. The fog appeared to be a solid wall and my words could not penetrate it. It felt unreal as though it was supernatural. Yet it looked and felt like fog. We all watched and I shouted. I had no idea how long had passed since he had fallen in. We had drifted and the rocks were no longer a danger. In fact, they had not been seen since Gruffyd had shouted. Were we in enchanted waters?

A sudden and frightening thought struck me. "Erik, Aiden, how close are we to Syllingar Insula?"

They looked at each other and Aiden shook his head, "*Wyrd*! We are so close that I should have seen this before. This is the work of the Norns." He put his hand on my shoulder. "I have not lost my powers but the witch has hidden Gruffyd from us. I cannot see what the witch wishes to hide. Your son is lost."

I knew he was right and I slumped to the deck. I was defeated. Assassins had taken one son and my second had been taken by the Norns. I could fight assassins but the Norns? "Erik, take us home."

Erik shouted, "Haaken, oars!"

This time as they slowly rowed the chant sounded like a dirge. It was a tribute to a warrior who had barely begun his life. He had been but a seedling and taken before he could become the tree.

Ulfheonar, warriors strong
Ulfheonar, warriors brave
Ulfheonar, fierce as the wolf
Ulfheonar, hides in plain sight
Ulfheonar, Dragon Heart's wolves
Ulfheonar, serving the sword
Ulfheonar, Dragon Heart's wolves
Ulfheonar, serving the sword

Slowly, imperceptibly, the fog began to thin. I was not paying much attention. I stared at the wolf cloak he had left behind. He had been so proud of it and his part in the wolf hunt. It had hardened his resolve to become a warrior and now he lay with Ran at the bottom of the ocean. He would not be in Valhalla! His sword lay on his cloak! He had not died with a sword in his hand. I would see Wolf Killer again but not his brother. I closed my eyes and lay on my cloak. I tried to picture Gruffyd.

How would I tell his mother that he had been lost? I had no idea how much time passed.

"In oars!"

Aiden said quietly, "Jarl the Weird Sisters have brought us here once more. It is her island. We have reached the witch's home."

I opened my eyes and stood. I peered over the side to the mysterious island which rose from the waters. A tendril of smoke rose from the earth as though there was a hidden volcano. We knew it meant the witch was in her cave. Haaken said, "Will you go ashore, Jarl?"

I nodded, "She may be able to let me speak with the spirit of my son. I would say farewell to him." My voice was flat for I felt drained of life. All my dreams and hopes were dashed and lay with the crabs on the ocean bed."

"Can I come? I would speak with my cousin's spirit." Ragnar's eyes pleaded with me.

I was going to say no when Aiden nodded and said, "It is *wyrd*. Let him come Jarl."

We were close enough to the shore to be able to wade through the shallow water and walk across the rocks to the beach. As we made our way to the steerboard side the Ulfheonar and the rest of the crew stood in silence watching. Their heads were hung. All of our success and our treasures meant nothing. Even the two women, who spoke not our language had their heads bowed. It was a moment when time stood still. This was the end of my hopes and dreams. I would speak with my son and then return to Cyninges-tūn and reflect on what might have been.

I took my sword with me. If what Aiden had said was true and this was a Norn perhaps I would slay her. I would end her torture of men's minds. Aiden's head flicked around, "You know you cannot kill a witch so how would you fare against a Norn.? Hide those thoughts, Jarl."

I nodded, "Stay behind me, Ragnar. If you cannot descend into her underworld then return to the surface and go back to the ship. There is no shame for this can be a fearful place."

"I will go with you." He sounded brave but I caught sight of a pair of widened eyes. He was terrified and I admired him even more at that moment for to face something which is your nemesis is the mark of a true warrior.

Aiden led the way. We were entering his world. We climbed up through the rocks until we spied the entrance. I took my hand from my sword. I could not trust myself. The path to her lair always seemed longer each time we visited. The first time we had come she had been a young girl or that had been the face she had shown us. Each visit had seen her age. I wondered if it would be the same on this visit. I could smell her seafood soup. It always seemed to be bubbling away and we would, as always, eat it and, I had no doubt, we would sleep and dream. Perhaps I would not eat this time.

We turned the corner and saw the glow from her fire. She was not alone. There was a hunched figure with a hood sitting next to her. Was it another of the Norns who was there to help? I saw no face for her back was to us. I saw that the witch's hair was now pure white but when she spoke, her back still turned towards me, I recognised it. "You will partake of the food, Jarl Dragonheart. It would be rude not to do so and besides, you wish to dream. You seek knowledge of the future and you cannot stay away. Sit and face me. Then you will see if I have aged."

I felt Ragnar's hand reach for mine. I gave it a squeeze, "Do not be afraid Ragnar. She will not hurt us."

I heard her cackle, "Your father, Wolf Killer, was afraid when he met me."

We sat down. I saw that the witch had aged. Her eyes were sunken into hollow cheeks and yet they belied her apparent age for they were the eyes of a young girl. Her long bony fingers stirred the pot with a wooden spoon. I glanced at her companion who was almost the same size as her but I could not see her face. The cloak which covered her from head to toe hid all her features. I saw that Aiden was smiling. For him this was a special moment. There were two witches! I wondered if he would bring Kara and Ylva here. Then I dismissed the thought for we were always directed by the witch. We had searched for the island but never found it. It was as though it appeared when she commanded it. Perhaps Aiden was right and she was a Norn.

"Do not worry who or what I am, Jarl. For you, I am a portal into another world. We have chosen you. The reasons why do not concern you. So long as you do our bidding then we will continue to give you help." She ladled the soup into a bowl. "Now eat and you can dream."

I shook my head and raised my voice, "I will not! At least not until I have some answers! You took my son and he died with no sword in his hand. Where is he now? I know he cannot be in Valhalla. Tell me so that I may join him there when my time comes."

"You wish to join your son?" I nodded. "The son you saw fall from your drekar?"

"Aye. I have lost one son. Is that not enough? Where is Gruffyd? I would be with him."

She shook her head and removed the hood from the figure next to her. It was Gruffyd. I was frozen. Was he dead? He spoke not and he looked as white as snow. The witch said as she passed her hand before his face, "Speak to your father."

"I thought I was dead, father. I was on the bottom of the sea and two women came for me. They lifted me from the water and when I awoke I was here wearing these clothes I recognise not. I was ordered not to speak until she said I could. Are you dead too? And Ragnar?"

Ragnar's hand gripped my arm. I dared not take my eyes from Gruffyd in case he disappeared. "We are not dead. At least I do not think that we are dead."

"You live as does your son. Now drink the soup. Our time here is limited."

Aiden said quietly, "We must do as we are ordered Jarl. This is not your world. We are in the world of the spirits and the gods. We must trust her."

I nodded and took the bowl. She filled three more and handed them to my companions.

"Now eat!"

I began to eat. I would just eat a couple of spoonfuls. That would have no effect on me. I would not play this witch's game. It was good soup. The shellfish were fresh and there were spices in the soup. I was enjoying it but I knew that it was drugged yet I could not stop eating. It was delicious. I cared not that I ate heads, shells and bones. I devoured it. I was going to ask for more when I saw that Gruffyd lay on his side and Ragnar too slept. The witch gave me a crooked smile and nodded. My eyes closed and I fell into a deep well of sleep.

I was a child again on the Dunum. Raldson, the son of the Saxon chief of the village was beating me again, as he did every day. He was shouting, "Your mother is a witch! You are the spawn of the devil." I could not fight back for my arms were being held. He punched me in my face. I felt blood flow and then I passed out. When I awoke I saw his butchered body and the bodies of the others who had held me but I was whole and I was alone. It was dark and I made my way up the river bank to my village. I saw that it was on fire. Women were screaming but I could not see my mother. I ran through the village but when I turned the bodies over they were not Saxons or people from my village.

They were Vikings. They were from Ketil's stad and Windar's Mere. I saw Harland. He had been given the blood eagle. Then I heard an evil laugh and turned around. I saw a Dane. He had golden hair save for one long hank the width of a man's hand. It was pure white but that was not the most alarming aspect of his appearance. Around his waist he wore skulls. From their size, they had to be women's or babies'. Then I looked at his hand. He held the skull of Erika, my daughter. Even as I tried to reach it his other hand struck me with his sword and I fell into a deep dark hole.

When I woke Aiden was staring at me and the fire had gone out. One tallow candle illuminated the cave. Ragnar and Gruffyd slept still. I was unwilling to speak of the dream in the lair of the witch. I shook the boys awake. Gruffyd's eyes were wide with terror. I guessed what he had seen. "You are safe now. We will talk later."

My words woke Ragnar and he too showed the same terror. We made our way out of the cave. To my surprise, it was dark when we emerged. How long had we been there? I saw the drekar. It was still offshore. Haaken and my Ulfheonar were gathered around a fire on the beach. When they saw us approach they ran to us.

"We thought you had been taken!" Haaken saw Gruffyd, "Allfather! You were dead! Can such things happen? Can drowned boys rise from the sea and appear on land?"

"We will talk of such things later when we are sea. I would be gone from here!"

When Erik saw us he had the drekar warped in to the shore. As we climbed aboard men's hands went to the protective amulets we all wore. Gruffyd should be dead and yet he walked and seemed alive.

When we were aboard I wrapped their wolf cloaks around them and they sat on my chest close by the steering board. Einar stood looking at the two of them as though they were ghosts. Erik pointed to the pennant, "The wind has returned and takes us home. The Norns have woven a web once more."

I put my cloak around my shoulders. I shuddered. It felt as though someone was walking on my grave. I wished that Erik had not said what he had but I could not undo it now. No one spoke until the islands disappeared into the black night. I did not need to ask Aiden what he had seen; he always dreamed my dream. I was no wizard. Whatever skills I had been given by my mother were limited. I sat between my son and grandson. "It will be good to talk of what you dreamed."

Gruffyd shook his head. Aiden said quietly, "If you do not talk of them then the dreams will return each night until madness follows. If you give them the air they will fly back to the spirits who sent them. The women who came for you were your grandmother and Wolf Killer's mother. They are the spirits who saved you. Speak."

"I was far from here and I fished by a river. It was a wide river." He suddenly looked around at Ragnar. "You were there too!"

"I was and we fished. I caught one."

Gruffyd managed a weak smile, "And mine fell from my line as I pulled it to the bank." Then his face darkened. "Warriors came and we ran."

Ragnar shook his head, "I am a coward! I should have stayed and fought."

"It was a dream and your mind was being shaped. Go on." Aiden's voice was filled with authority. I was pleased he had taken charge for the two boys needed this spirit exorcising from their minds.

"We hid and watched as they slew the men. All save one."

Ragnar said, quietly, "It was Harland Windarsson. They had laid his chest open and..."

"It is called the blood eagle. It is a harsh punishment."

Gruffyd nodded, "Then they took the heads from the children and the babies. There was a warrior... he had skulls about his neck. He came for us and then."

"And then you woke us."

I pulled them closer to me, "Good. You have behaved well. And you, my son, are alive when I thought you lost."

Haaken and the others had been listening intently. "Aiden, does this mean these things have happened or are about to happen."

He shrugged, "I know not. When we return home we will discover if we avenge Harland Windarsson or save him."

Gruffyd was piecing together all the pieces of this puzzle. I saw his mind working. "But these Vikings could be at Cyninges-tūn!"

"They could indeed but I doubt it. Aiden will tell you that the spirits who warn us are those of my wife and my mother."

Ragnar said, "I thought I saw my father but he did not speak with me. He carried me away from the river."

Aiden nodded, "He does not have as much power in the spirit world but he watches over you."

"Erik, we make for Dyflin with all speed. I would leave these royal prisoners and the holy books with Jarl Gunnstein Berserk Killer. I had thought to make the Franks and the priests sweat but now I will sell them back and give the Jarl a broker's fee. My land is in danger. We must return home."

Olaf Leather Neck said, "And we will take to the oars. Let us make this dragon fly!"

Part Three

Viking Enemy

Chapter 11

Dyflin hove into view. I saw many ships there in the harbour but none that I recognised. My drekar, however, was recognised and Jarl Gunnstein Berserk Killer was waiting for us on the quayside. He looked troubled. "Come to my hall we must talk."

"No Jarl. I have urgent business at home. My visit here is a brief one. What ails you?"

He took me to one side so that we could speak without being overheard. "I sent a message to you. I had need of your men. I was told you were in Wessex. Was I told a lie?"

"No, you were told what I told my men to say. I was in the lands of the Franks avenging Wolf Killer."

The relief on his face was clear. "I am pleased. I did not want to think that our friendship was broken."

"Why did you need me?"

"The High King came with his chiefs and kings. He had grown bold because he had gained power in the north. He brought many tribes and kings as well as chiefs and clans. They tried to defeat me. Jarl Gunnar Thorfinnson brought his Raven Wing Clan and we defeated them. Hrolf the Horseman and Ulf Big Nose slew two of their champions. The High King will threaten us no more."

"Then I am sorry that I was not at home when you needed me. I would have come." A sudden thought struck me. This was the Weird Sisters. I told him all, including the drowning and resurrection of Gruffyd.

He clutched his hammer of Thor. "I am sorry for any bad thoughts I harboured. I can see now that you and I were the victims of a mighty web. What would you have of me?"

"Hold the prisoners and the holy books until they are sent for. Take the payment and keep whatever share you feel you are owed."

"That is generous. Are you not afraid I might rob you?"

"If you did then you would not be the warrior I think you are. I harbour no such thoughts in my heart."

"And this trouble at home; do you need my help?"

"I think not besides if you leave it might encourage the Hibernians. If I need help then I will send to you. Hibernians and Franks are easier to deal with than an enemy who is a Viking. I have a face but not a name. I am just grateful that we still have an alliance. When Jarl Gunnar returns here let him know he can still count on my help."

As we headed across the short stretch of water to Úlfarrston I told Aiden and Haaken of our news. Haaken nodded, "So he has taken a wife. That is good but I am sorry about his brother. After the loss of his father, that must have seemed hard."

"Who is Hrolf the Horseman and Ulf Big Nose?"

"Ulf Big Nose is a scout. He is almost as good as Snorri but Hrolf served with me. He was a slave I rescued from the Franks. He was with me the last time I was in the cave with the witch. She told him that his destiny lay in the land of the Franks and that he would be a horseman."

"She always tells the truth then, father?"

"She tells us some truths. She does not lie but her words are like the fog we travelled through. They distort events. Remember we are the playthings of the Weird Sisters. They toy with us as a wild cat might with a mouse before he devours the creature." And that was how I felt. I was a mouse or perhaps one of those dancing creatures the entertainers at Miklagård used to entertain people. They danced on strings and did the bidding of those who pulled the strings. That was me. I fretted and worried all the way home that I might have delayed too long and yet I now knew that had I not visited with Jarl Gunnstein he might have brooded about my lack of support for him. Whatever happened I had been right to do this but I feared it would cost me.

We had lost no warriors but we had had an eventful voyage. None would forget the foggy journey home and the descent into the bowels of the earth. In many ways, it made us all that bit closer. We had been within touching distance of the spirit world and we had survived. I did not want to delay our journey home by a moment longer and I left Erik to organise our chests and treasures. He would see they reached our hall. We borrowed ponies from Coen and we rode as fast as we could for my hall.

I saw, by the light of the setting sun, the walls of my settlement standing. Aiden had not seen disaster but I was relieved that no harm had come to it. Asbjorn met us at the gate. "Did you not have a successful voyage, Jarl? Where is the treasure?"

"It will follow. Have you heard from Ketil or any of those to the east?"

"No Jarl. Is there danger?"

"We visited the witch. I had a dream of Harland Windarsson and he had suffered the blood eagle."

"We have heard nothing."

"Have as many horses and ponies gathered as you can. We leave in the morning."

Snorri said, "Jarl I can leave now. It is not far. I will be back by dawn."

"When we go we all travel together and we take many men. My dream was of a large warband. Besides, I would have Kara and Aiden give me answers. Our enemy is a Viking."

We reached my hall and both Elfrida and Brigid rushed out to see their sons. Brigid looked larger than when I had left. The baby was growing. She looked healthy. I had not told Gruffyd what to say about his experience. That would be his decision. After Elfrida had hugged her son she asked, "Did he behave as a warrior should, Jarl?"

"He did. He obeyed orders and was a credit to you and my son."

Brigid asked nothing. We went indoors. As much as I wanted to bathe and change I would be going to war the next day. I allowed myself the pleasure of taking off my mail. When I had done so I said, "I must see my daughter."

"But you have only just returned home. It can wait until tomorrow."

I would not lie. "Tomorrow I go to Windar's Mere."

I left and walked across to the house of women. The three of them were waiting for me as I entered. I had not mentioned to Aiden that I was unhappy with his lack of warning of the danger to Gruffyd but now that I was here in his house I hid it no longer.

"Why did you not see the danger, Aiden? Was it because you serve the witch and not me?"

He looked shaken, "No, Jarl, you know that is not true."

"I know that my son nearly drowned and you showed no regret."

"That is because I knew that he was not dead."

"But you could not tell me."

Kara shook her head, "If he had told you then would you have believed him? He told you he believed he was not dead. Aiden serves you, father. Ylva and I work for you too. But we also serve the spirits. Sometimes they choose to give us glimpses and no more."

"Well then, have they shown you a glimpse of Windar's Mere? Are we in time to save Harland or not?"

"We do not know. We will have to speak with the spirits."

"I leave for Windar's Mere in the morning. If you cannot tell me by then it will be unnecessary." I was annoyed and I made to leave.

Kara said, "When we speak with the spirits it takes much out of us. We cannot guarantee success."

I saw, in my head, Harland Windarson's body. "Then let us hope that my warriors are able to reach him in time. You have the luxury of sitting behind my walls knowing that my men defend you with their lives. It is my warriors who put their lives at risk. Think on that and seek the truth of this dream."

I was heading for my home when there was a shout from the gate. I drew my sword and ran to the walls. Karl One Hand peered out. "It is Bergil Rolfsson from Ketil's stad."

"Open the gate and admit him."

The noise had brought Aiden and some of my Ulfheonar forth. Bergil was wounded. His leg had been cut. "Jarl, Windar's Mere has been attacked. It is Danes."

I turned and saw Aiden, "See to his wounds. Fetch ale. Where is Ketil?"

"He pursues them east." He shook his head, "We found his brother Harland. He had been given the blood eagle."

I looked at Haaken and Olaf. Olaf nodded, "I will get the men."

"Tell me all!"

Ragnar ran up with ale and then knelt by my side. Bergil drank deeply. "Two days since a boy ran to our stad. He said that Windar's Mere had been surprised by Vikings and many slain. He said that Ulla's Water had also been devastated. The Jarl took our warband south and found that the men of Ulla's Water had been slain and the people were taken. We met refugees who had survived the attack on both places. The Jarl sent them to his stad. We hurried down to Windar's Mere and there we found his brother. The men had been slaughtered and the Danes had fled."

"You know they were Danes?"

"Those who survived said that they were Vikings and used the words of the Danes."

Aiden had finished and asked, "Why did Ketil not send to Ulf for help or send here immediately?"

"He thought you were still away and he was mindful of the Hibernians, Windar's Mere and Ulla's Water were his charge."

"And how many men has he with him?"

"No more than forty. He left men on the walls."

"You fought there?" he nodded, "How many men were there?"

"There had to be over a hundred."

"And yet Ketil followed with forty. Something is not right here. Uhtric, my mail."

Aiden said softly. "We could have done nothing to stop this. The attack came when we were sailing north. The crew rowed and the winds were with us. This was *wyrd*."

"I know but it does not make it any easier. I had thought I had planned for this. I took but one crew and yet an enemy succeeded in hurting us. I have failed."

Bergil said, "Jarl Ketil thought he did for the best, Jarl Dragonheart."

A sudden chilling thought struck me. "Where did you get these wounds?"

"A pair of Danes attacked me as I headed west. I slew them."

Bergil was an honest warrior but he could not see further than the end of his sword. "The Danes were west of Windar's Mere?"

"Aye, they were close to the bridge at Skelwith."

"Then we have enemies close to home. They are not all fled. Karl One Hand, send a pair of your boys to ride to the Rye Dale, the Grassy Mere and the Stad on the Eden. Warn them that there are Danes abroad. Prepare for war."

Haaken asked, "Is this a ploy to draw us east?"

"Perhaps but it is clever. We cannot go to Ketil's aid until we have made sure that there is no warband close to our walls. It ensures that this Dane with the skulls can evade us."

Bergil looked up, "Dane with the skulls? I did not mention that, Jarl Dragonheart, yet the refugees spoke of this."

I nodded, "They said he had golden hair and one white streak."

Bergil's hand clutched at Thor's hammer. "Aye Jarl!"

"I dreamed and saw this. The Norns are playing with us." Uhtric had brought my mail and I donned it. Gruffyd stood expectantly by his side. Brigid's arms were around my son, protectively. "Gruffyd, you will stay here for Karl will need warriors. You have done enough." I held his eyes and he nodded. He was growing. There would be no petulance and no tantrums. He had died a boy and been reborn almost a man.

Infuriatingly it was past the middle of the night when we were ready to ride. We only had half of Asbjorn's men. The ones who had not reached us would man the walls of Cyninges-tūn. We had ten boys with us and they would have to be messengers, archers and slingers. I had sent word to Coen ap Pasgen to warn him. His brother Raibeart was still raiding and Sigtrygg would be too far away to offer any help. Nor did we have every man mounted. A third would have to walk. I mounted the Ulfheonar and my mailed men. It was a perfunctory farewell. Brigid was stunned by the horror of the manner of Harland's death and her arms stayed around the shoulders of our son. She did not even tell me to stay. We headed north and east through the dark and along our own greenway.

I sent Snorri and Beorn ahead to look for signs of our enemies. I was not worried about the odd scout but a warband could wreak havoc amongst my farmsteads. Skelwith would be our first stop.

Einar and the hearth-weru were tightly gathered around my grandson. He was a warrior now. He had killed. It might have only been a priest but he had killed. I needed every man I could. I had but fifty men with me. A Warband that was large enough to destroy two well-defended stad would be large and I feared for Ketil. He was brave but he would be driven by revenge. I sensed something more than a simple raid. If the Danes outnumbered Ketil why had they not destroyed him? Harland Windarsson was different. Harland had been no warrior. The blood eagle was a terrible death but more so for those who were not warriors.

Our eyes flickered to the forests alongside us as we headed east. I was gambling that the Danes did not know my land. They would follow the roads and paths we had made. They had come on the Roman road from the east and that had allowed them to attack without the knowledge of Ketil. He kept a good watch. I wondered what news he had had from Prince Athelstan. A memory of a conversation came to mind. *'The Prince told me that they have set themselves up as warlords and petty chiefs.'* It had seemed insignificant before but now, after the cave, it seemed clear. There was a Dane living in the valley of the Dunum. It made perfect sense. The river allowed him the opportunity to use his drekar to raid upriver or further afield. No one had been a threat there since Magnus the Foresworn. The Norns' web was a complicated one.

We reached Skelwith just before dawn. Snorri was there and he and Beorn were tending to the wounds of the farmer and his sons. Aiden took over as Snorri told us what he had discovered. "There was a small warband. They attacked last evening but Arne son of Skel has a well-made home. They held them off. I think that the approach of Beorn and I made them flee."

"They were that close?"

"We waited for you for they are on foot. I thought it better to tell you and then pursue in daylight when it will be easier to spy their tracks."

"How many were there?"

"We outnumber them. I think that is the remnants of those that attacked Bergil Rolfsson."

"You did right." I turned to my men. "Prepare to move quickly. There is a war band ahead. Those with horses will pursue. Ragnar, you take your hearth-weru and those on foot. Go directly to Windar's Mere and wait there. There should not be any Danes but I need you to hold it for us and to protect the dead. We owe them that, at least."

"Aye Jarl."

It would be his first command and, I hoped, an easy one. It was not far to Windar's Mere. I needed to move swiftly to catch and destroy this warband and then catch up with Ketil who might, even now, be on the Dunum.

Dawn came as we were ready to ride. Snorri was like a dog with the scent of his prey. He soon found the tracks. They headed north, towards the Rye Dale. The greenway followed the beck which bubbled from the valley of the Grassy Mere and the Rye Dale. The Danes would keep to it for it was the easier route. Audun's farmstead guarded the col close to the Lough Rigg. I hoped we would catch them before they reached the old man and his family.

We found the wounded Danish warrior just a mile from Skelwith. He was lying in a ditch. Snorri had disarmed him. One of Arne's son's arrows had slowed him down. "Aiden, Cnut Cnutson, question him and then give him the warrior's death. Catch us up. Snorri, on. They may be closer than we think." He had been left because he was wounded and wounded men slowed you up.

I spied the smoke from Audun's farm blowing towards us when Beorn galloped up. "We have them Jarl. They are half a mile from Audun's farm. I think they plan to attack. They have not seen us for the wind is in our favour."

We rode hard and stopped four hundred paces later. We dismounted and tied our horses to the trees by the beck. We hefted shields to our front. There might be few of them but we would not risk a reckless attack. Beorn led us to Snorri who had his bow ready. He held up his hands twice. There were twenty men. He pointed ahead. Audun's farm had been built on a solid piece of rocky ground above the valley which sometimes flooded. The land gave him protection. I could picture the Danes as they ascended the slope hoping to have an easy raid, food and shelter.

The Ulfheonar led and we followed Snorri and Beorn. As soon as we climbed the bank and emerged from the gorse we saw the Danes as they crept closer to the farm. Audun's grandson, Egil shouted the alarm as he saw them. When the Danes rose, two arrows flew from the bows of my scouts and two Danes fell. There was a moment of indecision as they looked to see where the arrows came from. This allowed us to get closer to them. When they did see us they did the only thing they could. They formed a thin shield wall and began to keen their death song. They saw forty mailed warriors racing towards them and the wolf cloaks told them who we were. They knew they were dead men and would die with their swords in their hands.

"I want one prisoner alive!"

A shield wall one warrior deep, even though they were on a slope held no fears for my men. I raced to the centre of the line and hacked below the shield of the Dane whose spear thrust down at me. My shield took his blow while his leg was almost severed by the force of my blade. As he dropped I tore my sword across his throat and stepped over his body to plunge my Ragnar's Spirit into the side of the next Dane who was fending off Haaken. The two of us stepped into their line and stood back to back. Olaf Leather Neck and Rolf Horse Killer swung their axes as I had below the shields of the Danes. It had the same effect. Finni the Dreamer could be a quiet warrior but in that instant, he became a ferocious whirlwind of sword and shield. He spun and slashed deep amongst the disorientated Danes. His bloody blade was a blur.

In an instant, their line had been destroyed. I ran to the warriors who had had their legs taken by our axes. Their lives were pumping away down the slope. "Who is your Jarl?"

The two of them held their swords and smiled. One said, just before he expired, "He is your bane, Dragonheart! Your time is..."

"Are there any alive?"

"None Jarl, they fought too hard."

"Back to our horses, we must reach Windar's Mere." We had no time to see how Audun fared. We had destroyed the small warband and now we had a bigger one to catch.

We met Aiden and Cnut by the top of the Mere close to the old Roman fort and the charred remains of the ancient fort destroyed by the Saxons. The Dane was dead. He had been given the warrior's death.

"Well?"

"He was a hard man but the thought of dying without his sword loosened his tongue. The Dane is Eggle Skulltaker. From what the dying warrior said he has his stronghold on the Dunum where the river narrows. He had a warband of over a hundred men. They have four drekar on the river."

Haaken said, "There are twenty warriors less now."

I nodded. I had a name now. "Let us hurry." I began to fear for Ketil. He would be outnumbered by more than two to one. He was brave and I hoped that he would be wise. A man did not fight impossible odds. He used his head.

It was after noon when we reached Windar's Mere. It was a sad sight. The walls stood but within was a charnel house. Dismembered bodies were strewn around. The defenders had killed Danes and neither band of warriors had been buried or burned. It told me something of this Dane. He was ruthless and his men were to be used. There were at least twenty dead Danes. Einar had organised the men to begin to collect them and put them in one place. As I dismounted and walked around my eyes were drawn to the body of Harland Windarsson. He had not been a warrior. He had been a merchant, he had been a man who enjoyed the good life and yet he had suffered the most painful of deaths.

"Haaken, Olaf, bury Harland. He deserved better." I saw that he was surrounded by the hearth-weru of Arne Thorirson. The butchered body of the hersir was strewn around as though he had been torn apart.

"Aye Jarl. Ketil must have been angry not to have buried him."

"I think that he was keen to pursue our enemies. I hope his rashness has not cost him dear."

Most distressing of all were the babies and children. All that remained were their bodies. Eggle Skulltaker had lived up to his name. As much as I wanted to hurry after Ketil I could not leave the dead as they were. We had had no sleep and tired men make mistakes. "We will bury the dead and leave before dawn."

Aiden came over to me. "I am sorry Jarl. We did not see this. I was far away and Kara and Ylva were not seeking such danger this close to home."

"I know I was harsh with you. This is my fault. I relied on the power you have instead of the power of my warriors. With Elfridaby abandoned I should have strengthened Windar's Mere and put a strong warrior here. I have learned my lesson but it is Harland who has paid the price."

Einar had put men on watch around the walls. It was they who alerted us to the sound of men approaching. "Warriors, Jarl, from the north and east."

Every warrior stopped what he was doing and grabbed weapons. "To the walls." The gate had been destroyed but the low gates were still standing. I went with the Ulfheonar to stand in the gate. I looked to the sentry, "Where away?"

"I saw movements in the woods towards the Hawk's Head forest. The late afternoon sun glinted off metal. They are warriors."

I nodded, "You have good eyes Siggi. Keep them on the danger." I swung my shield around. I saw that Ragnar and his hearth-weru stood behind us. "Einar keep him safe. This Dane is a tricky and cunning warrior. He outwitted both me and Ketil. Watch for tricks."

"Aye Jarl. Ragnar Arturusson will be safe. You have my word."

"Jarl they are using the paths in the woods and avoiding the Mere."

It was a clever approach for we would only see them at the last moment. We had no idea of numbers save that they were warriors and using the woods and forests for cover.

Olaf Leather Neck said, "Well they will not find this gate as easy to destroy as the wooden one. Ulfheonar do not die easily."

"Aye!"

Haaken began a chant, "Ulfheonar! Ulfheonar! Ulfheonar!"

"They come!"

The warriors emerged from the trees just a hundred paces from us. To my great relief, I saw that it was Ketil's men but Ketil himself was carried on the back of a horse! Two other horses carried other wounded men. Disaster had struck once more. My Jarl was hurt.

Chapter 12

There were just twenty men with Ketil and many of them had wounds. His hearth-weru led the horse. "Aiden!"

We ran to help the Jarl from his horse. "He has a wound to his stomach lord!"

I could hear the concern in Oleg's voice. "Fear not Aiden is a good healer. He will look after him but I need you to tell me all." He handed the reins to Haaken and I took him to one side. "Speak and leave nothing out."

"We came as soon as the jarl received the message about the attack. There were still Danes here and we fought and slew the rearguard. Then we followed their trail. It was easy to find for they had captives, animals and treasure. They made no attempt to hide it. The Jarls' brother and his father had much gold."

There had to have been a spy in Windar's Mere for how else would they have known that Harland's stad was rich and unprotected?

"We caught up with their rearguard by the pass of Shap. We fought them. We slew ten but we lost the same number and the rest escaped. We rested only briefly for Jarl Ketil was determined to avenge his brother. We left at dawn and followed them. We found them again by the high pass over the moors. There were more of them this time. Jarl Ketil was reckless and he charged them. We broke their first shield wall but a mighty Dane wounded the Jarl. We dragged him from their clutches and lost more men. I decided that we had to fetch him home. We would have all been slain and..."

"And you did the right thing by coming back, but tell me if there were many Danes left why did they not pursue you and end it?"

"I know not and we have asked that question many times on the journey home. He even let us keep the three horses you see."

I knew the answer to this riddle but I would not tell him. He would be hurt that he had been duped."Were many of them mailed?"

"No Jarl. We had as many mailed men. That is how the jarl was able to break their shield wall. He laughed away their weapons and their blows. He fought as though he was immortal. It was just an accident that the Jarl's mail was breached."

I nodded. The Norns' work could be clearly seen. "You have done well. All of your men have fulfilled their oath and, fear not, we will avenge Harland Windarsson and those who were slain. We will bring back the captives."

He shook his head, "There were few of them, Jarl Dragonheart. We found headless bodies as we headed east. It was almost like a trail of breadcrumbs."

I saw even more clearly now the plan of this Dane. He was drawing us east. "Just so. Come we will see how he fares and you can have your hurts seen to." All of the survivors had wounds but Oleg's armour had protected him.

We found Aiden and the rest of Ketil's wounded in the hall of Harland Windarsson. It had been ransacked but not burned. Aiden looked up as we entered. "He might live, Jarl Dragonheart, but he cannot be moved. He is between life and death. The spirits are all around him and he sleeps in their world. I had to sew him. If we move him then the stitches might burst or the spirits might decide to take him. I have his sword in his hand in case they do."

I nodded and looked at the wounded. "How many are fit to move?"

Aiden looked at the wounded and injured men. He pointed to Sven the Bear, "He can go and those seven. The rest will slow you down."

"You will stay here and care for them."

"Will you not need me?"

"I think I have the measure of this enemy now. He needs a warrior to defeat him and not a wizard. I have seen his plan." I waved over Ragnar, Olaf, Snorri and Haaken. "We leave in the morning. Snorri I wish you and Beorn to ride to the Dunum. Scout out his home. It is on the high cliff over the Dunum."

Ragnar asked, "How do you know?"

"From the information which Aiden and Cnut Cnutson obtained. This Eggle Skulltaker is setting a trap for us. He is clever as well as cruel. He has not enough men to take Cyninges-tūn and so he attacks the weakest of my settlements to draw us to him. He could have defeated and slain Ketil any time he chose. He wishes to entice me over the high passes to the Dunum. He thinks he knows the land well and he will try to destroy us. With us dead, he could return west and claim the land of the wolf for his own."

My Ulfheonar nodded but Ragnar asked, "Could he not be just a raider who took a chance and was lucky?"

"He could have been but if he had been he would have destroyed Ketil and his men. He had the chance to do so twice. Instead, he hurt them knowing that they would return here and tell me. He expects me to go charging in and he will ambush us or lay a trap. Then he can return at leisure and walk into an undefended land. I have the journey east to find a way to defeat him."

I waved over one of the boys we had brought with us. "Harald Finnison."

"Yes, Jarl?"

"I have some important tasks for you. I want one of your boys to ride to the stad on the Eden and tell Ulf Olafsson what has happened. Tell him that I wish him to watch Ketil's stad as well as his own. I go to the Dunum." He made to run. "I have not finished. Then I want another boy to go to Cyninges-tūn. I need the rest of Asbjorn's men. They are to follow us to the Dunum. Your messengers can come with us then." He hesitated, "Now you can go."

I knew that I was risking my home by taking Asbjorn's men but I counted on Raibeart returning and coming to my settlement. When he heard of the disaster he would respond. If he did not then it would be up to Karl One Hand and my old men. That thought made me even more determined to succeed.

We buried the dead. They included one of the men who had been with Ketil. He could not be saved. We chose a piece of ground close to the mere. It was sombre for, as night fell, the rains began. Aiden said it was a good sign for the gods were showing that they were weeping for the dead too. We made a huge barrow over the top. By the time it was finished it was dark and we retired to the hall.

As we collected the food which their rearguard had intended to take I started to plan. I had a good idea where he would have fled. It was an old fort from before the time of the Romans. The first defenders of the valley, the ancients had lived there. It had no stone walls but earth ramparts above the river. I guessed that this Dane must have improved the defences. The river was just wide enough to turn a drekar around. It was the only place to do so that far up the river. We would travel along the greenway by the river. There were many trees and we had good scouts who would stop the enemy from seeing us.

Cnut Cnutson had been outside and he returned when the food was almost gone.

Olaf laughed, "You will learn that we do not keep food for those who cannot be bothered to turn up on time."

Cnut smiled, "I found some food myself." He pointed to the south. "I remembered that Arne Thorirson was a careful hersir. He had food and weapons buried south of here at Rayrigg Wyke. I learned of it when I was a ships' boy for he asked Erik to send some of us. He had an idea that he could fortify the island in the middle of the mere. He said that if enemies came the people could shelter on the island and be supplied from the hidden store. We came to help him sail the food down the mere. Arne was a clever man."

Haaken said, "If it was when you were a ship's boy then the food would have spoiled!"

Cnut laughed, "Did you not hear of the famous feasts they threw here at Midsummer? They ate up the previous year's food. It was seen as a bounty from the gods. Then they refilled the barrels which lay beneath the ground."

I shook my head, "I thought the feasts were because Windar liked his food. It was clever of Arne. I should have paid more attention to him." Even as I said it I knew that if Arne was before me now and alive he would have the sharp edge of my tongue. He had prepared food but not done as I had asked and improved the defences. If he had done so this disaster might have been avoided.

"We can take the food with us. I had men bring it and the weapons. The weapons are mainly spears and arrows but there are some swords."

"Then we will take them and this will be Arne's revenge as much as ours and Ketil's."

We were better armed than we had been as we left the village of ghosts. We used ponies to carry the food and spare weapons. There was little point in pushing hard. What we had to do was to arrive unseen. Snorri and Beorn had left before dawn and they would be halfway there as we began the climb towards the high pass. We had passed the dead at Shap and made a stone cairn around their bodies and then trudged eastwards climbing ever upwards. The carrion in the distance told us where the last charge of Ketil had taken place. If Oleg Strong Arm had not told us that it was our men we would not have recognised them. Their bodies had been stripped and chopped up as though a beast had torn them apart. Their eyeless heads were on spears stuck in the ground. It hardened the hearts of all of us. There would be no mercy. As with those at Shap we covered their remains with stones. We left as the sun began to sink in the western sky.

Rather than camping close to the dead, we crossed the high pass. The skies had cleared after the rain and we could see, with the golden rays of the setting sun, all the way to the eastern coast. The forests and the woods began just ten miles from where we camped and it was a green swathe with the dark line of the sea to the east. Then the sun dropped behind the mountains and all was plunged into darkness. It seemed ominous.

We ate the salted meat left by Arne and thanked him silently as we did so. Ragnar was taking it all in. He listened and rarely spoke save to have a question answered. He recognised the importance of this raid. My authority had not only been challenged but it had also been shaken to its very core. We had never had a settlement devastated. Now we had had two. We had not had captives taken before. Now we had a whole village taken. I thought back to the near death of Gruffyd and our visit to the witch. I had seen the start of my life as a Viking. Would this be the end? Was this the final demise of the land of the wolf?

"We will be outnumbered." Olaf Leather Neck made a statement rather than posing a question.

I nodded. "That is why he tempts us across with just a hundred warriors. Even if the four drekar were only threttanessa he would have more than a hundred men and would have far more if his drekar were bigger. From what Aiden and Cnut said he could have two hundred men or more. When Ketil attacked men who were not in armour it showed that this Eggle Skulltaker could afford to throw men's lives away. He has more waiting for us. He will keep men hidden to surprise us."

Olaf waved his hand at the men camped around us. "We will have more mailed men than he has but fewer men so what is your plan Jarl?"

"I did not have a solid plan until Cnut found the weapons. He was guided there by the Norns. The men who are not mailed can use bows and spears. If we have the archers, under Snorri, behind us then we can probe for weakness. Their arrows will fall as rain and thin their ranks. The men with spears can guard our flanks. If we take out the rivets holding the heads of the spears then we can throw them and they will not be able to return them. But in the end, Olaf, it will be down to us. We have thirty warriors who are either Ulfheonar or had once been Ulfheonar. Another thirteen have mail. I will give the banner to Ragnar so that Leif the Banner can fight in the shield wall and yet we can draw our enemies on. We make them bleed. Oleg told me that Ketil and his few men broke their shield wall for they did not have a large number of mailed warriors."

"My hearth-weru could fight with you, Jarl."

"They could but we would be better served if they guarded the banner and protected our rear. I know they will not retreat and their weight, even at the rear of the shield wall, can make the difference. Do not worry, Ragnar. They will be playing their part as will you. We will be fighting at night where our lack of numbers will be hidden. When Asbjorn's men join us then we will have another ten men with mail. With over fifty of our warriors thus armed we have a chance."

I had not told them all. I needed Snorri's information before I did so.

We made our way east heading, all the time, for the valley where I had spent the first years of my life. We were now in the land of Northumbria but from what I knew the King had little control outside of the far north, Din Guardi, and the walled city the Danes now called Jorvik. Eggle Skulltaker might not be the only warlord we might encounter and I kept scouts out in front of us as we moved closer to the river. We avoided the waterfall which invited death to the unwary and kept to the north bank of the river. The craggy and wild land gave way to areas where the trees had been felled and fields farmed. There were still precious few of them. We saw few people on our journey east. When the river began to loop and slow I knew that we were close and we made camp by a deserted and ruined Saxon village. It had a good site above the bluffs and I wondered when it had been abandoned. I guessed that we were no more than twenty miles or so from the sea. I knew that Eggle's stronghold lay somewhere between us and the sea. I would find it.

"I will ride with Haaken and we will head east. I will find Snorri and Beorn. Olaf, I wish you to make rafts. They can be crude. They only need to carry two men each. Build five of them and have kindling collected."

I could see that he did not understand but he knew me well enough to nod and say, "Aye Jarl."

Ragnar asked, "Why do you put yourself in danger, grandfather? Let others go."

"The day I do that is the day I let you or Gruffyd lead the clan. This was my valley. I am not so old that I cannot hide from our enemies. I have to see with these eyes what faces us then I can formulate a better plan that helps us to defeat this butcher and keep my men alive. That will not be easy. I will be safe and I will return by morning. Keep a good watch. The rest of our men may be arriving soon."

We were some way down the greenway when Haaken said, "Ragnar is right. We could have sent Rollo and Rolf. They are good scouts."

"You did not wish to come?"

"That is not what I meant. We cannot afford to lose you, Jarl Dragonheart."

"And you will not. I need to see where their drekar lie. I have been fermenting a plan as we came east. Their drekar is the chink in their mail. If they have their ships threatened it will weaken their resolve. Does this Eggle Skulltaker sound like a warrior who inspires men to follow him? Is he a Prince Butar? Gunnstein Berserk Killer?"

"No. He threatens and the men follow him because they fear him and there are no rules for them to follow."

"He has been successful. That is obvious. He has gathered the sweepings of the land under his hand. They stay with him because he gives them women, treasure and easy targets. If their drekar are taken or destroyed then his men will fear the wolf." Haaken nodded. "I blame myself for this. My grandson, Ragnar, could have taken Windar's Mere. I can see that now. When I asked Arne and Harland to make it like the stad on the Eden they did not. I should have made them do it! I did not do as I said I would. The Norns sent the snow and I stayed in my home, warm by my fire! It has cost them and their people their lives."

"But you are not a king. You do not order them. Men follow you because of who you are."

"Then I must find a way to make them follow me while they obey me. I will ask Ketil to become Jarl at Windar's Mere and to make it into a fortress."

"If he recovers."

"Aye."

"And if he will accept."

"Then if not I will ask Asbjorn. He is a strong leader and he raids. That breeds stronger men and they build better walls for their families. They know the danger of raiders. Arne and Harland were farmers and merchants. They had been kept safe by Wolf Killer, Ketil and me. The Norns have shown me the folly of my ways. It has been an expensive lesson but it is learned. It will become harder. When I give a command I will expect it to be obeyed."

Haaken said quietly, "Do not forget Jarl that you are the heart of your people. Do not become hard-hearted."

"And I will not. Kara and Brigid would not allow it. I will become like the blade I wield. Tempered in blood, water and fire I will guide my people in the right direction. A good sheepdog obeys its master and keeps its flock safe. Arne and Harland did not obey me and look what has happened to their flock."

The river path wound its way through bushes and trees. In places, people had built wooden walkways through the reeds. It meant we travelled hidden from view. It had been some years since we had travelled this path which meandered around the river. But I knew we were close to the enemy when I heard the sounds from their camp. There were screams and shouts. The smell of wood smoke and cooking meat drifted towards us. We dismounted and left the river path. Leading our ponies we headed up the steep bank, through the trees. The stronghold had to be there. Suddenly Snorri and Beorn materialized from the woods. Snorri put his finger to his lips and pointed west. He led us through the forest to a deserted farm. Their horses were tied up by a half-demolished barn. I saw two dead Danes.

"We can speak here. These Danes came by earlier this evening and we slew them. We were just having one last scout before we sought you out. The warband is down the river a short way from here."

"What else have you discovered?"

"He has about a hundred and thirty men. He keeps six on each of his four drekar. They are anchored beneath his stronghold on the north bank. They are close to the stronghold and tied in twos. He sends scouts out each morning. You were fortunate they did not see you."

I pointed to the two dead men. "From which direction did these Danes come?"

"The east."

"Then they may have seen us. If that is the case then he will have an idea of where we are."

"We slew two more yesterday but that was south of the river. We may have confused him."

"He doesn't seem to be the type to be confused." I handed my reins to Haaken. "Snorri take me so that I may see his camp and the river."

"But I have told you all."

"I know but I cannot get inside your head. I need to see the lie of the land. I will not rush into this without knowing I have a way out.

Remember I am Ulfheonar. I have not lost my skills." I hung my shield on my saddle and took off my helmet. I needed to see and hear. I hoped we would not need to fight. With our wolf cloaks, we would be hidden from view. I pulled the wolf skin over my head and became the wolf.

He nodded and led me back to where we had met. We slipped into the woods and moved stealthily. I followed this master of remaining hidden. I heard noises ahead. It was the enemy camp. I trusted Snorri to take us the safest route and to find somewhere we could view the camp without being discovered. The path dipped a little and Snorri held up his hand. I stopped and we edged forward until we were behind two large willows they had many trunks snaking up to the sky. Below us was the camp. Men were drinking, and fighting and women were being used but I only saw thirty or forty men at most. I looked at Snorri. He pointed to the walls of the stronghold beyond the camp. I stared and saw that there were men on the walls and they were alert. The walls were not high but men would die trying to scale them. Then Snorri pointed to the towers at each corner. There were men in those too.

Tugging my arm he led me along the edge of the wood down the slope towards the river. It became a jumble of bushes, rushes and reeds. Snorri took us by the edge of the water. He moved slowly and when I saw two ducks paddle quietly away from the bank I saw why. He did not wish to frighten the wildlife which might give warning to our foe. We crouched beneath an elder. He pointed up and I stared wondering what I was seeing. Then I caught the flicker of light and then another. It was a second camp and in the flickering lights, I saw that there were men walking through the camp and the fires. The first camp was there to deceive our scouts into believing that it was a drunken rabble we faced. The second camp held the ones we would have to fight. Hidden by the fort they would fall upon an enemy who attacked his drunken rabble. I guessed that Eggle Skulltaker allowed different men to enjoy the camp each night. It was a risk they took but I guessed they thought it was worth it.

As my eyes descended towards the river I saw the four drekar. Their masts were on the mast fish. One was a threttanessa but one was almost as large as my own drekar. They were tied in twos and moored to the shore fore and aft. If their ropes were severed then they would float down the river. The crews would have plenty of time to step their masts. I had seen enough and I tapped Snorri on the shoulder. Before I moved he gripped my arm. I saw two warriors walking along the path. The bushes and reeds meant that it was narrow and they would pass us. I did not wish to risk a noise. There was nothing else for it. We slipped into the water and hid among the reeds.

The two warriors drew closer. They wore their swords but neither had mail. They were young. They passed and went to make water. They chatted, amiably, as they did so. "Do you think this Dragonheart will come here? I have heard he is clever. Why would he risk a journey across the Saxon land?"

"I know not. Guthrum said that the blood eagle we left was a message for him and the chief knew he would come."

The sound of their water ceased. The air was filled with a sour smell and they began to walk back. "He has not made a mistake yet. We all have gold and as many women as we wish."

"Aye, it is easier than rowing and raiding. I just wish this wolf would come so that we can slay him and then take his land! There is no king there."

They were almost out of earshot but I heard one say, "And that is what Eggle wishes. He would be king."

"That is good for we will all be jarls and hersir. I will have slaves to do my bidding. When he is king he will not allow any to take it from us! It is the land filled with gold, iron, fish and game. I have heard it is Valhalla on earth."

When they had disappeared we climbed from the water. We would not take any more risks and we headed back to the deserted farm where we had left the others. I saw the relief on Haaken's face as we appeared. "You had me worried. Can we go now?"

"We can go now. I have my plan and I will explain it when we reach our camp."

I did not do as I said. Instead, I slept. I had seen the enemy and his dispositions. He had planned for everything. Or he thought he had. I slept and my mind improved and refined my plan even as I slept. It was not a dream; it was an imagining of how the battle would go. I awoke and felt the hard ground beneath my back. I opened my eyes to a grey sky. I smiled. I knew how to surprise this Eggle Skulltaker.

When I stood I saw Haaken. Olaf and Ragnar watching me. Snorri and Beorn slept on. Olaf said, "The other men arrived last night, Jarl."

"Good. And the rafts?"

"They are almost ready but what eight men on four boats can do is beyond me, Jarl."

"It will be one man and seven boys on four boats Olaf Leather Neck. Is there food? I could eat a horse with the skin on."

Ragnar smiled and said, "Come, we have made a stew of salted meat and river fish. It is an interesting taste."

"Lead me to it, grandson." As we walked I said, "You do not seem as inquisitive as you normally are."

"Last night I dreamed and I saw you. You were not in a wolf cloak, you were a wolf and you were terrible to behold. You slew all before you and they fled to the river which consumed them."

I smiled, "Where did you sleep last night?"

"The camp was noisy. Olaf Leather Neck should be called Olaf the Farter for he farts a lot and Finni the Dreamer snores and twitches when he dreams. I went alone to the river and slept alone."

"Then you were close to the river?"

"I was."

I knew now why he had dreamed so clearly, "Water is our friend and the spirits use it. You have been given a glimpse of what might be."

"You mean that was not what will happen?"

"Dreams do not work that way. If you had dreamed of the past then it would have been different. We all have a clearer picture of the path, especially in dreams but the present and the future are uncertain. That may be a future far ahead or it may be tomorrow. That is why there are three Norns. Urðr is the Norn who tells what happened in the past, Verðandi what is happening now and Skuld what could happen."

Ragnar nodded, "Then it was Verðandi who told us what was happening?"

"It was and I was wrong to chastise my daughter and Aiden. They were quite right. We could not have saved Windar's Mere unless we could have flown on the wind and even then we would have been too late. It was Skuld who showed you a possibility of the future."

Eystein Big Belly served me a bowl of food and I nodded my thanks. I went to a log and sat upon it. I started to eat. "This is good stew."

"You said a possibility. What do you mean?"

"There have been many kings, princes and jarls who have used those who can see into the future to help them and provide intelligence to help them win. It is dangerous to rely upon that for it is not ordained. Skuld can change what happens on a whim. It is better to hope for that outcome but to do all in your power to make it so. When you are a leader then treat these dreams with caution. They may happen. A good leader makes sure that they do. Your dream has hardened my resolve. I will be the wolf in the battle to come."

As I finished the stew he asked, "But you have a plan?"

"I do and I used my own dream, not that of the Norns or the spirits to devise it. If it goes wrong and we all die then it will be on my head and I will answer for it in Valhalla."

"But that will not happen."

"How do you know, Ragnar Arturusson?"

"I thought I knew you before, while my father lived, but I did not. I knew the legend, I knew the story. I did not know you. I still do not know you but I understand you more than I did for I have stood behind you and seen you fight. I have heard the men speak of you and I have seen how you lead. You care not if you live or die so long as your people are safe and prosper. I watched when Gruffyd sank beneath the waves. You would have offered to exchange places with him in a heartbeat if Ran had allowed it. When we fight, whenever that may be, you will use all your strength, skill and experience to see that we do not lose. I do not think this barbarian who wears skulls around his neck is a match for you."

"I wear the skin of a dead animal."

"Which you slew with your own hands. What does Eggle Skulltaker wear around his neck? The heads of warriors? No. He wears the heads of those who cannot fight back. He is no hero or leader to be admired. It tells me much about our enemies and I do not fear them. Their numbers do not make me tremble."

I was impressed. "You are learning."

"That is your son, Gruffyd. He beats me so many times at the game of war that I have made myself improve. He still beats me but not as often as he did. Karl and Einar train my arm. Aiden and Gruffyd train my mind."

"Good! You are becoming a leader. Let us go and speak with the others. I have teased them enough."

I gathered the Ulfheonar, jarls and hersir around me. "I have a plan." I pointed to the half-finished rafts drawn up on the bank. "The drekar in the river are tied close together. A warrior who wears no mail and seven boys who can swim will pile kindling on them and, after dark, let the river take them down to the drekar." I looked at Ragnar and nodded. "The river is our ally. Trust me on that. When they are next to the drekar they will fire the rafts and swim to the southern bank. If the rafts are placed at the steering boards of the two rear drekar then the current will hold them against the ships."

Olaf Leather Neck said, "But if there are two at the front will they not escape?"

"That is possible. I do not fire the drekar to stop them from escaping but to help us win. When the fire begins the natural reaction will be to save the drekar. They may well send men to man the drekar and put out the fires. That is when we begin the attack. Snorri, tell them what we saw." I was thirsty and I took a horn of beer and drank as Snorri told them of the camps.

"They have a small camp with men who drink and fight. That is the lure to make us think they are unprepared. Inside the stronghold they have the walls manned but on the far side they have the bulk of their warband and they are the ambush that will strike us. The jarl is right, this Eggle has thought things out well. We heard his men and he would be king and take over the land of the wolf."

I saw them taking in that information. "So Olaf if they do rush to save the drekar that is good. They cannot fight us and save their ships."

"Bergil Rolfsson and Oleg Strong Arm will lead the warriors without mail to attack those in the false camp. Both fought the enemy and will be recognised. I am hoping that Eggle launches his surprise attack on you for I will be waiting with the mailed warriors to the north of the stronghold. When the trap is spring we spring our own trap. We will be attacking in the dark and, while we know their numbers, they know not ours."

I saw them nodding. Haaken asked, "But we will still have to take the stronghold?"

"We will but if we defeat his surprise attack then that will be easier. Its strength is an illusion. From the river, it looks daunting but the walls are only as high as a tall man and it is the riverbank that makes it hard. To the north, there is no river. If they try to enter the stronghold then we will follow. The key will be those who fire the drekar and the men led by Bergil and Oleg. It is they who will draw the enemy within the length of our swords and spears!"

My men nodded their approval and Oleg Strong Arm and Bergil Rolfsson organised their men. Snorri and Beorn chose those who would use spears and those who would use bows. They would be as important as my Ulfheonar. It would be the spearmen who protected our flanks and the archers who would rain death from the dark. A warrior could see arrows in daylight and use his shield for protection. When it was dark then the first sign of an arrow would be the dead man who had just been standing next to you. Each spearman was given three spears. Two had the rivets removed so that they could be thrown and not sent back. The third would be to make a wall of steel. Each archer was given fifty arrows. When they were ready Snorri nodded. We had our own surprise for Eggle Skulltaker.

Chapter 13

Einar Grimsson, the young brother of my drekar captain, volunteered to lead the boys on the rafts. He had been a ships' boy on his brother's drekar and could swim. More importantly, he knew how to sail. We chose seven boys from those who volunteered. All could swim and most had experience at sea. We could have done with Aiden for he would have had some magic to help us make fire. We had to improvise. We found six jars in the deserted village. Some were buried in the huts with dried food in them and others had been discarded because they were chipped. We emptied them. Before they sailed we would make a fire in each one and put in charcoal. We used oiled sheep's wool with the kindling so that they would fire quickly. We would make a fire in the pots and carry that on the rafts. When they neared the drekar they would spill the fire onto the kindling on the rafts. Once Olaf had discovered my plan he added another layer of dried logs to the rafts. It made them heavier but there was more wood to burn.

"You will need one of you to stay aboard the raft until the fire has caught."

Einar was proud to have been chosen to lead as were his boys. "We will Jarl. This is an honour. We are serving the clan and we will not let you down."

"Leave after dark. We will not attack until the drekar are on fire."

We left Einar Grimsson and his sailors. It would be their attack that would initiate our own. It would not take long to sail the two large loops of the river. The current was steady. It was Einar who came up with the idea of tying the rafts together and he would sail when darkness had fallen. He and his boys would make their way back upstream and cross the river close to our camp. We left our horses tethered there and Einar would watch them for us. We had no one left to guard our camp. We gambled all on this throw of the bones.

The rest of us headed north. I intended to take us around any scouts and defences they might have to the west and north. Snorri and Beorn had chosen six scouts from the other bands and they would eliminate any Danes that they found.

The land over which we passed was flat with barely a rise but it was densely wooded. That suited us. We walked down hunter and animal trails. I knew that the river turned sharply north after the stronghold and so when we found the small beck I hoped that it would lead east to the river north of Eggle's fort. We followed it. When we found the two dead Danes by the side of the path then I knew that Snorri and his scouts were doing their work well.

Snorri met us where the beck turned back on itself. It began to head south, not west. "We have been to the river and there are no Danes between us and the northern loop." He pointed to the south of us. "If we follow this beck it will bring us close to their lines but I would wait until dark, Jarl."

It was good advice and I nodded. We would have an hour, perhaps longer until dusk. We prepared for war. Our weapons were sharp but some of us needed our war faces. Many men emptied their bowels or their bladders. It was a ritual like putting on cochineal. Ragnar had no such rituals yet and I saw him looking around as warriors prepared. I waved him over.

"What they do, Ragnar, is to prepare their minds for battle."

"I am ready!"

"Are you? When you first fought a priest surprised you and you slew an unarmed man unnecessarily. Your mind was not ready. You were excited and that is dangerous. These men do what they do to calm themselves and clear all from their heads. They must be cold when they fight. An excited man can go berserk. A berserker is as dangerous for his own men as for the enemy. Be cold and then your mind will be clear. Create for yourself a routine. For me, I would put your helmet on last. When your head is enclosed you are complete."

"What do you do, grandfather?"

"I first put on my cochineal. Then I check the straps on my shield and sword belt to make sure they will hold. I look at my helmet and ensure that it is whole. I tighten my wolf skin and slide Ragnar's Spirit in and out of its scabbard three times. Then I don my helmet and clutch my wolf and dragon tokens. I close my eyes and ask the spirits of my mother, wife and son to watch over my family if I should fall. When that is done I am ready for war and, if necessary, Valhalla."

"You think you will die each time you fight?"

"No, but I am prepared. There is a difference. If you are prepared to die and live then the air tastes sweeter after a battle. Now go. I have to prepare."

As I donned my cochineal I watch him as he debated what to do. He took out his sword and slid it back in. He did the same with his seax. When he began to examine his mail I concentrated on my own preparations. He was learning.

As darkness fell we split into our two groups. Oleg Strong Arm led the smaller number of warriors. They would have an easier task. They would fall upon the drunken warriors. We could already hear them as they enjoyed their night of debauchery. They would attack when they saw the flames from the river. He and Bergil Rolfsson would exact vengeance for their dead comrades and for Ketil who still lay between life and death in Windar's Mere.

Snorri led my men through a depression in the woods and then we climbed up the low ridge. From the edge of the trees, all that we could see were the walls of the stronghold. An occasional glint showed us a helmet as a sentry walked along the fighting platform but all was quiet. We waited. We were in the hands now of Einar Grimsson and the young boys he led. If he failed then we all failed.

It was hard to hear any noise from the real camp to our left. The fake camp was too lively with screams and shouts. It had been a clever plan. If Snorri had not persisted and discovered their actual camp then we would have invited disaster by attacking a handful of warriors. As we watched and waited there was one painful thought nagging in the back of my mind. There had to be at least two spies. One had been in Windar's Mere and told the enemy of its defences. They may even have let them in but more worryingly there had to be someone who had preceded us over the high moors and warned Eggle that we were coming. It was the only reason for the continued deception. He would not have kept up his false camp unless he knew that we had taken the bait. Where was that spy? When the battle was over I would search the field for someone I knew. They were the worst kind of enemy. They were an enemy within.

Snorri nudged me and sniffed the air. I turned my face. The wind had shifted and was now coming from the west. It would help us by sending any flames towards the drekar. We waited and then Einar Grimsson and his boys did as I had asked them. The only sign that the attack had begun was the sudden flash of light. It soared in the air and then quickly died down. It was the flaring of the first pot. The three others followed in quick succession and then we saw movement on the walls. Shouts could be heard above the fake camp's madness. Then an enormous flame shot into the air. We could not see the drekar for they had stripped their masts but the fire showed us where they were. Then we heard the shouts and cries as Oleg Strong Arm and Bergil Rolfsson led their men into the camp. They would take no prisoners. They were set on revenge! I pulled my shield around in anticipation of the second warband. I had worried that Eggle might send them through the fort but then I realised that would slow them down. He had to send them along the woods where we hid for that way he could bring his full force to bear quickly. Of course, the number they could bring was now fewer for he had to send some to save his drekar. If he lost those he was stranded here on the Dunum.

Snorri saw them first. They came from our left. The ones at the fore had no mail and each carried a spear. They ran quickly. This was not a wedge. They thought they were falling upon an unsuspecting warband. Behind I saw, from the flames of the burning drekar lighting up the sky, mail byrnies and helmets. The second wave was the better-armed warriors. I would let the lighter-armed ones pass and hope that Oleg and Bergil could deal with them. If we struck a mortal blow to the mailed warriors then we had a chance to defeat them. It was now in the hands of the men I led. Einar Grimsson had done his job. Oleg and Bergil were doing theirs. It all came down to this. My mailed men against Eggle; Viking against Viking. Leading such warriors as I did was a privilege. I knew that none would move until I gave the command. We would not be advancing as a shield wall; that was our normal formation. Instead, it would be a line of determined, mailed warriors each trying to hit the enemy as hard as we could.

I waited until the middle of the lumbering Danes had passed us and then I yelled, "Ulfheonar! Vengeance for Windar's Mere!"

I ran at the right-hand side of a shocked Dane. Even as he turned I brought my sword across his neck in a scything slash. I almost severed his head. I punched a warrior to my left with my shield as I stabbed at his leg. My sword bit into his knee. I felt it grate along the bone and when I twisted and withdrew it he fell to the ground. We had to kill as many of these mailed men as we could if we were to have parity of numbers. I gave him a warrior's death by stabbing him in the throat. Out attack had cleared a hole twenty men wide. We were almost at their walls and it was the time to halt. We had to use the strength of my men against a disorganized rabble.

"Shield wall! Ragnar, bring the banner here in the middle!"

I turned to my left and Haaken and Finni the Dreamer flanked me. I felt a shield in my back and a voice said, "It is Harald Fine Hair, Jarl. I will watch your back. Your banner is behind me. This is a good day to die!"

My men began banging their shields and the chant began.

The storm came hard and Odin spoke
With a lightning bolt the sword he smote
Ragnar's Spirit burned hot that night
It glowed, a beacon shiny and bright
The two they stood against the foe
They were alone, nowhere to go
They fought in blood on a darkened hill
Dragon Heart and Cnut will save us still
Dragon Heart, Cnut and the Ulfheonar
Dragon Heart, Cnut and the Ulfheonar

It mattered not what we sang. It showed that we were one. The Danes hurled themselves at us in a frenzy. They had been outwitted and twenty of their best warriors lay dead. Now the killing would begin and it would be bloody and without mercy. I could smell burning from my right and knew that Einar Grimsson had done as I had asked. The drekar were on fire. If Oleg and Bergil could do the same then we had a chance. Would Eggle risk the reserves he held in the fort? Would he try to save his drekar? None of that mattered yet and we began to kill. The arrows flew over our heads from the archers in the woods. Spears were hurled and the Danes died.

Their fury worked against them. They were in the dark and the ground was uneven and slippery with the blood and the gore of the dead. They were being attacked from the dark and the only enemy they could actually see was my ring of mailed warriors. I saw a Dane slip and as his arms flailed Asbjorn stepped from the line and took his head. He was back in the shield wall before any enemy could take advantage of it. A Dane wearing just a helmet and leather armour ran at me with a spear. He was fast and I barely managed to get my shield up to protect myself. My hands were fast too and my sword darted out straight and true. He did not get his shield up in time. His leather armour was good but my blade had a tip that could penetrate mail. My sword entered his upper chest. I twisted as I pushed. His spear clattered to the ground as he reeled backwards into a mailed warrior trying to get at me.

167

This was a mighty Dane. He had many warrior bands about his arms. On his fingers he wore rings and his helmet had golden cheekpieces. He opened his mouth and roared at me, "I will have that sword and then I will gut you like a fish! I will watch you squeal like a girl as I kill you! You are no Viking! You are the son of a Saxon coward and Welsh whore!"

I had him in that moment for he was trying to antagonise me into a wild attack. You did not do that if you knew you could beat your opponent. From his size, I guessed he normally used his strength and weight to win. I would have to use speed, guile and intelligence.

He took my silence for weakness. "The great Dragonheart is afraid! He has no wizard to help him this time!"

The men around laughed and that, too, was a mistake for my men lunged forward and with moves so quick that they were a blur those who stood around the giant fell. They had stopped concentrating on us and it cost them dear. In a fury, he brought his sword over like a sledgehammer. Had I stood my ground then any blow would have broken a limb. I stepped to my right and angled my shield as I sliced sideways with my sword. He was taller than I was and had his shield held high to protect his head. His sword slid down my shield but mine bit into his leg. I felt the edge slide along bone. He tried to punch me with his sword hilt but my shield came up so quickly that the metal rim rapped his knuckles. I saw blood but, more importantly, I knew that I had made them numb. Rings looked good but were no substitute for leather gloves.

As he stepped back I took in that we were holding our own. Some of the front rank had fallen but those from the second circle had joined us. I knew that Einar the Tall was my reserve. The six hearth-weru would be a shock to a Dane who thought they had slain the best.

The Dane was hurt and he was bleeding but he was still dangerous. I kept my eyes on his and when I saw them flick to my shield I knew what he intended. He feinted at my head expecting me to bring up my shield. I did not and he was committed to the stab at my middle. It was a good blow and it hit my shield hard but it hit it point first. It did not stick in the wood for I had too much metal upon it and when he pulled it back I saw that the tip was flattened and there was the slightest of bends in it. He could no longer stab and knowing that meant he had a limited number of strokes he could make. He would have to use the edge and slash at me.

It was my turn to attack and I lunged at his head. He brought up his shield and my sword scraped along the edge of his shield striking the gold on his helmet. When he saw the sliver of gold on my blade he became even more enraged. He threw himself at me. I was forced to step back. Harald Fine Hair's spear came over the top and plunged into his right shoulder. Harald twisted and I heard a shout of pain. Blood spurted and he stepped back. Now was my chance and I punched with my shield as I sliced across the top of his shield and into his throat. Weakened by the blood loss he could not raise his own shield to block the blow and Ragnar's Spirit tore across his throat.

As he fell my men gave a cheer and the Danes stepped back. When they did so I saw a wall of bodies they had left there.

"Reform the wall. Prepare to attack!" I turned and said, "Ragnar, see to the wounded."

"But the standard!"

"Men's lives are more important than my banner. This is not over yet."

I saw the Danes reforming their own lines. Haaken said, "They have few men with mail left. Yet we have only slain forty or so. Where are the rest?"

Those were my thoughts too. I worried that they would be emerging from the fort to fall upon Oleg and his men and then outflank us. I risked turning. I saw, on the other side of the circle of warriors, Cnut Cnutson. "Cnut are there many men before you?"

"No Jarl. They are falling back."

"Then lead the men on your side and rout them. Take the spearmen with you. Join Oleg and Bergil!"

"Aye Jarl."

I knew I was taking a risk but sometimes you have to gamble. This was just such an occasion.

"Are we ready?"

The men around me shouted, "Aye Jarl!"

"Archers use your last arrows on them and then draw your swords and follow me!"

"Aye jarl!"

"Then forward."

We did not run. It was dark and there were many obstacles below our feet. I did not want us to lose our footing as the Danes had done. They stood resolutely enough as we approached. They had almost the same number of men as we did but we had Ulfheonar in our ranks. I raised my sword and lifted my shield. I was tiring but we had one more push to make. Suddenly Olaf's axe swung in a long two handed arc. He had slipped his shield around to his back. Even as he swung Rolf Horse Killer did the same. Olaf's axe struck first, it smashed across two shields and was such a mighty blow that both shields cracked and split. The warriors had been hurt by the blows. Rolf managed to take the head of one Dane and then hack into the shoulder of a second. As Olaf and Rolf were standing together a gap appeared in the Danish line. With a roar, Olaf leapt into the gap followed by Rolf. All order went as we plunged deep into their ranks. I slashed at a warrior who had no mail. My sword took his right arm and bit into his side. With a stump spurting blood he ran.

He was soon followed by most of the survivors of the first rank and they took the second and third ranks with them. The one or two who stood were soon despatched. They all ran down the slope towards the river. The glow from the burning drekar had long since stopped. Our main problem was avoiding falling over the dead, dying and wounded who littered the river bank.

When we reached the gates of the stronghold I saw that they were open. "Asbjorn, search the stronghold."

As we reached the river I saw that two drekar had survived and the men who had fled us were flinging themselves into the dark water to reach them. The current was already taking them downstream. I saw Eggle Skulltaker at the stern of the larger of the two. His white-striped hair stood out, even in the dark.

I took off my helmet and shouted, "This is not over Eggle Skulltaker! I will find you. There is no place to hide. I am Jarl Dragonheart and I do not forget and I never forgive! Count your days on this earth for they are numbered!"

He laughed, "I fooled you once and I will do so a second time. You are not the great warrior the sagas say. You are a lucky one and everyone's luck runs out sometime. Yours will too!" Then he turned and shouted, "Run out oars! It is time to leave! We have the treasure of Windar's Mere and the women have served their purpose."

I saw men pleading from the water for their leader to wait for them but he turned his back and the two drekar began to slip down the river. I saw some men try to swim until the weight of their weapons dragged them down. A couple made the south bank and a few made it back to shore. I had been correct. Eggle Skulltaker was not a good leader. He was however a resilient one. He lived to fight another day.

I turned, "Bind the survivors. I will decide their fate later. Give the wounded a warrior's death. Olaf, take charge here. Haaken, Snorri, come with me."

I slipped my shield around to my back and held my helmet in my hand. I strode up the bank to the gate and entered the stronghold. As I walked through the gate I could see that it was not well made and we could have taken it had we had enough men. Asbjorn and his men had slain the sentries they had found and the fort was now deserted. When I reached the western gate I saw Cnut Cnutson, Asbjorn and Bergil Rolfsson. They were standing over the body of Oleg Strong Hand. Ketil's hearth-weru was surrounded by six Danes. It looked as though he had died well.

"How did he die?"

"It was after the battle proper had finished, Jarl Dragonheart. It was my fault." Cnut Cnutson shook his head. "I led my men to see if any of the Danes had fled west. I did not think to watch the gate. Ten Danes rushed from the gate and Oleg tried to stop them. He slew six. By the time we realised what was happening, he was dead. We killed his killers."

Bergil said, "Do not blame yourself. It was the end he wanted. He will be accorded great honours in Valhalla." He waved his hand, "But this is a more pitiful sight." I looked and saw what he meant. Most of the female captives and children had been slain. There were, perhaps, a dozen women who huddled together. "We came to save them, Jarl, and we failed. We have taken our revenge but that tastes sour in my mouth. I am sorry."

"You are right. It is a bitter taste. And it is not over. Take the women within the fort and see to them. Have the wounded brought within as well. It will take daylight to see who has survived."

I suddenly remembered Ragnar. I had left him tending to the wounded. There were Danes who lived yet with nothing to lose! "Snorri!"

I ran up the hill and Snorri followed me. I saw my banner. It had been planted in the ground. There were many men lying on the ground and some were moaning but I could not see Ragnar. If he had died then that would be my fault.

Snorri pointed, "There Jarl! He is tending to a warrior. He lives!"

I gripped my dragon and wolf, "Thank you Allfather, thank you."

As we approached the wounded Olaf Leather Neck said, quietly, "Jarl we should not leave the dead. There are animals who would despoil them and they all died bravely."

"You are right. Have them brought close to the shelter of the walls and we will have an honour guard over them."

Ragnar was covered in blood when I reached him but it was of the wounded. He had used torn kyrtles to bind wounds as best he could. Snorri and I joined him and we helped to staunch the bleeding from those who could be saved. Those that could not be saved were given a sword and a warrior's death. I did not ask my grandson to do that. He was not ready but one day he too would have to help a comrade to make the journey to Valhalla.

I was so busy that night, speaking with the dying before they were sent to Valhalla, receiving thanks from grateful captives and walking around my men to see that they lived, that it was dawn and I had not slept. I found myself at the river. I saw two or three bodies caught up in the driftwood on the opposite bank. Each time the current tugged at one branch the body attached appeared to wave as though alive. My walk during the night had shown the cost to us. We had lost over twenty warriors. The cost to the enemy was higher. We would be burning more than seventy of them. Our enemy's plan had worked against them. Their men playing the drunks were easy to kill and had fallen easily. Our sudden attack from the flank had killed their best warriors in the initial battle. But it was the burning of the two drekar which had been decisive. It had sent my enemy to his boats to try to save them. We had lost him as a result but we would find him again. I saw the two charred remains of the drekar. Their blackened timbers stuck from the water looking like the ribs of some giant sea beast. Einar Grimsson and his boys had done well.

I heard steps behind me and I whirled around. During the night we found a Dane playing dead. He had almost gutted Bergil Rolfsson with his knife but luckily others had been close by and the Dane had been slain. This was not a Dane, this was Ragnar. I was not certain he had slept and he was bloody, from head to toe. It was not his blood but those he had tended. He had been unable to save many. He was no healer but it had been a comfort to dying men for him to be there with them. Einar and the hearth-weru had joined him when the field had been scoured of Danes.

"I did not know if we would win or lose last night, grandfather. In the dark, it was hard to tell. I just saw the rise and fall of swords and heard the cries and screams of men. I think it is easier when you stand in the shield wall for you know what is going on."

"In many ways, it is easier but you never know how it is going unless you stand on a high place, with the sun shining and you watch the battle. That is how the warriors in the past fought. They were not in the front rank but they ordered men to do their bidding."

"Do we often fight at night?"

"We do for we are few in numbers and darkness hides us. But it is dangerous." I smiled at him. "You did well last night and warriors are speaking highly of you."

"But I did nothing! I killed no one! At least I killed no enemies. My lack of skill may not have saved the wounded."

"Aiden never kills and yet he is worth a warband on the field of battle. When Leif carries my banner then he rarely kills yet he is acknowledged as a brave man. My standard did not waver and you were like a rock. There will soon come a time when you fight and I have no doubt that you will acquit yourself well."

"What do we do now?"

"We spend a day or two letting warriors and captives recover. We will have a long journey home and I want us to travel safely. We burn and destroy this place as though it had never been. If Prince Athelstan wishes to build a burgh here then he can do so but it will be from bare rock."

"And Eggle Skulltaker? He should not live."

"No, he should not but he is beyond me for the moment. He has sailed and the world is wide. He could go anywhere. We will question the prisoners. They may have knowledge which can help us."

"But you will follow."

"I will track him down for I must. He thinks that he outwitted me. I know that is not true but he does and that will eat away at his mind. He will think that Cyninges-tūn is as weak as Windar's Mere and he will come to try to take my land again."

"Then why not wait for him to come?"

"If I did that then I risk every farmer who farms the high and lonely places. I risk having women and children taken captive or, more likely, losing their heads. We seek him and we destroy him. It may take many years but we shall search out this Viking enemy for there is no more dangerous enemy to us."

We walked back up the hill to the gate where my men stood guard over the bodies. Alf Jansson said, "Jarl we should burn the enemy dead. I heard animals feasting on them in the night. They were our enemies but they died as men. We should burn them."

"You are right. I will fetch men and we will use the palisades as a pyre."

I had laid down my mail and shield in the night, along with my helmet but I had my wolf cloak about my shoulders. I laid that down now for this would be dirty and hot work. I fetched men from inside the fort. I saw that someone had organised food. "Haaken, make sure that the prisoners are closely guarded. I would speak with them soon."

There were just twenty of them. Most had been plucked from the river when they had been abandoned. "We will watch them. You go to burn the dead?"

"We do. Then we will have these captives dig a grave for our dead and collect stones to make a barrow. They can atone for what they did. It might make their end easier."

It was as we were carrying the bodies to the wood we had placed by the river that Bergil Rolfsson called out, "Jarl! Come here!"

I dropped the torso I had been carrying and ran. He stood over a warrior who wore no mail and had been slain by having his throat hacked by a sword.

"I know this man. It is Arne the Smiler. He lived in Windar's Mere. When the jarl visited we often saw him. He was one of Arne Thorirson's men. The hersir was going to make him hearth-weru. That is how I know him. He always smiled which was how Harland Windarsson gave him the name."

I was relieved that we had found the enemy who had duped us. "Then this is our spy. This is the one who allowed the enemy into the walls. Do you know when he came?"

"No Jarl. It must have been in the last year. I do not remember him from before. He was always happy and that is how I knew him." He shook his head. "I liked him."

I put my hand around his shoulder. "They are the hardest enemies to fight. It is easier to kill a man who snarls and spits at you. The ones who smile can confuse a warrior. It is better to fight a warrior who faces you. The worst kind are those who wait in the background and plunge a knife when you least expect it."

As I watched the pyre of bodies burn I was relieved that we had found the spy but it would not stop me from searching the hearts of those who guarded my walls. Even as the pall of smoke drifted west I had the captives brought out to dig the grave. One warrior objected and refused. Olaf Leather Neck took his head in one blow and I said, "You live so long as I allow. I swear that I will give a warrior's death to those who cooperate. I may even give life but refusal will give you a death that sends you not to Valhalla but to Hel!"

They nodded and they obeyed. They had little choice. They dug and then they collected stones. Our men were buried with full honours. Those, like Oleg Strong Arm, who had mail and warrior rings, were laid with them. Those like Sven Alfsson from the Grize Dale, who just had a helmet, shield and sword, were laid with their possessions. They were laid side by side and then covered with stones, the earth and finally turf. When the walls of the fort had been destroyed that and the blackened earth where the bodies were buried would be the only reminder of the battle at Eggle's Cliffe.

Finni the Dreamer stood with me as we put the last stones on the barrow. "Jarl I know that this sits heavily with you but we could have done no more than we did. We have a good home and a good life. Men will envy that and desire it. They will want for nothing that we have worked for. This may happen again but it does not make you a bad leader."

"You may be right Finni but it does not stop me from trying to be a better one."

Chapter 14

We left the next day. We had set fire to the wooden walls of Eggle's stronghold and made sure they were burning well before we headed along the greenway to the river. We had to walk for we had found a few horses in the fort. When we reached Einar Grimsson and his seven heroes we were able to move much faster. We put the captives who had survived on the horses and ponies and headed west.

"You did well Einar. Did you lose any boys?"

"No Jarl. I am sorry that we did not burn all their drekar but we were seen as we fired the first one. I had intended to take one raft to the two drekar anchored downstream."

"You helped us to win the battle. I am grateful."

"But Eggle Skulltaker escaped."

"He did but we will find him."

"Then I beg the opportunity to serve when you do find him. I would be there at the end."

"And you shall be for I will need warriors like you."

It took four days to reach our home. We had to pass by Windar's Mere and the captives we had recovered keened and wailed when they saw the desolation which remained. I had yet to speak with my jarls and I had not thought what we would do about Windar's Mere. The water there teemed with fish and the land was fertile. Cyninges-tūn was a wasteland by comparison. I would hold a Thing to discuss the matter. Neither Aiden nor the wounded were there. He must have moved them to Kara's hall.

Bergil Rolfsson led the men of Ketil's stad north to their home. They had with them, as we all did, many weapons and much mail. It did not compensate for the lost warriors but it would help us to become stronger. Bergil would act as hersir until Ketil if he lived, returned. The captives were reluctant to leave the protection of my men and they came with us to my home. Riders had warned them of our approach and all came to greet them.

Kara met us at my gate and hugged me saying, "We have come through a hard time, Father but it will become better. We have dreamed."

I nodded. I was now more cautious and sceptical about the power of those dreams.

Kara turned and said to the captives, "We have places for you in the hall of women. Stay here until you have decided what you wish." Deidra and Macha opened the doors to admit them. I was grateful. They would be cared for and women understood how to talk. Men did not.

"I am sorry I failed you, Jarl Dragonheart."

I turned and saw Ketil. He was standing but he did not look healed, "You did not fail me. Your brother and Arne Thorirson made mistakes and that has cost our people dear but they paid for it with their lives. We will talk about this later. I am pleased that you are still alive. The last I saw of you made me wonder."

"It is thanks to Aiden. This is the first morning I have left your hall."

Aiden put his arm around him and turned him, "And the last for some time. This exertion was more than enough."

Elfrida and Brigid approached with Gruffyd, "Your son did well Elfrida. There are warriors alive now because he was on the battlefield."

Elfrida nodded her gratitude and hugged Ragnar, "Thank you Jarl. I knew that he would be safe with you."

I embraced Brigid. She was noticeably bigger. "And I am returned safely."

She shook her head, "So few captives."

I nodded, "Aye and I fear they will all be carrying children for the Danes used them."

Brigid's hand went to her mouth, "I will pray for them."

I went into my hall. "Uhtric, I will go and bathe."

Gruffyd asked, "Could I join you?"

"Of course."

I turned to my servant, "It is fine Uhtric, I will take the drying blanket, soap and clean kyrtle." He nodded and went to fetch them.

"I am keen to know what went on. I want to hear from my cuz of the great battle in the east."

"Of course. I shall enjoy sharing my Water with my son and grandson."

Ragnar had changed on this campaign. He was more thoughtful and measured his words. Gruffyd suddenly seemed much younger. I had thought they were almost the same but they were not. Perhaps that was what war did. Ragnar answered all of my son's questions. He had watched the battle and knew more about it than I did for I had been engaged too closely.

As I dried myself Gruffyd asked, "Where will we find this Eggle then father?"

"I questioned the men we captured. I think he will head for the coast and Streanæshalc or as it is called by the Danes, Hwitebi. It is a small port on the Esk, just south of the Dunum. There is an abbey there. His men all seemed to think that would be where he would go. It can be defended and yet he can raid."

"And we will go there?"

I smiled, "I will take my drekar there, yes but only when we have discovered if that is where he hides for it is a long voyage around the coasts of Wales, Wessex and East Anglia."

Ragnar asked, "Will he not attack the abbey?"

"No, for he is no fool. He might be tolerated by those who live in Eoforwic and the King may allow him to live there but not if he slays priests. It is a good base from which to raid. He can reach Frisia easily and he will know the waters."

"But you think, grandfather, that he may not stay there long."

"He has warriors to reward. The kind of men Eggle attracts are drawn by the lure of riches. The gold of Windar's Mere will only last so long. He may take his men and find another lord who will pay him. I would expect him to offer his services to the Danes who now protect Frisia. And we now know the names of his drekar: *'Serpent's Tongue'* and *'Skull'*.

Gruffyd asked Ragnar, "Did you get to fight any?"

He shook his head, "I guarded the banner and tended the wounded. I was honoured to do so."

Gruffyd nodded, "Then I could have come for I would not have been in danger."

I laughed, "I can see that when you do go to war you will always look for a solution to a problem. That is good."

That evening the mood around my table was quiet. We all had much to reflect upon. Elfrida and Brigid now knew that we were the frontier. Until we had a strong jarl in place then we would be in danger from raiders to the east. I saw Ragnar wrestling with what he had witnessed. He had seen things that were truly horrific. Gruffyd was trying to come to terms with the prospect of travelling with the army but not actually fighting. I think he had thought that war would be one long battle. He was wrong.

"How is our child?"

"Kara thinks that our child will be here by the next moon." I nodded and ate. "Will you be here then?"

"That depends upon our enemy. If Eggle can be found then I need to bring him to account for his misdeeds. He is still a threat to us. He is not afraid of me and that is dangerous. He gained great riches from Harland's stad. He knows or he believes that there is more treasure here."

"Then, husband, stay here and defend your land. If you are here then we cannot fall!"

"I hold a Thing in three days. I have summoned all of my jarls. They will make the decision."

"But this is your land."

"And I lead the people but they have a say. They may agree with you in which case we will wait here. I would counsel against it but this will be a decision made by the Thing."

I was anxious to know what had resulted from the dream and I reached the house of women by first light. Both my daughter and Aiden looked weary. Ylva, in contrast, looked fresh and alert. I was led to the large table where food was laid out. I noticed that Aiden drank more than he ate. "It was a difficult dreaming. Eggle is a Dane and he must use his own volva for he was hidden from us but we saw his drekar. The gold he took is there and the fresh skulls of his captives rest in his ship. He cannot hide the spirits who await release to the Otherworld."

"Will he not be haunted by them?"

"He may be but some men can ignore such things. However so long as the spirits are in torment then we can find where he is. We saw a river spilling out between high cliffs and there is a church of the White Christ high on the southern ones. They have men and women in the church."

"Hwitebi." I nodded. "He still has gold to buy his men. He will seek new ones and then decide where he will raid." Where is Ketil?"

"He rests here."

"I must speak with him. We need the help of Prince Athelstan."

Aiden looked intrigued, "You would use Saxons? How?"

"The Prince does not like these Danes in his land. I do not want Eggle to bolt. If the Thing decides that we sail to end his life then I do not want him wriggling away when my drekar sail into the Esk. If there are

Saxons waiting to deliver their justice then he will be forced to fight or to flee. I back my drekar and men against him."

"You will leave soon?"

"He is there but it will take time to prepare three drekar and the men to row. It is a long way."

"Then come and we will speak with Ketil. He should not go himself. He was only allowed out of the hall yesterday to speak with you."

"I know but he has knowledge which I need." Ketil tried to rise as I entered. "Keep your bed. I just need words with you." He sat. "I need your advice and your knowledge. Tell me how stands Prince Athelstan to offer us help against Eggle?"

"The Dane is a thorn in the Prince's side. He would have him removed."

I wondered why he had not already done so but I answered myself immediately. The men of Northumbria feared Vikings because of us. His father had never bested me. "Eggle is at Hwitebi. I intend to trap him in the river but I do not want him fleeing overland. I need the prince to bring warriors and stop him from fleeing."

He smiled, "And you would have me as a messenger."

"To be blunt that was my intention but Aiden tells me you cannot travel. I will send a messenger from here instead."

He forced himself to his feet. "I thank you, Aiden, for what you have done for me. I owe you a life. But I am a warrior and I am a jarl. Jarl Dragonheart will avenge my brother. The least that I can do is to mount a horse and ride to Din Guardi." He turned to me. "I will do as you ask. I shall send a messenger back to give you his answer."

"Tell him to scout out Eggle and not to move until he sees my drekar enter the river." He nodded and I put my arm around his shoulder. It was partly so that I could have a quiet word with him and partly so that he did not fall over. "Windar's Mere; what are your thoughts on the resettlement?"

He turned and looked at me with sad eyes. I saw pain reflected in them. He sighed. "Are you asking me, Jarl Dragonheart, if I would be jarl of a newly built Windar's Mere?"

"It was your father's. You allowed your brother to be jarl... yes I am asking you."

"It would be too painful Jarl Dragonheart. I think that it is *wyrd* that I stay where I am. My wife comes from the valley and I know the people. It is a hard land and a wild land but I know it. I decline."

I smiled, "In my heart, I knew that you would but I had to ask. I will choose a new jarl when we hold our Thing. You will not be there. Would you like me to delay it until you return?"

"Jarl my mind is a maelstrom at the moment. I have lost family, hearth-weru and warriors. I trust you and the other jarls. I will become Ketil again but it will take some time to find him."

As he left and took his wounded warriors with him I felt hope. Even when half-dead and with a family slaughtered my people fought against the enemy- no matter who the enemy was. We rarely held Things. It was mainly because I did not feel that my people were unhappy with my decisions but Windar's mere was different. I could not force people to go to that settlement of ghosts. I needed their advice and their words. Ulf Olafsson came from the stad on the Eden. Sigtrygg came. All the rest lived in Cyninges-tūn. Our Viking enemy had destroyed two communities. How could we replace them?

Kara, Brigid, Elfrida and the women stood to one side while every man gathered in the middle of Cyninges-tūn between my hall and the house of women. The children found every vantage point they could so they could see and hear all that went on. This was a rare event.

I stood and spoke simply. "We have lost two parts of the land of the wolf. Ulla's Water and Windar's Mere had thriving communities that farmed and prospered. They are gone and have yet to be avenged. I swear that they will be avenged but we need to decide if we wish people to live there any longer. I have spoken with Jarl Ketil Windarsson. He has given me his thoughts and, if needs be, I will speak them. Any man who has seen eighteen summers may speak." Uhtric had brought out my chair and I sat.

I hoped that my Ulfheonar would hold their tongues. It was important that others spoke first. Eventually, Beorn Bagsecgson stood. He had a deep, rolling voice that carried well. "I have been with Jarl Dragonheart since we left Hrams-a. I was there when that village was devastated by the Hibernians. I am happy here. Cyninges-tūn is a good place to live. If others wish to live here there is room for all. This is a rich valley and we have all that we need here. I do not know why we need to live in the valley of Ulla's Water or Windar's Mere."

Men nodded. Einar the Tall stood, "I lived in Elfridaby and we gave that up. I understand the reasons. It was far from those who might help. Windar's Mere is but a little way away as the crow flies. It is fertile and it is beautiful. If we give that up because of a nithing then I say it is sad."

Siggi the Fisherman said, "But would you live there?"

"I am hearth-weru. I follow Ragnar Arturusson."

It was a warrior's answer and I saw all my warriors nodding. Siggi knew fish. That said it all. Individual conversations broke out. I stood again, "You know the rules. One man speaks and all hear his voice! If you have an opinion, then give it to us."

Rolf Horse Killer stood. He was young and he came from Cyninges-tūn. "I hear the words and I agree with Einar the Tall. If we do not rebuild at least one of those homes then we have been defeated. I am Ulfheonar and I have never tasted defeat. If this is the taste then I am glad that I have not. Beorn Bagsecg is right. Cyninges-tūn is a good place to live but how many more people can it house? Windar's Mere has more land and a larger Water. I say let us rebuild. Let us appoint a Jarl and this time defend it! I will not speak ill of the dead but can anyone here say that this could have happened here at Cyninges-tūn? Karl One Hand watches our walls and sets his watch and we are safe. Why could that not have been done at Windar's Mere?"

Haaken stood, "We know we have people who wish to live in our land for we are well-governed and we are rich. That is why Eggle Skulltaker came here. He used a spy! The spy is dead. I say we put a Jarl to rule the valley and he will build a better and more secure home for those who choose his valley." He waved a hand around the assembled warriors. "I know that we have hersir and jarls here who could do the job. Is there any here who says we should not?"

Silence filled the space and men looked at one another. Haaken had asked for a decision. I stood and waited. "Does no one oppose Haaken One Eye's suggestion?" Men shook their heads. Then we rebuild Windar's Mere." There were cheers and shouts. I held up my hand. "That is the easy part. Who will take it upon himself to rebuild? Who will tie himself to the earth? Who will be like Ulf here or Ketil or even Sigtrygg and guard the frontier because, make no mistake, Windar's Mere is the new frontier." I scanned every face. "Rolf Horse Killer has spoken wisely even though he is young. He has thought of the future. There are many people who wish to live in our land. Newcomers can be given land in Windar's Mere but I cannot see one who will choose that rock upon which to tie himself."

This time the silence seemed to reach back as far as Man. I wondered if any of my Ulfheonar would choose the task. I did not think so. Eventually, Asbjorn the Strong stood. "I chose to leave the Ulfheonar because I wished to raid. I still wish to raid but I also want to repay the jarl and every other warrior here. It is time I laid down roots. I have a woman and will marry soon. I want a home with a wall to protect my children. Sigtrygg Thrandson has shown that a warrior can rule and still raid. I have a crew of warriors who are the best that can be found. Some have families. If Jarl Dragonheart will have me I will be jarl of Windar's Mere. I will choose a new place upon which to build a stad like Ulf's and I will be the new frontier."

The silence lasted a heartbeat and then cheering erupted. I barely had time to say, "Asbjorn is the new Jarl of Windar's Mere. He will be lord of the eastern march," before my voice was drowned out.

Haaken came to me. "This is *wyrd*, Jarl Dragonheart. We have an Ulfheonar who will rule Windar's Mere. He will build a strong wall and defend it with his drekar crew. He is no Harland nor Arne Thorirson. We still have his drekar to raid and yet we are more secure."

"I will not use him when we attack Eggle."

"You are right. It will take time to make a stad like Ulf's."

Every wagon and cart was used to take Asbjorn's people to their new homes. Many of his warriors had families. Most lived on the eastern shore of the Water and so that became deserted. I found it sad for that had been where my first hall had been. Then I put that sadness from me as I spent all my time with Haaken and Olaf Leather Neck planning our raid.

Raibeart travelled from Úlfarrston to help us plan. He also brought news. King Egbert had finally defeated Mercia and was now the overlord of both kingdoms. I had no doubt that his eye would turn to us. For the moment I had the more immediate problem of Eggle Skulltaker to deal with.

"I know the waters well, Jarl. It is a good anchorage but it is narrow. You say you take three drekar?" I nodded. "Then they can block the entrance so that none may escape."

I knew the place well for when Harold One Eye had taken me as a slave he had raided there and captured a princess who drove me from my home with Ragnar. *Wyrd*.

"When can you be ready?"

"When I get back I can tell Erik and Olaf. So we can leave in three days' time."

"Then we will do so."

Aiden had been present the whole time both in the Thing and when we were alone he said, "This is a moment in time Jarl Dragonheart. The Norns have brought us here but it is your decisions that will decide our course. King Egbert will come and he will fight you. Can you afford to lose warriors fighting Eggle that you might need to fight Egbert?"

"Your words are wise, Aiden. But I have no choice in this and you know it. The Norns have spun their webs and the threads of Eggle the Skull taker, King Egbert and Jarl Dragonheart are so closely entwined that I cannot differentiate between them. If I deviate from this course then I am damned. If we lose warriors then it is meant to be. We will find new ones." He nodded. "I want you to stay here. Asbjorn will need your advice and I will be away for some time. Brigid will need you."

"But what of you?"

"Eggle needs a warrior and not a wizard. This will be bloody. It will be drekar to drekar and warrior to warrior. Your magic cannot help and I do not think the Norns wish it. You did not see Eggle before. You and Kara are searching in smoke. I will rely on Ragnar's Spirit and the Ulfheonar."

"Then you gamble all."

I shook my head, "No for I leave the future here. Gruffyd and Ragnar will not be coming with me. If I fail to return then you will guide them and make them great leaders."

He nodded and, clutching the red stone he wore about his neck, said, "*Wyrd*." He hesitated, "This Eggle has a witch. Be careful. I sense a danger we have not met before."

"Then I will meet that danger."

Chapter 15

Ragnar took the news that they would not be going with me better than Gruffyd but I was not willing to risk my heirs. Even though I would have another child by the time I returned, I wanted Ragnar and Gruffyd to be safe. It was a long and dangerous voyage on which we embarked.

A messenger returned from Ketil, "The Jarl has spoken with Prince Athelstan. He sends thanks for what you have done. He will take a mounted warband to Hwitebi and block the road west."

"Thank you Eystein. How is he?"

Eystein Einarsson laughed, "He is busy making the stad as strong as Ulf's on the Eden. He might not be able to fight the Danes yet but he will make us much stronger should they return."

There had been no shortage of volunteers for the two drekar I would man from my people. Most people had suffered a loss when Eggle Skulltaker had raided; cousins, sisters, brothers, sons and daughters. There had been many who had died and it seemed that the whole of Cyninges-tūn was united in its desire for vengeance. As we headed down the Water towards the ships I saw many new and young faces who would be coming with us. That was inevitable for many of those I knew lay in barrows far from home. Asbjorn and his crew had all been older and more experienced warriors. They would be hewing logs and digging ditches. They would not be slaughtering Danes. I would have many new men to lead and we would be fighting a battle on the water. Just over one in three of those who marched had a mail byrnie but in all other respects, they would be ready for war.

Kolbjorn of Torver would lead the men on *'King's Gift'*. He was a hersir and had sailed with me before. He had mail and had fought the Danes when, many years earlier, a band had ravaged the land which he now farmed. He had been a child then and his parents had been killed. He hated Danes but he had a cool head. I needed that for the young men he would lead. I would have the youngest of warriors with me. The Ulfheonar would be my rock. The new young warriors would learn on this voyage. The youngest, Karl Stensson, was just sixteen summers old. I would not have brought him save that he was huge and his mother's brother and his family had been killed at Ulla's Water. I owed the family the chance for weregeld.

My three drekar would be ready at Úlfarrston. This was not a short voyage. It could take half a month or more to sail around to a place that could be reached in two days of hard marching across the land. We had plenty of supplies. We were now well endowed with spares for the drekar which meant that we would be laden. I did not worry. I had good captains and it was unlikely that any would threaten three drekar filled with Vikings.

As I boarded I said to Coen Ap Pasgen, "Have the captains of the knarr keep their eyes and ears open for news of Egbert of Wessex. Now that he has Mercia I have no doubt that his eye will be drawn north."

"Aye Jarl. It will come through Dyflin. Since Jarl Gunnstein Berserk Killer defeated the High King it has become even more prosperous and there are more ships plying the seas."

"Then I pray that we can hold this part of the world and bring prosperity to our people."

The winds were in our favour for the first part of the voyage at least and we did not need to row. As we were sailing around three sides of this island there would be many times when we would. We headed south and Olaf and Haaken organised the new rowers and assigned them their oars. I stood and looked astern at my other two ships. Raibeart would bring up the rear with *'Red Snake'*. She was the smallest of my drekar and had the least oars. She was however very quick and had a very experienced crew. Raibeart had something which every captain envied. He had luck and he rarely lost a man. If danger threatened he could be at my side in a flash of oars. I was content that he was there. Olaf Grimsson had the hardest task. He rarely had the same crew for two consecutive voyages. I would have to be tolerant. Kolbjorn was a good warrior but it would take time for the two of them to meld the crew into a single being. They would have a long voyage to do so.

The winds took us south of Ynys Enlli and Ynys Môn. We put in, late at night, to a small sheltered cove in the land of the Welsh. The three captains gathered on the beach to talk of the drekar they sailed and their plans for the next day. I went with Haaken to speak with Kolbjorn.

"How are the men I gave you?"

He grinned, "They are young and seem desperate to prove that they are warriors."

"It is always so."

Haaken laughed, "When they have spent a day or two at the oars it may change their mind."

"Remember, Kolbjorn, that we will probably end up fighting Eggle at sea. I want your drekar to be the stopper in the jar. The entrance to the Esk is narrow. You need to place your ship so that the enemy cannot easily flee. Force them into the shallows if they manage to evade our drekar."

"Do you think that is likely Jarl Dragonheart?"

"I thought we had them at Eggle's Cliffe but the slippery snake wriggled away. I take nothing for granted. Unless we plan to spend the rest of our years pursuing this butcher then we end it at Hwitebi."

"The young men I lead may not be happy to sit and watch others fight."

"Then it is up to you to make sure that they obey your orders. You are not there to be their friend. You are there to be their leader."

"I know Jarl and I will not let you down."

We left early for none of us wished to be drawn to the witch's lair at Syllingar. As luck would have it as we turned to pass An Lysardh, the southernmost point of Britannia, the wind changed. It dropped and we had to take to the oars. That helped for Haaken was able to use one of his chants to put steel into men's hearts and our oars powered us through waters that were calmer than I had known and well to the north of Syllingar. We had a chant about another who thought himself safe from the Dragonheart. He had found, to his cost, that there was nowhere to hide.

> *The Saxon King had a mighty home*
> *Protected by rock, sea and foam*
> *Safe he thought from all his foes*
> *But the Dragonheart would bring new woes*
> *Ulfheonar never forget*
> *Ulfheonar never forgive*
> *Ulfheonar fight to the death*
> *The snake had fled and was hiding there*
> *Safe he thought in the Saxon lair*
> *With heart of dragon and veins of ice*
> *Dragonheart knew nine would suffice*
> *Ulfheonar never forget*
> *Ulfheonar never forgive*
> *Ulfheonar fight to the death*

Below the sand they sought the cave
The rumour told by wizard brave
Beneath the sea without a light
The nine all waited through the night
Ulfheonar never forget
Ulfheonar never forgive
Ulfheonar fight to the death
When night fell they climbed the stair
Invisible to the Saxons there
In the tower the traitors lurked
Dragonheart had a plan which worked
Ulfheonar never forget
Ulfheonar never forgive
Ulfheonar fight to the death
With Odin's blade the legend fought
Magnus' tricks they came to nought
With sword held high and a mighty thrust
Dragonheart dealt death and an end that was just
Ulfheonar never forget
Ulfheonar never forgive
Ulfheonar fight to the death
Ulfheonar never forget
Ulfheonar never forgive
Ulfheonar fight to the death

The new men seemed almost sad when two hours later the wind sprang again from the north and west and we took in our oars. When they had unfurled the sails and tightened the sheets the ships' boys went around with beer for the rower's thirst and Aiden's salve for the hands of the new rowers. They would not need it again for the skin would become hard, like leather.

I stood with Haaken and Olaf Leather Neck. "We will have to put ashore in Wessex, Jarl." Olaf pointed to the sun lowering in the sky to the west.

"I know. Erik, is there anywhere safe close by?" I pointed to the rocky coast. "I know that this is still On Walum. Is there anywhere there?"

"The only places are guarded by men and the rest by savage rocks that would eat my dragon. There is a cove just north of here. On Aiden's map, he says it is near the arch called Durdle. I do not think it is guarded but it is in Wessex now. Raibeart told me where it was when we spoke of our voyage. He had marked it as a refuge should he need it."

"Then we try this cove and we keep a good watch."

Erik Short Toe knew how to sail and he knew how to read Aiden's charts but like all good sailors, he had a sense of where he was and he took us unerringly towards the land of our enemies and this hidden refuge. Sometimes the gods are kind and the Norns are asleep. Whatever the reason we were able to see the last light from the west shine upon the arch carved by the gods. It dwarfed many strongholds and burghs I had seen. It made me feel insignificant but I took it as a good sign that the cove we found was deserted save for a few huts on the headland. We went ashore and set guards.

The ships' boys foraged and found berries and crab apples which augmented our salted fish and meat. Haaken asked me about the arch. "Why do you think the gods carved that arch? Does it serve a purpose?"

I shrugged, "I do not know."

Finni the Dreamer said, "Perhaps it is a portal into their world. Maybe if we sail through it we would find a shortcut to Valhalla." Finni was the most thoughtful of my warriors. He saw beauty in many things and yet he was a fierce warrior. I was lucky to have him on my side. He was reliable and always there when you looked around. He never wavered in battle.

"You are a dreamer Finni. There is only one way into Valhalla. You die with a sword in your hand and I for one would not sail through the arch for a shipload of treasure."

From the nods, I saw that most would agree with Olaf Leather Neck but I wondered what it would be like to sail into another world. Unlike Olaf, I had been in the cave of the witch. I had been in another world. I had survived many times. I did not think there would be a risk but we would not sail through it this voyage. We had Eggle to find.

Finni said, "I for one would travel such a portal. Who would not wish to see what lay beyond?"

The next day we kept the men at their oars. Often they just rested them in their oar holes but we were vigilant with sharp-eyed lookouts watching for Saxons. Often they lurked close to Vectis and rowed out to take unsuspecting ships. Three drekar were too big a mouthful and we passed Vectis. We did not want to risk landing in Wessex and, with the wind changing direction, we took to the oars to make for the marshes of Essex and Kent. Haaken used the heroic song of Eystein's death to inspire the crew. The new men were finding the voyage harder than they had expected.

Through the stormy Saxon Seas
The Ulfheonar they sailed
Fresh from killing faithless Danes
Their glory was assured
Heart of Dragon
Gift of a king
Two fine drekar
Flying o'er foreign seas
Then Saxons came out of the night
An ambush by their Isle of Wight
Vikings fight they do not run
The Jarl turned away from the rising sun
Heart of Dragon
Gift of a king
Two fine drekar
Flying o'er foreign seas
The galdramenn burned Dragon Fire
And the seas they burned bright red
Aboard 'The Gift' Asbjorn the Strong
And the rock Eystein
Rallied their men to board their foes
And face them beard to beard
Heart of Dragon
Gift of a king
Two fine drekar
Flying o'er foreign seas
Against great odds and back to back
The heroes fought as one
Their swords were red with Saxon blood
And the decks with bodies slain
Surrounded on all sides was he
But Eystein faltered not
He slew first one and then another
But the last one did for him
Even though he fought as a walking dead
He killed right to the end
Heart of Dragon

Gift of a king
Two fine drekar
Flying o'er foreign seas
Heart of Dragon
Gift of a king
Two fine drekar
Flying o'er foreign seas

The narrow seas between the land of the Franks and Kent were always a dangerous place for many ships plied that route. The river led to Lundenwic and there were powerful burghs there. All of the men on the river were our enemies but the Norns were benign and we reached the marshes north of the Tamese without incident. We moored amongst the reeds. None went ashore but we could all get some rest for we were now just two days from our prey. Even if the winds were against us we could row there in two days. In my mind, I prepared for war and I became more silent than normal.

Haaken recognised the signs, "You worry that he will escape us?"

"I worry that he will have gone already and this voyage will be for nothing. At least when we war with Wessex we have an idea of what Egbert will do. He will come by land and from the south. This Eggle is a Dane. He is a Viking. Just as we are unpredictable so is he. He could go home to the land of the Danes. He could sail to Jorvik or Dorestad. Who knows where he might flee? I have wrestled with his mind. What would I do if I were he?"

"And that is where you go wrong, Jarl. You are not like Eggle. You do not kill without reason and you do not abandon your men. You cannot see into his mind. If you wish my opinion then it is this. The Norns sent you to the witch and you dreamed of Eggle. Your task was appointed to you. We failed the first time and the Norns have given you a second opportunity. I cannot fault your plan. Three drekar against two in a narrow river with the warriors you lead should give us the victory. I confess that I would not have thought to use Saxons to stop them from escaping and that is why you are jarl and I sing songs of what you do. We cannot change our plans now. You have cast the bones and we will soon discover where they fall."

"You are right, old friend. It is the loss of two stad which has made me doubt myself."

Chapter 16

It took two days to beat up an east coast which was filled with dark threatening skies and winds which were trying to push us to the land of the Danes. It was hard going. We laid up in marshy land close to the old Roman town of Lindum. The road north to Jorvik lay there but any port which might have been there in Roman times was now silted up. It was a swamp and a marsh as empty as in Essex. We shared it with wildfowl and fenny snakes.

We anchored next to each other so that my captains, jarls and hersir could come aboard and I could give them their final instructions.

"I know not when we will reach Hwitebi tomorrow but we are so close now that we can almost smell the blood on Eggle's hands. Whenever we reach the river I intend to attack immediately. We will not scout. We will attack. *'Heart of the Dragon'* and *'Red Snake'* will close with Eggle's drekar and we will board it."

"Suppose he is not on his ship?"

I smiled, "Then, Kolbjorn, the task will be easier. If he is not aboard then we can destroy his drekar. Without his ships, he is trapped in Hwitebi. You and *'King's Gift'* will guard the entrance to the river until we have grappled the two drekar. Then you will go to the aid of *'Red Snake'*. She has the smaller crew."

Raibeart asked, "And if he is ashore?"

"Then we sink his ships, land and find him." They nodded. "Have our men prepare for war. Unless they have sentries on the cliffs then the first they will know of us is when we appear in the mouth of the river. I expect that the water will be calm but tell your new warriors how hard it is to fight on a ship!"

We sailed north at dawn. Erik nodded as we set sail, "The gods are working for us Jarl. This wind is from the east and the south. It will take us north swiftly."

Haaken said, "I know it helps us but it must come from the east for it chills me to my bones!"

"You are getting soft, Haaken. This wind makes me ready to use my axe and hew heads. It invigorates me!" Olaf Leather Neck stroked his axe much as a father cuddled his newborn.

There was one village between us and Hwitebi. It was Falgrave and housed a few fishermen. They were Saxon and would not bother us. The high cliffs were empty. The rocks which lined them kept us well out to sea. Our first sight of Hwitebi was the abbey that dominated the south cliffs. We saw it as we approached. It was a clear landmark. I was ready for war and just needed my helmet but I was nervous. It was at times like this that I missed Aiden. I did not know if we would spy two drekar or an empty river. My plan assumed that he would not have left his new home so soon. The favourable wind meant that we did not need to row. Indeed, when we turned west the wind would rush us through the narrow entrance. It would be a test of skill for Erik but Eggle's ships would be unable to sail out for my three drekar would fill the entrance. I resisted the temptation to race to the prow and be the first to see if there were boats in the harbour.

Arne Eriksson shouted from the masthead, "Two drekar in the river. They are preparing to sail!"

Haaken turned to me, "They did have sentries on the cliffs."

Erik Short Toe shouted, "It matters not Haaken. They have the wind against them."

"Aye, Erik. Sail us so that we take out the oars on one side."

"It will mean we have to repair our ship."

"It will be worth it for it means Eggle will not escape us." I hoped that Prince Athelstan was where he said he would be. If not it would not be a disaster. I would follow him wherever he went and if he was on foot then I would find him. A drekar was different for the seas were as vast as the star-filled sky. But I was anxious to be back in my home.

As we turned I saw the two drekar. They must have been moored next to the huts I could see on the south bank. They were rowing and rowing hard towards the river mouth. I saw that '*Skull*', Eggle's drekar, was leading. That would be the Dane's way. It was a large drekar. It looked to have twenty oars on each side. That could mean as many as eighty men on board. I did not think it would. His men would have to have slept aboard to ensure that it was fully manned and Eggle's warband did not seem the type to endure hardship when they did not need to.

"Go for the leading drekar, Erik. Ulfheonar, to the steerboard side." I left my shield around my back. I would need my left hand to help me aboard the drekar.

"Reef the sail!" Erik's voice made the ship's boys race up the lines to the masthead.

"Snorri see if you can hit a few with your bow!" Snorri and Beorn began to loose arrows at the drekar as it approached. The half dozen arrows they would send would hardly change the outcome but it would distract the attention of the crew.

The wind astern was pushing us swiftly towards the *'Skull'* which was desperately trying to get out of our way. I looked astern and saw that Olaf had put *'King's Gift'* on our steerboard side. He was preparing to turn to fill the river mouth with his drekar and Raibeart was darting, like a greyhound, towards *'Serpent's Tongue'*. Whatever happened we would have a battle in the Esk. Erik's crew timed it perfectly. As our bow began to slice and slide through the oars the sail was furled and we lost way. The crash was so violent that, had I not been clinging to a stay, I would have been thrown from my feet.

I drew my sword. Three of my warriors threw ropes with grappling hooks on them and held us against *'Skull'*. I used the stay to pull myself up and then, shouting, "Revenge for Windar's Mere!" I leapt aboard the drekar. Some of those who had manned the oars now lay with terrible wounds where the broken oars had been rammed into their bodies as we had collided. Others lay stunned. This was no time for mercy. Those who could still fight were fair game and I hacked and slashed around me so that those behind could board safely.

I saw that Eggle Skulltaker and his hearth-weru were gathered around the stern. They were a solid wall of shields and mail. He had twenty men with him. The rest, the ones through whom we passed, were without mail. As they had before some of them took their chances with Icaunus and leapt into the sea. I hoped that Kolbjorn had remembered my instructions and was heading towards the side of *'Serpent's Tongue'* where he could aid Raibeart.

"Ulfheonar! Shields!" I began to move towards the mast. A knot of warriors had gathered there. It was mainly because they had nowhere else to go and they had the protection of the mast behind them. They were brave men for I could see, in their eyes, that they expected to die. I would not prolong their end. With Haaken on one side of me and Cnut Cnutson on the other, I brought my sword over my head and swung it down at the Dane who thrust his sword at my head. I moved my head to my right and his sword slid off my helmet to tangle in my cloak before striking my mail. My sword smashed into his helmet. It was poorly made and he had no skull protector beneath. I saw the life leave his eyes. Cnut Cnutson brought a backhand stroke to slide into the neck of a second Dane. His hot blood spurted over us making us look like butchers. Haaken had punched his shield into his opponent's face and smashed it to a pulp. Unable to see he was relieved of his pain by Haaken's sword in his chest.

A spear darted towards me and I fended it off easily. The Dane had used two hands. I swept a backhanded stroke and it tore across his throat. Behind me, I heard my crew as they fought those at the bows. Behind me I had Ulfheonar and we faced Eggle Skulltaker and his hearth-weru. He was not in the front rank. There were men before him. His helmet was a full-face helmet and the top was adorned with a metal skull. I stored that information.

As I had expected he taunted me."So, old man, you seek to end the life of Eggle Skulltaker. You will not find it so easy without your wizard. Let us see how you deal with my magic!"

From behind him, a girl with wild limed hair and a red-painted face stood up. He had his own witch. I remembered what Aiden and Kara had said. This witch had hidden him from their thoughts. I had been warned of danger. I just had not expected this. The witch took a small stick doll and began to chant. She was cursing us and me in particular. I stepped forward for I was not afraid but the Ulfheonar had not followed me. The sight of the witch had done the impossible. It had made the Ulfheonar falter.

Eggle laughed, "So Dragonheart, your men are afraid without your wizard. Perhaps when I have slain you I will go to your land and see if he has the same powers as my witch!"

Just then an arrow flew from behind my shoulder and struck the witch squarely in the middle of her forehead. She was thrown backwards and tumbled over the steering board into the river.

Snorri's voice sounded, "No, Eggle baby killer! We are not afraid! The Ulfheonar did not want to get in the way of my arrow!" He released a second one and it clattered off the side of Eggle's helmet then bounced into the neck of the hearth-weru next to him. It stuck in the mail.

I could see that Eggle was shaken both by the death of his witch and the arrow which had hit him. "You will be cursed for killing a witch! I would not be you!"

"And for that I am grateful." Snorri loosed a third arrow and it struck the Dane who was trying to pull the arrow from his mail. Snorri's arrow went through his cheek. Blood gushed.

"Ulfheonar, let us end this now!" I raised Ragnar's Spirit and raced forward.

Haaken and Cnut locked shields with me. We would advance as a wedge. There would be no quarter given and on a narrow drekar, a single mistake could be fatal. It was Finni the Dreamer who made that mistake. He was next to Haaken and as we stepped forward he was looking at the Danish line and not his feet. Perhaps it was the Norns who punished him I know not. Some said it was the witch but whatever the reason his foot slipped on some blood and gore which covered a rope. As he fell forward a Dane brought his axe over and it struck Finni in the nape of the neck. He fell to the ground and a second Dane half severed his head from his body.

Rollo Thin Skin had begun to move forward even as Finni slipped and his sword took first the axeman, slicing across his forearms and then stabbing the killer in the thigh. The death of one of our own was a mistake on the Danes' part. We leapt forward all thoughts of a shield wall gone as we closed with our Viking enemies. I was oblivious to the swords and spears which clattered and rang off my helmet and shield. I stabbed blindly forward as I head-butted a Dane with an open-face helmet. As his nose spattered I felt my blade sink into his leg.

Eggle Skulltaker saw his chance and he brought his mighty sword overhand to end this by killing me. I barely had time to bring my left hand up and block the blow with my shield. My sword was still embedded in the thigh of his heath-weru. He pulled his hand back and stabbed it towards my chest. He had quick hands and my shield did not move fast enough as it came towards me. It struck me but, unbelievably it did not sink through my mail or my flesh. It found the golden dragon. My talisman saved my life. The dragon had saved the Dragonheart! I saw his eyes widen in disbelief that his killing blow had failed.

I finally tore my sword from the hearth-weru's leg. I must have torn something vital in the Dane as blood spurted high in the air. It showered Eggle Skulltaker! I brought my own sword around in a wide sweep. Although he managed to block it, the blow I struck was so powerful that he reeled as it struck. Before he could strike me again I punched high with my shield and caught his hand. I pulled back and punched again. He was off-balance now and he was forced back to the steering board. Around me, my Ulfheonar were fighting to the death with Danes who had no thoughts of surrender. I only had eyes for my enemy.

He recovered his balance and brought his shield around tighter to his body. I pulled back my shield and feinted another blow. I swung at his head. He ducked but my blade caught the skull on his helmet and knocked it from his head. It rolled along the tilting deck. I pulled back my hand and this time swung not at his shield but his hand which had been struck twice by the boss of my shield. He brought his shield across but not quickly enough. Ragnar's Spirit sliced across the back of his hand. It began to bleed heavily.

"That, you treacherous Dane, is Ragnar's Spirit. It was touched by the gods. I need no wizard to help me for the gods themselves send their power through this sword. Soon you will join your bitch of a witch but I will send you to Hel and not Valhalla!"

I saw fear in the eyes for he had lost his helmet. I punched again with my shield. His hand was hurting and when I brought my sword over my shoulder he had no defence. I chopped off his hand and it fell to the deck still gripping his sword. He slumped to the deck and sat looking at me. I was dimly aware that we were now lower than my drekar. We had sprung the strakes of '*Skull*' and we were sinking. Eggle was sprawled over chests that stood stacked at the stern. It meant his shoulders were above the sheerstrake.

I stood over him. "I will not see you in Valhalla for you will not go there. This is for those you butchered!" I swung my sword and took his head in one blow. It flew from his head and into the water. It seemed appropriate for Eggle Skulltaker to die thus.

I heard cheers behind me. Turning I saw that all the Danes were dead. Erik shouted, from my drekar, "Jarl you are sinking!"

I pointed to the chests, "This is the treasure from Windar's Mere. We have time. Strip the dead and get all aboard."

Slinging my shield over my back I said, "Haaken, help me with Finni the Dreamer. We will bury him with honour."

Using his cloak we lifted him to the side of the drekar. My own ship now rode higher in the water and we needed help to lift him up. Erik had his boys throw more ropes for us and we followed the body of my Ulfheonar. The deck of '*Skull*' was almost underwater as we hauled the last of the mail and the chests aboard *'Heart of the Dragon'*. I looked over and saw that the second drekar still floated. I went to the side and shouted, "Sink her!"

Raibeart nodded and I heard the sound of axes as they hacked and chopped through the deck and into the hull. Erik had the sail half-lowered to give us way against the current and we sailed to the wooden quay a thousand paces upriver and close to the huts. I saw no one as we approached. I knew that there had to be Saxons living there but the sight of a sea battle would have driven them hence. As we tied up I heard the sound of hooves and I looked up to see Prince Athelstan and his men riding towards us.

He dismounted and clasped my hand, "Well met, Jarl. I do not think that my father believed that a Viking would help us rid this land of a Dane."

"He was an enemy to all. It is good that he has gone and we have not broken the peace."

"No indeed. If anything you have strengthened it."

I gave him a wry smile. I pointed to the two sinking ships. "I do not think the fishermen hereabouts will say that. We have blocked the channel for them."

"They can mark it and it is a small inconvenience. The headman told me that Eggle had abused the women here. He was afraid that you were cut from the same cloth and he and his people have taken shelter in the abbey."

"I do not blame them. We are a frightening-looking band. With your permission Prince, we will bury our dead by the river. I hope their grave will be respected."

"I will give commands. It will be so."

It was dark by the time the grave had been dug, the dead and their weapons laid within and stones, soil and turf placed upon them. The Prince asked as we walked away, "Are there no words you use? Do you not leave a marker?"

"There will be words. Haaken One Eye will sing a song about this battle and when we sing it then we will remember them. As for a marker... we know where the grave lies and that is all that matters."

Before Haaken and I left I said, "Well Finni, you have found your portal now. You were oathsworn unto death and we will remember you."

We shared a camp with the Northumbrians and the nuns and villagers fed us. I could see that they were petrified of us Norsemen. They clutched their crosses and the nuns chanted prayers as they fed us. I think it was as close to us as they wished to come.

I turned to the Prince after the nuns and villagers had departed, "You know that we are your allies so long as the peace holds."

"I do and I am grateful that Ketil brokered this peace."

I pointed to the water where the masts of the two drekar stood proud of the low tide. "The Danes are not your allies. They are your enemy as much as they are mine. I confess that I would not have stirred had not my people been attacked. I speak honestly for that is my way. You could have stopped Eggle before he gained power. The Dunum is not far from Din Guardi. The valley is now empty of people. When we marched west we saw none until we reached our home. We did not destroy the people there. Eggle and Danes like him did. They are not like my people. They do not come to settle and to grow. They are like leeches living off the blood of others. I say this as an ally. Unless you are stronger then you will lose the Kingdom of Northumbria. Your land is filled with Danes. They are like fleas on a dog and like those fleas they suck your lifeblood. Destroy them or die!"

He smiled.

"Have I said something funny, Prince?"

"No, but is like hearing myself talk to my father." He lowered his voice. "I will be as honest with you as you are with me. He fears Vikings. That is your fault, Jarl Dragonheart for he has never defeated you. He thinks the Danes are the same."

"Your father knows how to defeat Danes and Vikings. Your home at Din Guardi is an example. Build high walls with deep ditches. When the men of Strathclyde came to my land it was a stronghold on the Eden which defeated them. You could do the same. Eggle showed you the way with his fort on the river." I pointed towards the glow from the abbey. "If that is not protected then the Norse and the Dane will come. They will enslave the priests and steal the treasures. It needs a wall. If you want strength and protection from Vikings then build walls."

"You would raid yourself?"

"No, Prince. I gave my word and I will keep it. But I am a Viking and I know a soft and weak target when I see it. A good Jarl does not waste his men in fruitless attacks on a wall."

He nodded, "And you have entered Din Guardi have you not? Could you take it?"

"I could but I would lose many men and what would I gain? I am sorry, Prince Athelstan, but there are greater treasures to be had in Wessex burghs than in Northumbria. We will raid and Saxons and Franks will fear us but we choose targets which reward us." I pointed to our drekar. "The treasure we took from Eggle was our own. That was why he attacked us. I made a Saxon mistake. I did not protect the stad he attacked. He took our treasure. I learn from my lessons. I hope that you do too."

We left on the morning tide. We could not see the sunken drekar but we knew their position. Some bloated bodies floated to the surface in the night and as we sailed south we saw them coming with us. My men believed they would return to their home in Denmark. I knew they would not. There were many sea creatures that would feast on their flesh long before they crossed the sea.

The winds which had brought us here swiftly now worked against us. Whilst not in our faces they slowed us. Haaken was able to compose the saga of Finni's end. By the time we reached Kent the crew were chanting it to help us beat west.

The Danes they came in dark of night
They slew Harland without a fight
Babies children all were slain
Mothers and daughters split in twain
Viking enemy, taking heads
Viking warriors fighting back
Viking enemy, taking heads
Viking warriors fighting back
Across the land the Ulfheonar trekked
Finding a land by Danes' hands wrecked
Ready to die to kill this Dane
Dragonheart was Eggles' bane
Viking enemy, taking heads
Viking warriors fighting back
Viking enemy, taking heads
Viking warriors fighting back
With boys as men the ships were fired
Warriors had these heroes sired
Then Ulfheonar fought their foe
Slaying all in the drekar's glow
Viking enemy, taking heads

Viking warriors fighting back
Viking enemy, taking heads
Viking warriors fighting back
When the Danes were broke their leader fled
Leaving his army lying dead
He sailed away to hide and plot
Dragonheart's fury was red hot
Viking enemy, taking heads
Viking warriors fighting back
Viking enemy, taking heads
Viking warriors fighting back
Then sailed the men of Cyninges-tūn
Sailing from the setting sun
They caught the Skull upon the sea
Beneath the church of Hwitebi
Viking enemy, taking heads
Viking warriors fighting back
Viking enemy, taking heads
Viking warriors fighting back
Heroes all they fought the Dane
But Finni the Dreamer, he was slain
Then full of fury their blood it boiled
Through blood and bodies the warriors toiled
With one swift blow the skull was killed
With bodies and ships the Esk was filled
Viking enemy, taking heads
Viking warriors fighting back
Viking enemy, taking heads
Viking warriors fighting back
Now Finni has passed through portal high
He waits for us up in the sky
Valhalla toasts his mighty tales
The hero with the gods now sails
Viking enemy, taking heads
Viking warriors fighting back
Viking enemy, taking heads
Viking warriors fighting back

The fact that it was so recent made each verse and word poignant. We took it as a sign when we stopped singing that the wind sprang from our steerboard quarter and we were able to stop rowing. Finni had reached Valhalla. We rested once more at Durdle. I was reminded that Finni the Dreamer had thought it a portal to Valhalla. He was there now and would know the truth of it. We had been given two barrels of beer by the monks of Hwitebi. I think they were glad to see the back of us. We finished the second barrel on the beach and we drank to the memory of Finni the Dreamer. He had died oathsworn.

We were silent as we sailed west, the next day. The crew were all aware that we were close to the islands. The death of the witch had played on many warriors' minds. Snorri did not regret killing her. Had she cursed us who knew that might have happened but we all knew that the killing of a witch was a serious matter. Would the Norn, Verðandi, punish us? Erik took us well to the north of the islands so that we would not risk her wrath. I saw many of my warriors fingering their amulets and chanting. They were afraid.

Snorri saw it too and he approached me, "Jarl I would not bring bad luck to this ship. Let us go to the island. If I have offended the Norns then I will be punished. So long as we do not know then the ship is cursed. It is as bad as though the witch herself had cursed us."

I saw Erik clutch his Thor's hammer. "We may not find her."

"In which case, we will be safe."

I could not argue with that logic. Once more I wished I had brought my wizard with me. "Very well. Erik, steer for Syllingar. Let us find the witch."

I knew that only Snorri and I went willingly and the rest were petrified but none argued with us for Snorri had made a good case. It did not take long for the islands to hove into view. We had passed them before and not seen the island of the witch. We had never seen the witch when she did not wish to. I think that Haaken and the Ulfheonar thought we would not see her this time. They were wrong. I saw a tendril of smoke. The witch was there.

I pointed and Erik put the steering board over. Every man on the ship, save myself, clutched at their amulet. We were poking the dragon!

We hove to and Snorri prepared to clamber over the side. "Take off your helmet and wolf cloak." He nodded and did as I said. I copied him.

"What are you doing, Jarl?"

"I am coming with you. You did not think that I would allow my oathsworn to go alone into the cave? Besides, you do not know the way. Haaken, take charge until I return."

"And if you do not?"

"Then you have a long voyage home to explain to Brigid why I am not returning and to compose Snorri's Saga."

He laughed and gave me a mock Roman salute.

I led the way for Snorri knew it not. We climbed up to the cave and I descended into its glowing bowels. I went slowly to help Snorri. If he fell then he would not be in the right frame of mind to face Verðandi, the witch of Syllingar. When we turned I saw her there. It had not been long since I had seen her but she had aged. She smiled a toothless smile, "Come Dragonheart and bring this killer of witches so that I may see his face."

I took him to the log upon which we normally sat. Snorri was a fearless warrior. He was the best scout I had ever known and yet, seated next to me, he shook.

Her eyes bored into him. "So Snorri son of Harald Snorrison, you killed a witch. Do you repent of your action?"

Snorri's voice came out higher than he intended, "No, I would do it again."

"You come here and tell me that you killed a witch and would do so again. You do not sound penitent."

"I am not."

"Then why did you come here?"

"If there is a punishment then it should be for me and not for my shipmates. I am here for my punishment."

"And if that punishment is death?"

"Then so be it. I have had a good life and my arrow stopped us from being cursed."

"And if you died and did not go to Valhalla?"

"Then that would be a cruel punishment but I would bear it for the Ulfheonar and for Jarl Dragonheart."

She nodded and looked at me, "Now you see why we chose you Garth, son of Myfanwy. You make warriors willing to forego Valhalla. He is a brave man. He is terrified of my judgement and yet he faces me. He does not even think to kill me!"

Snorri looked around at me. I shook my head, "You cannot hide your thoughts from her. So what is to happen? Do we drink your soup and wake up to an empty cave?"

"No. There is no dream. The witch chose a bad leader. It happens. He deserved to die and so did she. But, Snorri son of Harald Snorrison, do not make a habit of killing witches. It could prove fatal for your health. Now go. We are done and you have a new child, Dragonheart. If you hurry you will meet her when she enters this world!"

Snorri was like a drunken man as I led him up to the sun and sky. He said not a word. We walked across the beach towards the drekar which was in the shallows. We climbed aboard and my Ulfheonar looked at him as though he was a ghost returned from the dead.

Haaken said, "Was she not at home?"

Snorri found his voice, "She was and I am not to be punished." He looked at me. "She is the same witch you see each time you visit?"

"She is."

"Then Jarl Dragonheart you truly have the heart of a dragon for I would not descend there again for all the treasure in Miklagård. Once was enough."

I turned to Haaken, "Well you have no saga but at least you do not have to face the wrath of Brigid!"

"Then I am grateful too, Jarl, for that is an equally terrifying prospect."

"Erik, let us sail home. I would see my new daughter."

Epilogue

It took a long five days to sail up the west coast. Some thought it was the witch punishing us but Snorri and I knew it was not. When we reached Úlfarrston it was dusk. I was anxious to return home. Snorri came with me as did half of my Ulfheonar. The rest either headed to their farms or stayed in Úlfarrston to enjoy the pleasures it offered.

As we rode north Snorri said, "Jarl, was I in the presence of a Norn?"

"I think so but I do not know. Perhaps this is a time to be happy and ignorant than wise and in pain."

"We have enjoyed a journey you and I." He looked at Cnut Cnutson, "Your father must be enjoying his time in Valhalla. The tales he can tell will keep everyone listening. Now that Finni is with him and Eystein the Rock they will have company. When we were in the witch's cave I thought my time was come and now I feel reborn. I have wasted time. My wife needs to bear me children. I have tales to tell them that they will not believe and my blood must go on."

Cnut nodded, "You are right, Snorri. I wish my father was here now. There is so much that I would ask him. I cannot but listening to you and the Jarl helps. I will tell my son everything from the moment he is born."

"Do you have a child, Cnut? I did not know."

"No Jarl Dragonheart but when I get home I will make one. I fear our world is ending and I would have my son enjoy the moment. Harland Windarsson died as did Arne Thorirson. They left no issue. I want my father's name to resonate through the ages. He might not be Jarl Dragonheart but he came from good stock. He was there when the sword was touched by the gods."

I nodded, "You are both right. We are here for a blink in time. We must make our mark while we can. Eggle Skulltaker made a name but it is not the name that I would wish for. If I died tonight I would be happy with what I have achieved."

Snorri shook his head, "I have served you since Man, Jarl, and I would be happy if I had done a tenth of what you have. But jarl, you are too reckless. There are others like Olaf who can go berserk and can fight impossible odds. We need you to lead us. Prince Butar was a good leader but you have exceeded him."

"That is the finest compliment that any has paid me and I am honoured. I do what I do for my family and my people. I will let my grandchildren say if I was worthy."

Cnut looked at Snorri and they both shook their heads.

We rode through the gates. It was well after dark. Elfrida ran to me, "Jarl you are a father!"

"I know I have a daughter and her name is Myfanwy!"

For the first time since I had known her, Elfrida was stuck for words. When she finally managed to speak she said, "Aye but how do you know? The bairn was born but an hour since and we just named her."

I smiled, "We visited the witch and she told me I would have a daughter. She called me Garth son of Myfanwy. No one has used that name since I crossed the sea. It is *wyrd*. We have rid the world of the Viking enemy and now we bring some order. I am happy for another daughter. I see the future and it is good."

The End

Glossary

Afon Hafron- River Severn in Welsh

Alpín mac Echdach – the father of Kenneth MacAlpin, reputedly the first king of the Scots

Alt Clut- Dumbarton Castle on the Clyde

An Lysardh - Lizard Peninsula Cornwall

Balley Chashtal -Castleton (Isle of Man)

Bardanes Tourkos- Rebel Byzantine General

Bebbanburgh- Bamburgh Castle, Northumbria also known as Din Guardi in the ancient tongue

Beck- a stream

Beinn na bhFadhla- Benbecula in the Outer Hebrides

Belesduna - Basildon

Blót – a blood sacrifice made by a jarl

Blue Sea- The Mediterranean

Bondi- Viking farmers who fight

Bourde- Bordeaux

Bjarnarøy –Great Bernera (Bear Island)

Byrnie- a mail or leather shirt reaching down to the knees

Caerlleon- Welsh for Chester

Caestir - Chester (old English)

Càrdainn Ros -Cardross (Argyll)

Casnewydd –Newport, Wales

Cephas- Greek for Simon Peter (St. Peter)

Chape- the tip of a scabbard

Charlemagne- Holy Roman Emperor at the end of the 8th and beginning of the 9th centuries

Celchyth - Chelsea

Cherestanc- Garstang (Lancashire)

Corn Walum or Om Walum- Cornwall

Cymri- Welsh

Cymru- Wales

Cyninges-tūn – Coniston. It means the estate of the king (Cumbria)

Dùn Èideann –Edinburgh (Gaelic)

Din Guardi- Bamburgh castle

Drekar- a Dragon ship (a Viking warship)

Duboglassio –Douglas, Isle of Man

Dun Holme- Durham

Dún Lethglaise - Downpatrick (Northern Ireland)

Durdle- Durdle door- the Jurassic Coast in Dorset
Dyrøy –Jura (Inner Hebrides)
Dyflin- Old Norse for Dublin
Ēa Lōn - River Lune
Ein-mánuðr - middle of March to the middle of April
Eoforwic- Saxon for York
Falgrave- Scarborough (North Yorkshire)
Faro Bregancio- Corunna (Spain)
Ferneberga -Farnborough (Hampshire)
Fey- having second sight
Firkin- a barrel containing eight gallons (usually beer)
Fret-a sea mist
Frankia- France and part of Germany
Fyrd-the Saxon levy
Garth- Dragon Heart
Gaill- Irish for foreigners
Galdramenn- wizard
Gesith- A Saxon nobleman. After 850 AD they were known as thegns
Glaesum –amber
Gleawecastre- Gloucester
Gói- the end of February to the middle of March
Grendel- the monster slain by Beowulf
Grenewic- Greenwich
Gulle - Goole (Humberside)
Hagustaldes ham -Hexham
Hamwic -Southampton
Haustmánuður - September 16th- October 16th (cutting of the corn)
Haughs- small hills in Norse (As in Tarn Hows)
Hearth-weru- The bodyguard or oathsworn of a jarl
Heels- when a ship leans to one side under the pressure of the wind
Hel - Queen of Niflheim, the Norse underworld.
Here Wic- Harwich
Hersey- Isle of Arran
Hersir- a Viking landowner and minor noble. It ranks below a jarl
Hetaereiarch – Byzantine general
Hí- Iona (Gaelic)
Hjáp - Shap- Cumbria (Norse for stone circle)
Hoggs or Hogging- when the pressure of the wind causes the stern or the bow to droop
Hrams-a – Ramsey, Isle of Man
Hwitebi - Norse for Whitby, North Yorkshire
Hywel ap Rhodri Molwynog- King of Gwynedd 814-825
Icaunis- British river god

Issicauna- Gaulish for the lower Seine
Itouna- River Eden Cumbria
Jarl- Norse earl or lord
Joro-goddess of the earth
kjerringa - Old Woman- the solid block in which the mast rested
Knarr- a merchant ship or a coastal vessel
Kyrtle-woven top
Lambehitha- Lambeth
Leathes Water- Thirlmere
Legacaestir- Anglo-Saxon for Chester
Ljoðhús- Lewis
Lochlannach – Irish for Northerners (Vikings)
Lothuwistoft- Lowestoft
Lough- Irish lake
Louis the Pious- King of the Franks and son of Charlemagne
Lundenburgh- the fort in the heart of London (the former Roman fort)
Lundenwic - London
Maeresea- River Mersey
Mammceaster- Manchester
Manau/Mann – The Isle of Man(n) (Saxon)
Marcia Hispanic- Spanish Marches (the land around Barcelona)
Mast fish- two large racks on a ship designed to store the mast when not required
Melita- Malta
Midden- a place where they dumped human waste
Miklagård - Constantinople
Mörsugur - December 13th -January 12th (the fat sucker month!)
Nikephoros- Emperor of Byzantium 802-811
Njoror- God of the sea
Nithing- A man without honour (Saxon)
Odin - The "All Father" God of war, also associated with wisdom, poetry, and magic (The Ruler of the gods).
Olissipo- Lisbon
Orkneyjar-Orkney
Penrhudd – Penrith Cumbria
Þorri -January 13th -February 12th- midwinter
Portesmūða -Portsmouth
Pillars of Hercules- Straits of Gibraltar
Pyrlweall -Thirwell, Cumbria
Ran- Goddess of the sea
Roof rock- slate
Rinaz –The Rhine

Sabrina- Latin and Celtic for the River Severn. Also the name of a female Celtic deity

Saami- the people who live in what is now Northern Norway/Sweden

Samhain- a Celtic festival of the dead between 31st October and 1st November (Halloween)

St. Cybi- Holyhead

Scree- loose rocks in a glacial valley

Seax – short sword

Sheerstrake- the uppermost strake in the hull

Sheet- a rope fastened to the lower corner of a sail

Shroud- a rope from the masthead to the hull amidships

Skeggox – an axe with a shorter beard on one side of the blade

South Folk- Suffolk

Stad- Norse settlement

Stays- ropes running from the mast-head to the bow

Strake- the wood on the side of a drekar

Streanæshalc- Saxon for Whitby, North Yorkshire

Suthriganaworc - Southwark (London)

Syllingar Insula, Syllingar- Scilly Isles

Tarn- small lake (Norse)

Tella- River Béthune which empties near Dieppe

Temese- River Thames (also called the Tamese)

The Norns- The three sisters who weave webs of intrigue for men

Tilaburg - Tilbury

Thing-Norse for a parliament or a debate (Tynwald)

Thor's day- Thursday

Threttanessa- a drekar with 13 oars on each side.

Thrall- slave

Tinea- Tyne

Trenail- a round wooden peg used to secure strakes

Tynwald- the Parliament on the Isle of Man

Tvímánuður -Hay time-August 15th -September 15th

Úlfarrberg- Helvellyn

Úlfarrland- Cumbria

Úlfarr- Wolf Warrior

Úlfarrston- Ulverston

Ullr-Norse God of Hunting

Ulfheonar-an elite Norse warrior who wore a wolf skin over his armour

Vectis- The Isle of Wight

Volva- a witch or healing woman in Norse culture

Waeclinga Straet- Watling Street (A5) Windlesore-Windsor

Waite- a Viking word for farm

Werham -Wareham (Dorset)

Wintan-ceastre -Winchester
Withy- the mechanism connecting the steering board to the ship
Woden's day- Wednesday
Wulfhere-Old English for Wolf Army
Wyddfa-Snowdon
Wyrd- Fate
Yard- a timber from which the sail is suspended
Ynys Enlli- Bardsey Island
Ynys Môn-Anglesey

Historical note

The Viking raids began, according to records left by the monks, in the 790s when Lindisfarne was pillaged. However, there were many small settlements along the east coast and most were undefended. I have chosen a fictitious village on the Tees as the home of Garth who is enslaved and then, when he gains his freedom, becomes Dragon Heart. As buildings were all made of wood then any evidence of their existence would have rotted long ago, save for a few post holes. The Norse began to raid well before 790. There was a rise in the populations of Norway and Denmark and Britain was not well prepared for defence against such random attacks.

My raiders represent the Norse warriors who wanted the plunder of the soft Saxon kingdom. There is a myth that the Vikings raided in large numbers but this is not so. It was only in the tenth and eleventh centuries that the numbers grew. They also did not have allegiances to kings. The Norse settlements were often isolated family groups. The term Viking was not used in what we now term the Viking Age beyond the lands of Norway and Denmark. Warriors went a-Viking which meant that they sailed for adventure or pirating. Their lives were hard. Slavery was commonplace. The Norse for slave is thrall and I have used both terms.

The coastlines were different in the eighth and ninth centuries. The land to the east of Lincoln was a swamp. Indeed there had been a port just a few miles from Lincoln in the Roman age. Now Lincoln is many miles from the sea but this was not so in the past. Similarly, many rivers have been straightened. We can thank the Victorians for that. The Tees had so many loops in it that it took as long to get from Yarm to the sea as it did to get down to London! Similarly many place names and places have changed. Some had Saxon names which became Norse. Some had Old English names. Some even retained their Latin names. It was quite common for one place to be known by two names.

I used the following books for research

Vikings- Life and Legends -British Museum
Saxon, Norman and Viking by Terence Wise (Osprey)
The Vikings (Osprey) -Ian Heath
Byzantine Armies 668-1118 (Osprey)-Ian Heath
Romano-Byzantine Armies 4th-9th Century (Osprey) -David Nicholle
The Walls of Constantinople AD 324-1453 (Osprey) -Stephen Turnbull

Viking Longship (Osprey) - Keith Durham
The Vikings in England Anglo-Danish Project
Anglo Saxon Thegn AD 449-1066- Mark Harrison (Osprey)
Viking Hersir- 793-1066 AD - Mark Harrison (Osprey)
Hadrian's Wall- David Breeze (English Heritage)

Griff Hosker August 2016

Other books by Griff Hosker

If you enjoyed reading this book, then why not read another one by the author?

Ancient History

The Sword of Cartimandua Series
(Germania and Britannia 50 A.D. – 128 A.D.)
Ulpius Felix- Roman Warrior (prequel)
The Sword of Cartimandua
The Horse Warriors
Invasion Caledonia
Roman Retreat
Revolt of the Red Witch
Druid's Gold
Trajan's Hunters
The Last Frontier
Hero of Rome
Roman Hawk
Roman Treachery
Roman Wall
Roman Courage

The Wolf Warrior series
(Britain in the late 6th Century)
Saxon Dawn
Saxon Revenge
Saxon England
Saxon Blood
Saxon Slayer
Saxon Slaughter
Saxon Bane
Saxon Fall: Rise of the Warlord
Saxon Throne

Saxon Sword

Medieval History

The Dragon Heart Series
Viking Slave *
Viking Warrior *
Viking Jarl *
Viking Kingdom *
Viking Wolf *
Viking War
Viking Sword
Viking Wrath
Viking Raid
Viking Legend
Viking Vengeance
Viking Dragon
Viking Treasure
Viking Enemy
Viking Witch
Viking Blood
Viking Weregeld
Viking Storm
Viking Warband
Viking Shadow
Viking Legacy
Viking Clan
Viking Bravery

The Norman Genesis Series
Hrolf the Viking *
Horseman *
The Battle for a Home *
Revenge of the Franks *
The Land of the Northmen
Ragnvald Hrolfsson

Brothers in Blood
Lord of Rouen
Drekar in the Seine
Duke of Normandy
The Duke and the King

Danelaw
(England and Denmark in the 11th Century)
Dragon Sword *
Oathsword *
Bloodsword *
Danish Sword
The Sword of Cnut

New World Series
Blood on the Blade *
Across the Seas *
The Savage Wilderness *
The Bear and the Wolf *
Erik The Navigator *
Erik's Clan *
The Last Viking

The Vengeance Trail *

The Conquest Series
(Normandy and England 1050-1100)
Hastings
Conquest

The Aelfraed Series
(Britain and Byzantium 1050 A.D. - 1085 A.D.)
Housecarl *
Outlaw *
Varangian *

The Reconquista Chronicles
Castilian Knight *
El Campeador *
The Lord of Valencia *

The Anarchy Series England
1120-1180
English Knight *
Knight of the Empress *
Northern Knight *
Baron of the North *
Earl *
King Henry's Champion *
The King is Dead *
Warlord of the North
Enemy at the Gate
The Fallen Crown
Warlord's War
Kingmaker
Henry II
Crusader
The Welsh Marches
Irish War
Poisonous Plots
The Princes' Revolt
Earl Marshal
The Perfect Knight

Border Knight
1182-1300
Sword for Hire *
Return of the Knight *
Baron's War *
Magna Carta *
Welsh Wars *
Henry III *

The Bloody Border *
Baron's Crusade
Sentinel of the North
War in the West
Debt of Honour
The Blood of the Warlord
The Fettered King
de Montfort's Crown

Sir John Hawkwood Series
France and Italy 1339- 1387
Crécy: The Age of the Archer *
Man At Arms *
The White Company *
Leader of Men *
Tuscan Warlord *
Condottiere

Lord Edward's Archer
Lord Edward's Archer *
King in Waiting *
An Archer's Crusade *
Targets of Treachery *
The Great Cause *
Wallace's War *
The Hunt

Struggle for a Crown
1360- 1485
Blood on the Crown *
To Murder a King *
The Throne *
King Henry IV *
The Road to Agincourt *
St Crispin's Day *
The Battle for France *

The Last Knight *
Queen's Knight *
The Knight's Tale

Tales from the Sword I
(Short stories from the Medieval period)

Tudor Warrior series
England and Scotland in the late 15th and early 16th century
Tudor Warrior *
Tudor Spy *
Flodden*

Conquistador
England and America in the 16th Century
Conquistador *
The English Adventurer *

English Mercenary
The 30 Years War and the English Civil War
Horse and Pistol

Modern History

The Napoleonic Horseman Series
Chasseur à Cheval
Napoleon's Guard
British Light Dragoon
Soldier Spy
1808: The Road to Coruña
Talavera
The Lines of Torres Vedras
Bloody Badajoz
The Road to France
Waterloo

The Lucky Jack American Civil War series
Rebel Raiders
Confederate Rangers
The Road to Gettysburg

Soldier of the Queen series
Soldier of the Queen*
Redcoat's Rifle*
Omdurman

The British Ace Series
1914
1915 Fokker Scourge
1916 Angels over the Somme
1917 Eagles Fall
1918 We will remember them
From Arctic Snow to Desert Sand
Wings over Persia

Combined Operations series
1940-1945
Commando *
Raider *
Behind Enemy Lines
Dieppe
Toehold in Europe
Sword Beach
Breakout
The Battle for Antwerp
King Tiger
Beyond the Rhine
Korea
Korean Winter

Tales from the Sword II
(Short stories from the Modern period)

Books marked thus *, are also available in the audio format. For more information on all of the books then please visit the author's website at www.griffhosker.com where there is a link to contact him or visit his Facebook page: GriffHosker at Sword Books or follow him on Twitter: @HoskerGriff or Sword (@swordbooksltd)

If you wish to be on the mailing list then contact the author through his website.

Printed in Great Britain
by Amazon